GASPING FOR AIR

BOOK TWO IN THE 'BIG DOGS SERIES'

S.L. DITMARS

WILD BLUE
PRESS

WildBluePress.com

GASPING FOR AIR published by:
WILDBLUE PRESS
P.O. Box 102440
Denver, Colorado 80250

ISBN 978-1-957288-73-4 Trade Paperback
ISBN 978-1-957288-74-1 eBook
ISBN 978-1-957288-72-7 Hardback

GASPING FOR AIR

PREFACE

Welcome back, readers, and thank you for choosing *Gasping for Air*, the second book in the Big Dogs series. The publishing world is full of options, and I am grateful you chose this book to read. That said, if you are new to the series, welcome. If you have not read Big Dogs, I strongly recommend reading that first. While this can be read as a stand-alone story, I feel you will enjoy it more if you have the background provided in the first book.

As I write this, I am inside my study at my home in Prescott, Arizona. We are deeply immersed in the COVID-19 pandemic. Thousands of people worldwide are ill, and many have passed on. Our doctors, nurses, and scientists are currently fighting a major battle in the war against this virus. Yet, they return to their jobs every day, battling an adversary just as scary as any criminal I have ever faced. They do so because of their sense of duty to help the sick and try to make a difference. Unfortunately, some of them will fall to this enemy, and we owe them our thanks and prayers.

This book is dedicated to my friend, Jennifer Murphy. My wife, Barbi, and I met Jennifer and her husband, Steve, shortly after we moved here to Prescott, Arizona. After Barbi, Jennifer was the first person to read *Big Dogs*. To be honest, I didn't think she would like the book, but she did. She also gave me a lot of constructive criticism. The most important thing she provided was encouragement.

Throughout the time I knew Jennifer, she was always optimistic about the book, asking how it was doing and how long before the next one came out.

About a year after meeting Jennifer, we learned she had cancer. I will not go through the details with you; those are private for her and her family. The one thing I will say is she was always positive. She never gave up and continued to fight right to the end. Cancer can be relentless, and in this case, it was.

I guess my one regret with this book is that Jenn will not have the chance to read it and tell me how she felt about it. We love and miss you, Jenn.

S.L. Ditmars
Prescott, AZ

"You feel the last bit of breath leaving their body. You're looking into their eyes. A person in that situation is God!"
—Ted Bundy

"Do what you can with all you have, wherever you are."
—Theodore Roosevelt

PROLOGUE

February 2020—A Truck Stop near Forest, Mississippi

Floyd Hansen sat in the driver's seat of his tractor-trailer rig. He had started driving a truck at an early age. After working for a major trucking company for ten years, Hanson had finally saved enough to become an independent. He spent a lot of time on the road, so he had purchased a used big rig with a large sleeper unit in the back. This add-on saved him a lot of money on hotels and allowed him to stop and rest when needed.

His sleeper unit was a special one. It had been very nice when he purchased it, but then he added a "special" space that allowed him to secure his guests. He sat in his truck with the engine running. It had been a cold winter, and even as far south as he was, it was still chilly outside. The big diesel rumbled quietly while providing heat inside the cab. His eyes swept the parking lot. It was full of trucks, most of them occupied like his was. It was late and many drivers were catching a few hours of sleep.

Floyd looked down at his bible. His mother had given him the family bible as she prepared to meet her maker. She told him how important it was as it not only contained the word of the Lord but also their entire family history. Floyd admired his mother and protected the family bible with everything he had. The leather cover was well worn and showed the extensive use that he gave it. The book was open to one of his most important verses, Leviticus 19:29: "Do not prostitute thy daughter, to cause her to be a whore; lest the land fall to whoredom, and the land become full of wickedness."

He had a dream the night after he had first read that verse. The Lord came to him and told him that the land was full of wickedness, and he must become his soldier. He was to remove all the whores from the land, or the Lord would cleanse the earth himself with fire. Floyd had thought about this message the next day, and when he went to work, he gave his notice and began shopping for a rig of his own. He wasn't sure how to accomplish his new goal, but he believed the Lord would provide.

He raised his eyes from the good book and scanned the parking lot. He spotted her across the way. He knew immediately she must be a whore. There was no other good reason for a woman to be out in the parking lot at this time of night, especially in such cold weather. He flashed the truck's yellow marker lights quickly. The rapid flash caught her attention, and she smiled and started walking toward him.

The prostitute walked to the driver's door, which opened a crack as she approached. She looked up and saw a large man with a bushy beard wearing a plaid shirt and jeans. He had a solemn look and simply asked, "How much for head?"

It has been a slow night for Sunnie Conrad. There was word among the drivers of a new type of flu from Asia. Because of that, the drivers were reluctant to have contact with strangers. She needed some cash but feared her John might balk if she asked for too much.

"Twenty-five," she replied.

The man nodded and said, "Get in," motioning to the passenger side.

As she settled into the seat, he asked her, "What's your name?"

She found this somewhat unusual. Her Johns typically did not want to know who she was; they simply wanted sex and then for her to disappear.

"Sunnie."

"Well, Sunnie, let's go into the back so we can take care of business," he said as he pointed to the sleeper space of the truck. She heard him get up and follow as she moved past the curtain and into the back. Once in the back, she took a quick look around and started to say how nice it was when she felt a powerful arm slip around her neck and apply pressure. She struggled, but the man was strong and had mastered the chokehold. Her vision began to dim almost immediately.

Sunnie woke with a start. She could tell by the engine noise and movement of the truck that they were on the road. She had no idea how long she had been unconscious, but as Sunnie tried to move, she realized that her hands were bound behind her back, her feet were tied together, and there was duct tape over her mouth. She was in the dark in some type of a container, no longer on the sleeper bed. She wondered if there was enough air inside and immediately began to panic.

She kicked out against the side of the cabinet with a loud bang. She heard the man call out to her from the front, "Quit making such a racket. If you keep that up, I will make it much harder for you." With that, Sunnie began to think, trying to find a way out of this. She was afraid. What would this guy do to her? There were stories among the girls about Johns who liked to beat up hookers. She began to steel herself against what was to come.

Sunnie felt the big truck brake and then pull off the highway. They drove on for another ten minutes until she felt the truck slow again and turn onto another road. This one felt rougher, like a dirt road. The semi slowed again, this time coming to a stop.

The driver shut off the engine and came into the back. Floyd unlocked and opened the metal box that also served as the base of a bench. He reached down and grasped the zip tie that bound her legs. The man pulled her legs up, lifted her out, and set her on the floor. The move was practiced as if he had done it many times. He smiled at her and said, "Time to get to work." He didn't want to give her too much information. It would be harder for both of them if she knew his true intentions. He then pulled her to the side door of the sleeper. He got out, dragged her out, and tossed her onto his shoulder like she weighed nothing. He walked away from the truck to the edge of the woods, beside a large tree that had lost its leaves for the winter. There was a full moon. He could hear the rushing of a small river nearby.

Floyd reached into a pocket and pulled out a wad of rope. He tied one end to the zip tie between her feet and tossed the other over a large limb from the tree, hoisting Sunnie until her head was about waist high.

She realized the man had intentions far worse than rape and a beating. She began to buck wildly, trying desperately to get loose.

"Your whoring has brought a blight onto the land, and the Lord has commanded me to remove your kind from this earth." Panic overcame Sunnie; she kicked even more violently, trying to scream through the duct tape.

Hansen again reached into another pocket and pulled out a large, clear plastic bag. He slipped the bag over her head and then threaded another zip tie around the bottom. As he snugged it around her neck, he told her, "I release you from this hell and commit you to the Lord. God will decide whether you spend eternity in heaven or hell, but I wouldn't get my hopes up if I were you."

Sunnie felt the zip tie tighten, sealing off her air. All she had left was what was in the bag. Her fear intensified her swinging, but after a few moments, the bag began to fill with carbon dioxide. As her swaying slowed, she could see the man watching her, smiling. Finally, a corner of the duct tape broke free, and she screamed, "Fuck you—burn in hell," as her vision began to dim. Floyd Hansen noted her passing without any emotion. After several minutes of watching her hang there, he checked her pulse to confirm what he already knew. She was gone. He untied the rope and removed her restraints, duct tape, and the plastic bag, putting them in his truck's secret compartment for now. He would dispose of them later. He picked her up and again tossed her over his shoulder to carry her down to the stream. He chuckled to himself while he worked. *Burn in hell...not likely. I'm doing the Lord's work.*

He set her down on her back by the stream and arranged her carefully, folding her hands in front of her as if praying. He dropped to his knees and silently prayed with her. His work done, Floyd dragged her to the river and pushed her corpse into the flowing water. He returned to his truck and carefully maneuvered it to turn around.

Floyd Hansen returned to the highway and drove back to the truck stop, where he hooked up his rig to the trailer he had left. He decided to get some food before returning to the road. As he entered the building, he paused and quickly looked around. No one was paying any attention to him. They were too busy preparing for their busy days.

1

JW North was asleep in a deluxe suite in the Ultima hotel in Las Vegas. He and his partner, Ben Kellum, had driven to Las Vegas two days ago on orders of the Long Beach Police Department's (LBPD) chief of police. He sent them there to help Las Vegas Metro Police search for a killer.

Just under a year ago, on his last day of service to the City of Long Beach, JW was seriously injured in a shooting by a serial rapist known as the Shadow. JW had recovered from his injuries—well, truth be told, he was still recovering. His near-death experience severely shook his mental state and confidence. To help him regain his sense of self, JW had restarted a K9 human scent detection and trailing program. The program, or "the project," as most people called it, had been a big deal almost ten years ago at LBPD. Ben Kellum had been the primary liaison and handler. They'd had several successes but had not had the big win to give the program the kickstart it needed. As a result, the department ultimately terminated the project.

North knew he needed to do something, and working with dogs was his key. He had been a K9 handler and supervisor at LBPD and that time represented some of his best days as an officer at that time. There was just something about a dog—working with them and hunting bad guys. It was an incredible experience, and JW needed to recapture that. Also, somewhere deep down inside, he knew that, eventually, it would bring him back to the man who had shot him. That man had stolen a piece of JW North. JW intended to take it back.

As soon as he was healthy, JW returned to work at LBPD only long enough to retire. He then signed on as a reserve officer working directly on restarting the human scent detection and trailing program. While he worked with the LBPD, Big Dogs was JW's project and he would ensure its success. Ben had been a huge part of getting them to where they were today.

JW tossed in the bed. He was sweating heavily, and his breathing was rough. He was deep in a dream state and was reliving yesterday's bloody shootout. He and Ben came to Las Vegas to track down a suspect who had already killed two local prostitutes and savagely cut up their corpses. The suspect's trail brought them to the same place he was now sleeping but in another tower of the massive Ultimo resort.

In the dream, JW was in an elevator with Ben and a team of Las Vegas Metro SWAT team members. The numbers above the door moved slowly and changed to 47. As the doors opened, he restarted Addy, one part of his two-dog German Shepherd team, on the scent trail. He had two dogs that work with him, but Ares, Addy's brother, was outside in their police K9 vehicle, waiting in case he was needed. The interior of the hotel was what JW and Ben would characterize as a neighborhood trail, one that was full of the suspect's scent because he had been here several times. Addy was much better at this type of work, whereas Ares had greater endurance and his skill set was better in more open areas.

As they exited the elevator, JW passed a table in a small lobby area. He looked down and saw fingerprints on the glass top. *Oops, housekeeping missed that one.* There was a picture above the table, an artistic impression of a large white Victorian-era home with a large garden in front. They had already worked 46 floors of the north tower and the fatigue was beginning to wear on them all.

They worked their way down the hall, Addy pausing to sniff at each door. She was on scent; the suspect had been here, and the dog knew it. Finally, Addy stopped in front of a doorway and put her nose down to inhale deeply. She turned her head to look at JW and smiled at him. Bingo! Jackpot! Whatever you want to call it, this was it.

The door exploded outward, shattering into a thousand pieces. As the smoke cleared, JW was the only one left standing. Blood was everywhere, and everyone was dead, including his precious Addy. He heard movement inside the room without a door. Something was coming for him; he could hear it. He reached for his Springfield Operator in the holster attached to his right leg, but it had been blown away in the blast. The sounds in the room were getting closer, and he could hear something else, like a deep growling. His heart rate quickened, his breathing was shallow, and a cold sweat broke out on his body. Something was coming…

JW jerked awake and sat on the side of the bed. He was still exhausted; it felt like he had never been asleep. A look at the clock on the nightstand told him it was three a.m. He had been sleeping for several hours. His heart was pounding, and he was drenched with sweat. *WAIT ONE FRIGGIN MINUTE! That is not what happened! Las Vegas Metro SWAT made entry into that room, confronted the suspect, and killed him. True, Addy and he were both hurt—Addy seriously—but they were both going to be OK. Addy was still at the vet here in Vegas, but she would be fine.*

JW looked up toward the heavens and said, "OK, enough of that crap. No more dreams like that, please." That said, he needed to know about the rest of his family. Ares was on the bed, at the opposite corner, looking at his pack leader and wondering whether there was something wrong. His nose told him there were no threats, but he sensed something else. JW looked into Ares' eyes; he could see the concern there. "I'm OK, boy; you good?" Hearing his voice calmed the large dog; he put his head down and returned to rest.

Where the hell is my wife? Where is Bonnie? He moved silently to the bedroom door. Ares watched quietly, assessing whether to get up too. Finally, he decided to watch and wait; no need to rush into things.

JW came out of a short hallway into the hotel suite's living room. It was dark except for a single table lamp that was on next to a comfortable-looking chair. Here he found Bonnie, writing on a yellow legal pad, but sensing his presence, she looked up and smiled. "You're up early. You should go back to sleep. You still look exhausted."

"I will. I was just checking to see how you were."

"Oh, I started out trying to read and make myself tired, but that didn't work. I have a lot of things on my mind, so I started jotting them down."

"Anything we need to talk about?"

"Yeah, but not now. I'm still organizing my thoughts. You should go back to bed and get some more sleep." She didn't bother to tell him about the call that came in earlier. The one telling her JW and Ben needed to be downstairs at one o'clock for a press conference. She knew how he felt about the media, and informing him would not help him get any sleep. JW nodded and went back into the bedroom. Ares was rewarded with the return of his pack leader, and they were soon both sound asleep.

Bonnie North continued to write on the yellow pad. Things were changing rapidly with their dog program, which they referred to as "Big Dogs"; changing faster than she was comfortable with. When JW first introduced the idea to her, she realized it would change their lives forever.

She understood that and also knew it was something her husband needed. The day before, JW had been in the middle of an emotional crisis as both he and Addy recovered from the shooting. She had been hard on him, in the form of an intervention, and it seemed to snap him out of it. Big Dogs had great potential; if they could all hold it together, society's innocents could benefit and sleep a little better at night.

She knew that JW and others in law enforcement liked to use the sheepdog analogy. Society, the sheep, was full of people who did not recognize the threat posed to them by criminal predators. Cops, the sheepdogs, were there to watch over the sheep and protect them from the wolves that hunted them. In her mind, it was about time someone started hunting the wolves instead of just watching the herd.

She believed JW was the right person at the right time to do just that. She loved her husband dearly but also recognized his weaknesses as well as his strengths. She and JW were well matched, each compensating for what the other lacked. Bonnie North was deeply religious and she thanked God for placing JW in her life and giving them the opportunity that lay in front of them. Then, another thought occurred to her and she quickly wrote it down.

The phone rang at six a.m., waking Bonnie from a brief nap. She answered it quickly, hoping it would not wake JW.

"Excuse me, ma'am, this is Matthew, the night manager. The front desk just received a call from the veterinarian taking care of your other dog, Addy. They say the doctor came in early to examine her and she is doing well. She will be available for release at seven a.m. I can send someone over there to pick her up if you like?"

Bonnie thought for a moment. "No, she was seriously injured and I'm not sure how she will react to a stranger, but thank you. We appreciate everything you've done."

"It is our pleasure to serve you, your husband, and the other officer, Mr. Kellum. I hope it's alright that I woke you."

"Absolutely, this is great news. Thank you very much."

"You are more than welcome, ma'am. Also, we have temporarily closed the atrium here at the Ultimo to provide a quiet place for your dogs to relieve themselves."

Bonnie had to suppress a laugh. When the owner of the Ultimo, Maddox Christensen, said he would extend every courtesy to them, he meant it. "Thank you again for that. Can you please have my husband's car brought around to the front so we can go get Addy?"

"Certainly, ma'am, and if there is anything else we can do, please do not hesitate to ask."

Bonnie got up from the chair and quietly checked on JW and Ares. They were both asleep, which was good. They needed to rest. She returned to the living room, took out her phone, and dialed Ben's cell phone.

"Ben? This is Bonnie. Can you please open the common door between the suites? I need to talk to you."

Ben Kellum was startled out of a deep sleep but was still awake enough to understand Bonnie and detect a sense of urgency in her voice. *What on earth had gone wrong now?* He moved quickly to the door, and as he opened it, he was greeted by Bonnie's smiling face.

"Ben, the vet called. Addy will be ready for release at 0700. Your call: Do you want to stay here and keep an eye on JW, or go and bring her back here?"

Ben thought for a moment and considered asking her why JW's rest was more important than his. But that would most likely set her off, and after seeing her yesterday, he was not ready for that.

"I'll get Addy. I know where the animal hospital is and most of the staff there."

"Great! Oh, and you'll love this—the Ultimo has reserved the atrium for the dogs' use while we are here."

Ben laughed and said, "Well, first class all the way. I was hoping to get out of here today."

"Probably not gonna happen. We have a press conference at 1300 hours. The Tahoe is out front. If you bring both of the go bags you packed back to the room, I'll see about getting your uniforms pressed."

"Press conference? We were kind of hoping to slip out of town quietly. JW is not going to like the idea of a press conference. Has anyone told Long Beach PD about that?"

"I assume they have since it was Chief Estrada who called me late last night and told me. He'll be there, so I guess it's OK for you guys to be there."

Ben said goodbye and went back into his room. He changed clothes quickly, went downstairs to get the Tahoe, and left to pick up Addy. She was happy to see him and wagged her tail excitedly. He thanked the veterinary staff for taking good care of her and then returned to the Ultimo. It had only taken him an hour to pick up the dog, including travel time. He knocked lightly on the door of the North's room. When Bonnie answered, Addy almost knocked her over in excitement.

Ben said, "Uh oh, she's not supposed to get too excited or rambunctious." He laughed as if it were a joke.

Bonnie scowled at him. "Yeah, right. Don't tell me; tell her."

Ben eased the door shut and went back to grab another hour or two of sleep. Addy was so excited to see Bonnie; she literally licked her face clean. Then, suddenly, she lifted her head and caught some scent. Her nails clicked on the floor as Addy walked toward the bedroom and pushed the door open. She nuzzled her brother for a moment and then jumped up on the bed and snuggled into her usual spot against JW's lower leg. He must have sensed her presence as he let out a quiet sigh. Addy burrowed in deeper and was asleep in moments.

2

JW was roused from a deep sleep by his wife's voice saying, "Reveille, Reveille!" He scowled at Bonnie and both dogs looked at her like she was out of her mind. "What the hell is this all about?"

"Darling dearest, you and the dogs need to get up. You need to shower, and I need to feed and break them, and then we need to get breakfast. We have a press conference in three hours."

"Press conference? Who signed me up for a press conference?" JW did not care for the media, although he recognized they served an essential role in society. If only they could stick to the facts instead of their agendas.

"That would be the chief of the Long Beach Police Department."

"Huh? Why is the chief ordering me to a press conference? I thought the idea was to come into town quietly and then leave. You know, like the Lone Ranger. 'Hi-Yo Silver! Away!' What happened to 'away?'"

"Well, all that went down the drain when you and Addy got hurt. Now you guys are part of the story. I've been told there are now Las Vegas Metro officers downstairs to ensure we are not disturbed by the media. It's probably better if we go to the press conference, answer a few questions, and then they will leave us alone."

JW nodded, acknowledging the logic of what Bonnie said. "Well, at least it appears we made some friends here. I can't believe how this place is taking care of us." JW raised his arms, indicating he was talking about the Ultimo.

"Mr. Christensen is a big fan of yours. He is very interested in Big Dogs. I think you should spend some time with him cultivating a relationship."

"I like the man, Bon, but you know me, I'm no politician. Maybe you should handle that. Wait, what do you mean, 'he is very interested' in us?"

"He flew to Long Beach to pick me up and bring me here, and we had a chance to talk on the flight. He is interested in potentially supporting the program as we need it. But I know he wants to speak with you in more detail before he makes that kind of commitment. I am more than happy to take the lead on this, but you will have to put some time in too. I spent a lot of last night thinking about this—Big Dogs is going to take off. This deal in Vegas will be huge, so a little media exposure might work in our favor. However, our tiny little enterprise will soon overwhelm us and we need to prepare for that."

Bonnie continued, "Look, I know we are OK with money. But we are going to need more dogs. We're going to need more space. We need to get a commitment from Ben as to whether he will sign on when he retires, and he may not be enough. That said, here is what concerns me: there will always be more demand for your services than you can meet. We need to figure out a way to keep this under control so you are not trailing every criminal in America. The FBI will come knocking now that this is a proven concept. You were smart when you talked to Long Beach PD and told them we would pay for the entire program. We need to be able to tell that to the Feds too because they're gonna want to own you—to control you."

"You know I was damn lucky when God put you in my life. You are thinking so far ahead of me on this, and you know what? You're right. And I guess my concern with Mr. Christensen is, what does he want? My first impression of him is very favorable. Still, you know me, I'm always suspicious of people wanting to do things for me for no reason. I know that can be a failing, but it also has served me well over the years. So, I will have to spend time with Christensen and get a better feel for him and his motivations. And as for the FBI or any federal money for that matter, there are always strings attached. So, what do you see that I'm not? Where are we going to spend so much money?"

"I think we are going to have to move. I've mentioned this before, but when I look at what we're doing and how we will meet the anticipated demand, we will need a lot more space. I don't think there's anything in Southern California that will meet our needs. I could be wrong, and we will have to spend a lot of time discussing what our needs are, but I don't think I'm wrong. If anything, I may be underestimating things."

"OK, I see where you're going. I haven't thought this far ahead. My focus has been on getting the dogs, training them, and proving the concept. This is kind of embarrassing, but I hadn't even considered that we might be successful. As this takes off, we'll also need a lot more people just to keep this thing moving."

"Yeah, as I said, this will require a long discussion. I think I'll fly back to Long Beach when we leave. You can use the time on the road with Ben to discuss this and see where he stands. So, grab a shower and get dressed. I'll take the dogs down to the atrium and give them a break. I need some food before I fall flat on my face."

JW nodded, but before leaving, he walked to his wife and hugged her. "Thank you. I know you probably think I'm crazy, but I appreciate you standing by me in this."

Bonnie hugged him with all her heart. "Oh, I know you're crazy, but that's one of the many things I love about you."

JW was dressed and ready when Bonnie returned with the dogs. They settled the dogs in and quickly left the room, both hungry. Ben met them at the elevator. As they arrived on the first floor, they were met by the concierge. The security officers watching the video cameras must have seen the group boarding the elevator and reported they were on the way.

"Good morning, everyone. Looking at you, I would guess you are in search of food. There are several nice restaurants here at your disposal. If you can tell me your preference, I would be honored to make the arrangements for you."

JW looked at Bonnie and Ben and said, "Thank you, sir. You're right; we are all hungry, but we are on a tight timeline, and something quick and easy is what we are looking for. Is there something along the lines of a nice buffet?"

"I have the perfect place for you. Please follow me."

The group was escorted to one of the nicest buffets they had ever seen. When they arrived, the concierge spoke quietly to the maître de. He turned to the group and said, "If you give us just a moment, we will arrange a private table for you."

JW frowned, "That's not necessary. I have no issues with sitting with other people. There's nothing special about us."

The concierge looked like he disagreed with this statement but arranged for them to be seated. JW wandered with Bonnie, looking at the various serving stations and planning his meal. Finally, he broke away and started gathering eggs, sausage, and fruit. He arrived at their table at the same time as Ben. Ben had most of the same food as JW and said, "Looks like we have similar tastes in food. This place has everything. I almost couldn't decide what to eat. Where's Bonnie? Should we wait for her to come back?"

"Bonnie may take fifteen minutes to decide and select the exact same meal as you. Before she can choose, she needs to see everything there is. So, go ahead and eat. We'll be on our second plates before she comes back." With that, they began shoveling food in.

After breakfast, they returned to their rooms to change for the press conference. They exited their rooms, along with Ares and Addy, thirty minutes later. They arrived early at one of the largest meeting rooms JW had ever seen. Their intention was to get the lay of the land before all the VIPs arrived. They had picked up two security guards from the hotel as an escort, so they were not concerned that the media would bother them. The camera operators were also there early, but they were busy setting up microphones and doing tests of their equipment.

They waited and soon were greeted by Maddox Christensen.

"Good afternoon, one and all. Thank you for coming. I appreciate that you may not enjoy these types of things, but they are our lifeblood. I spoke with Las Vegas Sheriff Carroll, who mentioned he wanted to hold a press conference to 'wrap this all up and put a bow on it.' I offered up this place in the spirit of cooperation. Of course, I have my own reasons. I have an important announcement. Closure is important, you know. Anyway, I would love to invite you to have dinner with me tonight at Belle Vue. I believe we have much to talk about."

Maddox hustled off to discuss things with his staff just as Long Beach Police Department Chief Michael Estrada walked into the room with his chief of staff and public information officer. The chief spotted them in the almost empty room and walked their way.

As he approached, JW noticed a quick glance from the chief at their field uniforms. JW quickly guessed what that was about and said, "Sorry about the uniforms, Chief, this is all we had. We didn't bring our dress uniforms."

Chief Estrada smiled and then hugged North.

"No worries, JW. Congratulations on another great job. Just one request—can you please do these ops without getting yourself or one of these beautiful dogs hurt?"

He smiled as if this was a joke, but to JW, it was a bit too close to home. He was still stinging over Addy's injury.

The chief handed JW a piece of paper and said, "We pulled some information from the proposal you brought me when we started all of this. The PIO put this together for the media, so you don't have to stand up there and try to explain this to them." The PIO referred to the Public Information Officer.

JW started reading it and immediately saw some errors.

"Chief, do you mind if I ask Ben to work with the PIO on this? I see a couple of minor changes I think we should make. I see the value in this, but I don't want to give away all of our secrets yet."

The chief nodded his approval, and JW handed the note to Ben. He asked one of the security guards about a business center. The guard said there was one, but it would be more private if they went to the administrative offices. Ben, the guard, and the PIO all left to work on the document.

As the group walked away, JW turned back to the chief and said, "Sir, I understand your concerns about officer safety and the program. Getting people hurt is not what I had in mind when we started this. That said, you know law enforcement is a dangerous business. I can tell you the trailing part worked just like we thought it would, possibly better. The ad hoc team we put together with Las Vegas Metro SWAT protected us, and the vest we purchased for the dog did its job. The one person we had a problem with was the suspect. Unfortunately, he got a vote in all this too. Everything I've read on these types of suspects, serial killers, says most of them will not stand up to an armed officer. They typically don't fight; they run or surrender. Apparently, this guy didn't read the same books I did. There will always be exceptions, and we must prepare for the unknown."

The Chief looked down for a moment, deep in thought. "First of all, great work. I am proud of what you and Ben have accomplished." He turned to Bonnie and said, "You too, Bonnie. I know this can't be easy for you, and I also know you are the person who runs all of this behind the scenes. You all have done a great job on this." He turned back to JW, "How about this, can you guys take an extra day here and hold a debrief session with their SWAT guys? Maybe try to think of new ways to improve the tactics. We know the trailing component works, but we have to find a way to do that without getting others hurt."

"That, sir, is an excellent idea. I was thinking of something along those lines, but I like the idea of getting the whole team together. These guys are outstanding, and I developed a bit of a relationship with their Lieutenant, Tak Van Geffin. I think he would be agreeable."

"Well, the sheriff is a friend of mine from the NA. If you need me to grease the skids, let me know."

The NA referred to the FBI National Academy, a ten-week leadership course held in Quantico, Virginia. This international program provided valuable training and education to law enforcement managers. Still, perhaps most importantly, it created lifetime friendships between agencies and the FBI.

As Chief Estrada and JW finished their conversation, the doors to the room opened and a large contingent of Las Vegas Metro officers and the sheriff entered. JW spotted Tak and went over to him.

"Hey, Tak, how are you and your guys doing?"

"We're all good; how about you and your dog?"

"We'll be fine." JW bent down to pet Addy on the head. "Tak, I know you guys are busy, but it would be a great help to Ben and me if we could have a debrief with your guys. Nothing major, but this is the first time we have deployed outside Long Beach and with a tactical team. Everything went well, but I want to have outside input on how we can do things better."

"I was thinking the same thing. The team has already done a 'hot wash' and you guys came up a lot. I think there would be a lot of value to sitting down and going over the trailing work specifically. The sheriff mentioned that he was really impressed with what you guys did and that he might be interested in starting a similar program here. I think he will mention it to your chief, so I wanted to give you a heads up. With that in mind, I'd like to invite some of the K9 supervisors to the meeting to sit in as observers."

JW nodded as he listened to Tak. *Maybe, but I might have someone else in mind.*

3

As the room began to fill for the press conference, Ben and the PIO returned from rewriting the news release. JW scanned it and nodded his approval. He backed up and leaned against a wall, dropping into deep thought as to how he got here.

It was amazing how much time you could cover in a short daydream. JW thought of the night he was shot, the long hours of therapy, and the work with Ares and Addy. Then, he was jerked out of the dream by Bonnie, who elbowed him back to reality.

"Hey, cowboy, you here with anyone?"

"Well, my wife is around here somewhere, so you should probably be careful."

"You mean to tell me you found a woman who would marry you?"

"Yeah, I guess I'm the luckiest guy alive."

Shifting gears, "You figure out what you're gonna say yet?" asked Bonnie.

"Not a clue."

"Well, maybe you should think about that instead of staring at that reporter's butt," and then she walked off.

JW focused his eyes and saw that he was looking directly at the back of a female reporter. "Hey, wait, Bonnie, I wasn't looking at her." He did recognize her, though—she worked for FOX News. He remembered her from several news stories he had seen on television.

As JW started to go after Bonnie, the press conference started. JW noticed an empty seat at the speakers' table with his name on a placard. He moved quickly and sat down while the room settled.

The Las Vegas Metro public information officer opened the meeting with thanks and some quick introductions. Next, Sheriff Carroll provided some background information about the incident and a brief synopsis of everyone's actions leading up to the shooting of the suspect. He also summarized the injuries to everyone, including JW and Addy.

JW learned that the one SWAT officer who was shot received minor injuries to his right arm and had already been released from the hospital. He was lucky; his ballistic vest had taken most of the hit from the double-aught buck in the suspect's shotgun. The sheriff raised the vest from a table to display the damage.

JW was impressed with the presentation. The sheriff did a great job of putting it all together. At the conclusion, he reminded the media that the event, specifically the shooting, was still under investigation.

Maddox Christensen gave a very general statement. No one associated with the Ultimo had any knowledge of the suspect or his actions. He did say that the 47th floor of the North tower would be closed until further notice. There would be no access to the crime scene except for law enforcement. JW could tell that Christensen was comfortable in front of the cameras, but not with this subject. He wanted to get the name Ultimo out of the media as soon as possible.

A local reporter asked JW, "What is the condition of the injured dog?" It was the one question left unanswered on the handout Ben had prepared.

Nodding toward Addy in the back with his wife, he said, "Addy is doing well after undergoing lifesaving surgery. I want to take this opportunity to thank the staff of Las Vegas Pet Emergency and Las Vegas SWAT team member Michael Perea, who provided first aid to Addy that allowed us to get her to the vet."

As the press conference started to break up, the reporters rushed to the front of the room to try and get individual interviews. Seeing that no one was interested in talking to him and very thankful for it, JW moved to the back of the room to get together with Bonnie and Ben. As he arrived, he was intercepted by the reporter he had spotted earlier. She was even more attractive in person, with beautiful blonde hair, piercing blue eyes, and a smile that had probably melted hearts her entire life.

She walked up to JW and said, "Hi, my name is Melanie Hitchens. I'm with FOX News."

JW nodded and said, "I recognize you from TV." Then, realizing he could help dig himself out of the hole he was in earlier, he added, "This is my wife, Bonnie, and my partner Ben Kellum."

Melanie smiled and shook their hands. She then turned to a fit-looking man that JW assumed was with her news crew and said, "This is my husband, Kyle."

JW felt Bonnie relax and said, "A pleasure to meet you both." He nodded at the throng of reporters clamoring for the attention of the sheriff, Tak, and the others and said, "Seems like you're missing the story, Melanie."

"No, I think the real story is right in front of me. I love dogs. May I pet them?" As she kneeled to pay attention to Addy, she asked, "Could I ask you some questions about what you do with the dogs and how you found the killer?"

"Sure, but I have a question for you first. How do you get to bring your husband along on the job?"

She laughed. "Oh, Kyle's on leave from his unit, but then I could ask you the same question."

"Trust me, I think she would rather not have come to Vegas this time." The reporter looked confused, so JW continued, "She wouldn't be here if Addy and I hadn't been injured. But truth be told, Addy is her dog, and I'm not sure if she would have come if it was just me."

Bonnie glared at JW and said, "You'll have to excuse JW. He sometimes says things that make no sense to the rest of us."

Melanie laughed again. "Well, I don't want to get myself into trouble, but I'm kind of familiar with that. Now, if I could ask just a couple of questions, I'm sure you guys want to get out of here."

JW nodded. "Sure thing."

"OK, first off, can you explain in simple terms how the dogs can follow someone."

"The dogs have a much more highly-developed sense of smell than we do. They smell things we don't know are there and they can break down complex smells into their elements. As an example, think apple pie. When a dog smells apple pie, he smells flour, sugar, cinnamon, apples, and whatever else is there. Plus, he smells something delicious, and that is the apple pie itself."

"OK, that makes sense, but what are they following?"

JW drew a deep breath, "We believe they are tracking human scent. Every person is constantly shedding skin cells from their body. These cells have an odor, which we believe is as unique as a fingerprint. The dog is given a scent to start, and they follow that odor until they reach an end. Sometimes that is the suspect, but sometimes things intervene, making it impossible to continue."

"Can you give me an example of something that would make it impossible to continue?"

"Sure. Scent can deteriorate over time. Heat, rain, and high winds can all have an effect. The scent seems to last longer in grass or other natural terrain but can also be detected on artificial surfaces."

"So, you can follow a suspect on streets and sidewalks?"

"Yes, that's what we did here in Las Vegas; we followed the suspect over a parking lot, sidewalks, a couple of escalators, more sidewalks, and finally, into the Ultimo. We trailed him to his room on the 47th floor of the North Tower where he opened fire on us through his door."

"But the murder was the day before. How could a dog do that? How long was the trail?" she asked, quickly picking up JW's terminology.

"The trail was a little over a mile. As to how, that goes back to that sensitive nose the dog has and their ability to use it to find what we want them to look for. Law enforcement uses dogs to find drugs, explosives, and hiding suspects. They can also use them to trail suspects."

"But how do you *know* the dog can do this? Isn't there a chance the dog will follow the wrong person?" She asked this question with particular emphasis on the word know as if she were incredulous at the very idea that law enforcement could arrest someone because a dog said so.

The reporter's husband, Kyle, stepped forward and lightly touched her elbow. He could sense the conversation might get out of control. He looked JW in the eye to assess his emotions.

JW made eye contact with Kyle and decided he liked him. He could sense they both had some things in common—they were protectors.

"No worries. We're used to people doubting what we do. I actually expect it. We don't know if the dog is correct, to answer your question. Although we use science to help determine reliability, this is just as much an art. We have worked with research teams from universities in double-blind studies to develop science that corroborates what we are doing."

"OK, but how can you be sure?"

"You are never one hundred percent sure. The courts are never going to convict based on scent evidence alone. You do your work and then turn the results over to an investigator. Scent evidence can point an investigation in a direction or provide focus on a particular area. Still, it never proves someone is guilty of a crime. You must see the dogs work to understand, to become a believer."

Melanie's face lit up at this last statement. "Would that be possible? Could I observe the dogs working; watch them run a trail?"

JW considered the question for a moment and wondered what her motivation was. Was she a seeker of truth, or was she looking to make a name for herself? He took a moment and asked himself, *If you believe in this, what do you have to hide? If it won't stand up to some questions from the media, how will you handle the pressure of a courtroom?* Deep down, JW just didn't trust the media. He had been to too many incidents where he wondered if he'd been at the same scene when he later saw the coverage. It seemed to him that some members of the fourth estate had no difficulty using the public trust for their own agenda. The question was, who was Melanie Hitchens?

"I'm sure we can work something out down the line. Addy is on the mend right now and we need to get these dogs home."

That evening the Norths and the Kellums met with Maddox Christensen in a private dining room. Earlier in the day, Bonnie had suggested to Ben that he have his wife, Lucy, catch a flight to Las Vegas and join them. She knew Ben had been talking with her on the phone, but she also knew Lucy was reluctant to have Ben participate in the program in the future. Bonnie felt that bringing Lucy here to enjoy some of the rewards of all the hard work might change her mind.

JW had ordered a steak and was chewing quietly. *This is the best steak I have ever had.* The rest of the group was also quietly eating, although Bonnie and Lucy occasionally said something to one another. After refilling their wine glasses, their waiter walked away. Maddox asked, "So, JW, what are your plans for your program?"

JW paused, thinking about how to answer. "Well, I think we need to hear from the FBI and learn their intentions before we can go further. They have shown interest, and I believe this trail qualifies as 'the big one' that Special Agent Gaurdia is looking for. But they haven't contacted us yet."

Bonnie chimed in with, "JW, we need to consider what we're going to do when they call. You know as well as I do that Lauralynn Gaurdia wants access to your dogs. Look what you accomplished here in Las Vegas. Can you imagine how many more poor girls that guy would have killed before someone got lucky and stumbled onto him? She's going to call; I know it."

Ben was now drawn into the conversation. "Bonnie, what do you mean, 'what are we going to do when the FBI calls?' I thought that's why we have been busting our butts for almost a year."

"OK, I know JW will think I'm getting ahead of myself, but thinking and planning is part of my job in all this." Bonnie paused to make sure everyone was listening. JW leaned back in his chair and gave her the go-ahead nod. "I believe this will be big—much bigger than we are prepared for. I chatted with Dr. Gaurdia at the certification party for Ares in Long Beach. She didn't want to give me all the details, but I got the impression the FBI may be changing direction on how they deal with these types of cases."

"I'm not sure I follow what you mean, Bonnie," said Christensen.

Bonnie mentally thanked him for the soft toss question. "When we spoke, Dr. Gaurdia mentioned a new approach. She didn't get into specifics about what they were doing.

Still, it involves computers and a more aggressive approach to assisting police departments with these types of crimes. She said, historically, they have had a more laid-back approach and wait for a call before becoming involved. She believed by using this new technology, they might be able to identify a serial killer before local law enforcement is even aware."

JW listened quietly. *Hmmm, she knows more about this than I do.*

"OK, Bonnie," Ben interjected, "back to the original question. What more do we need to do?"

"I don't think you guys," looking at JW and Ben, "need to do anything more or different. You did a great job with Ares and Addy. What I'm talking about is our ability to meet the demand. Right now, it is just two guys and two dogs against all the bad guys in the world. We need a place where we can have more dogs and support staff with the ability to train new dogs and handlers. We need a big place, but it has to be in an area where we can train in the different environments you two have told me about: rural, urban, neighborhoods."

JW decided it was his turn to chime in. "OK, Bonnie. Where is the new world headquarters of Big Dogs going to be?"

"I don't know, JW. That is something we need to work on."

Ben looked down at the table. His face showed disappointment and sadness. When he raised his eyes to Bonnie, she could tell he was in pain. He looked at his wife, Lucy, and said, "I don't know, Bonnie. We're pretty tied to Southern California with our kids and family."

Bonnie smiled at Ben and said, "Oh, I know that, Ben. Lucy and I talked about that already. I haven't completely talked this through with JW or figured it all out. Still, as I see it, you would become a satellite to the headquarters and be responsible for callouts in California and maybe Nevada.

That way you wouldn't have to travel too much. I don't like to rush big decisions, but you and Lucy need to talk and decide soon, OK?"

"Lucy and I will sit down and discuss this as soon as we get home. How does a week sound for an answer?"

Maddox Christensen took this opportunity to make his offer. "This all sounds very expensive. Now, I know you have substantial resources of your own, but I would like to offer to help with the financing of this venture."

JW knew this was his cue. "Mr. Christensen, I don't want to seem ungrateful. But why?"

"Why? My answer to your simple question is a bit complex. First of all, gratitude. What you did here at the Ultimo was magnificent. By locating the killer, you saved me from a substantial financial loss. A loss of far greater value than I believe will be needed to support your cause.

"The second part is more personal. Because I have properties all over the world, I have had the opportunity to see a great deal of the victimization of humanity. I am aware of an evil that feeds upon the innocent and I feel an obligation to help you to eliminate that in whatever way I can. Since we are in Las Vegas, I will use a gambling analogy. 'I am all in.'"

4

The drive home allowed JW and Ben to discuss the trip's events, including their plans for the future. Ares and Addy slept quietly in the back of the Tahoe. Bonnie and Lucy flew back to Long Beach on Maddox Christensen's private jet. *All in is, after all, all in.*

The meeting with Las Vegas Metro SWAT went well. The team appreciated the work done by all and was apologetic for JW's and Addy's injuries. JW told them that was appreciated but unnecessary. "It's a dangerous job, and sometimes the good guys get hurt. SWAT provided some helpful suggestions on equipment and tactics, but the suspect controlled the end game."

"I saw you talking with Officer Perea at the debrief. What was that about?" asked Ben.

"You remember Tak saying their sheriff wanted to possibly do something similar to what we do?"

"Yeah, sure."

"And do you remember him mentioning that their K9 division would have some handlers who might be interested?"

"I do, but I was watching those guys. They didn't seem all that interested."

"I know, they didn't. Once the handlers realized how much work was involved, I think they decided they were having too much fun with a patrol dog. Anyway, even I can take a hint, so I moved on to plan B."

"Plan B?"

"Yep, you know I always have a backup, right?"

"Sure, you usually have a backup to the backup and then something else in reserve."

"That's what I was talking to Perea about. Ben, I owe that guy. He saved Addy, plain and simple. I think he would be a good addition to the team and I told him so. I asked him if he was interested."

"And what did he say?"

"I gave him a lot to think about. I don't know. He's young, and he loves the SWAT thing. I get it; it's fun, it's sexy. But there is nothing like working a dog and having him trail right to a suspect. I was about a mile high when we found that guy… right until the door blew up and Addy was hit."

"Yeah, that scared the crap out of me," said Ben, looking over his shoulder at Addy in the rear. "And you scared me to death, little girl."

"Anyway, Perea said he would think about it. I couldn't get a read on him one way or the other. Bottom line, I think we'll be driving to Las Vegas occasionally."

Ben thought for a moment and added, "Well, at least the next time, we should receive a more friendly reception. The SWAT guys seemed to appreciate what we can do for them."

"How do you feel about our discussion last night, Ben?"

"Part of me wants to jump on board without even thinking. Do you realize how cool this could be?" Answering his own question, he continued. "It could be incredible. But, of course, that scares me. Am I reading too much into this? What if we fail? I mean, there is so much to think about. AND I need to really talk this over with Lucy. If she isn't behind it, all my enthusiasm means nothing. But I gotta admit, I really want to do it."

JW reached across, patted his friend on the shoulder, and smiled.

Almost two thousand miles away, John Joseph Flannery, the Shadow, was just finishing another night at work. After shooting Lieutenant North, the Shadow had relocated from Long Beach in a rush. Attacking a police officer tended to wear out one's welcome in any community. Long Beach was like a kicked-over hornet's nest after the shooting.

He had been a serial rapist, but that had all changed on the road to Kentucky. At a rest stop in Wyoming, he had raped and murdered a young woman and then dumped her body in the North Platte River. He considered it the culmination of his work to date, as he had grown less satisfied with the results of each rape. While he found the act satisfying, it lacked something. As he neared his destination of Bowling Green, he discovered what was missing.

The Shadow was a planner. He spent hours upon hours doing reconnaissance of his potential victims. He wanted to know everything about them. He liked to plan his hunts to create maximum satisfaction for himself. He didn't care about the victim at all. All he wanted from them was their terror, submission, and soul. He hadn't realized how satisfying killing was. To him, he was harvesting their essence for his personal pleasure. Planning his next hunt heightened and focused his desire. The act itself was merely the conclusion of it all. A release of sorts would begin the process over and over.

The Shadow knew he needed to make changes when he arrived in Bowling Green. If he started out using the same method of operation that he used in Long Beach, he would draw too much law enforcement attention. He wanted to change some things to disguise who he was but also retain his core identity. After all, he was The Shadow. He moved through the darkness and claimed his prey. No one knew who he was—no one could touch him.

Upon first arriving in Kentucky, the Shadow found a place to live near a restaurant where he could scout for future victims. Next, he got a job at a shipping railyard as an overnight security guard. He preferred to work in the dark. But this type of geography was utterly foreign to him. Things were more spread out and green. He could approach homes under concealment, which was a big advantage, but he needed more mobility.

Sitting in his new favorite restaurant, having breakfast, and reading the local paper, he came across an opportunity. There was an ad in the Daily News for an overnight delivery man. If hired, he would deliver parts to auto repair shops all over the area. He called and scheduled an interview. This could be perfect.

Floyd Hansen, the Truck Stop Killer (TSK), was a completely different personality. Unlike the Shadow, the TSK did not want sex with his victims. There was no way he could lower himself to that. Merely pretending to be interested in sex with them turned his stomach. He did not want to dominate these women; he saw them as a blight upon the land that needed to be eliminated. This was his calling. He had stopped for the night in a small rest area near Ruston, Louisiana and was reading his bible. Proverbs 23 said, "For a prostitute is like a deep pit; a harlot is like a narrow well. Indeed, she lies in wait like a robber and increases the unfaithful among men." Fortunately for him, this rest area seemed to have no prostitutes.

Although the TSK had no issue killing whores, he found it stressful. He understood that no one would comprehend his rationale if he was caught. They would think he was crazy. Society had, on some level, accepted prostitution. There were popular movies where the hooker was made to be sympathetic. TSK did not see it that way; they were a scourge and God had given him the responsibility to cleanse the earth.

Floyd was troubled by the last whore he had killed, Sunnie something or other. It was what she had said at the very end, about burning in hell. He read through his family bible, looking for answers. Finally, he found them in Matthew 13:50—"and will throw them into the furnace of fire; in that place, there will be weeping and gnashing of teeth." This verse gave him some peace. He now understood what he had known all along. He was the Lord's servant, not a minion of Satan. The devil had possessed the woman's soul in her final moments and she had tried to deceive him. Satan's minions were all deceivers and must be smiteth, just like the Lord had done in the land of Egypt.

TSK drifted off to sleep, humming the old rock and roll song, "Fire," by The Crazy World of Arthur Brown. Feeling renewed by the Lord, tomorrow he would find another Jezebel and smite her from the land.

5

After arriving home in Long Beach, JW unloaded his vehicle and wished Ben well in his discussions with his wife. Inside, he was smiling. He knew Bonnie had been talking to her the whole time she was in Las Vegas with them and on the trip home on Maddox Christensen's private jet. After getting Ares and Addy fed and everyone settled in, JW went to find Bonnie. As usual, she was seated in her office, but the door was blocked by sleeping dogs. "You know, I'm starting to take this personally."

Bonnie turned from her computer screen and said, "What? Oh, the dogs. They're just doing what dogs do, sleep wherever they want and block the door. Is that a problem? I'm sure they're happy to return to their normal home life after the bright lights and big city of Las Vegas."

"Well, I was going to come in and say 'hi,' maybe get a 'welcome home' kiss."

"Oh yeah, welcome home, Honey! Just give me a second to shut down the computer. After that, we should probably debrief what happened in Vegas, especially my conversations with Lucy."

"That sounds excellent. I'm going to make some coffee. Would you like some?"

"Yes, decaf, please."

"Decaf? What's the point? You might as well have a glass of water." JW walked down the hall to the kitchen, nearly tripping over the dogs as he went. "Come on, dogs. I'm too tired to negotiate a dogstacle course." The dogs, of course, not understanding what JW said, ignored him and went back to sleep.

When Bonnie entered the dining room, JW handed her a cup of decaf coffee and leaned back in his chair to await Bonnie's presentation.

"OK," she said, glancing at the bandage on his forearm. "First things first. Can you possibly do your job without getting shot? This is getting a little stressful here. I mean, I know I signed up for this, but come on. Do you have to get hurt every time? Not to mention Addy! Sheesh!"

"I know. But it's not like we tried to get hurt. The guy shot us through the door. Who knew the guy was going to commit suicide by cop?"

"I understand, JW; I really do. It just makes it hard for me to send you and the dogs out on trails with me here at home, waiting for the chief to show up on my front porch. When I opened the door and Chief Estrada was standing there, I almost had a heart attack. I just want you to be sensitive to the anxiety this causes me."

"Sensitive? You know me, Honey, I am all about the sensitivity. As a matter of fact, the guys all call me 'Mr. Sensitive.'"

"Ha! What guys? Yes, I know, you don't do sensitive. Just try to be conscious of how this makes me feel. Please."

"I understand, Bonnie, I really do. But you need to know that police work is a dangerous profession. I am always working to be safe. That was drummed into my head from the first day of the academy. Suppose you screwed up on a training scenario. In that case, you were doing pushups if you were lucky and writing a ten-page memo on officer safety if you weren't. When I graduated and went into field training, it was more of the same, except it was real. Someone was watching you—every minute. If you screwed up, their safety was in jeopardy too. Of all the things I learned, what every cop learns, officer safety is the single most important thing. You can't serve the public if you are injured. You do no one any good if you get hurt."

"I know all that. So, what is it you're trying to tell me?"

"We've had this discussion before. It's simple—I can't do this without you. I can't chase bad guys unless I know you're behind me. So, if what happened in Vegas has made you change your mind, you need to let me know. Then, I will drop the project, and you, the dogs, and I will learn to live the quiet life."

"Does that mean you'll be home more often? You'll be around to help me do things?"

"Yep."

"Oh, hell no! I love you dearly, JW, but I don't know if I can take that. You and the dogs go play and have a good time. Drop me a line now and then. Have lots of fun. Just please be safe."

They both laughed. JW knew, or at least he hoped, that she was kidding. He understood the importance of these difficult discussions even if, in the end, there was no perfect solution to their problem. *Police work was dangerous; sometimes, cops died in the line of duty. Sometimes police dogs did too. All you can do is use sound tactics and learn from the mistakes of others.*

JW decided to slightly change the subject. "You weren't at the Las Vegas Metro SWAT debrief, but one of the recommendations was for us to get better body armor. They said the stuff we used for the dogs was good; it's the same equipment their dog guys use on their K9s. They were polite about our soft armor, but basically, they thought it was a joke. They said we needed to look at a more tactical body armor, something like what the SWAT teams or the military use. They gave me some contact information for a company in Arizona that makes a new lightweight armor that might be better suited to our work."

"That sounds expensive, not that you're not worth it," she said with a smile and a wink.

"Not as much as you would imagine. Hey, wait a minute. What do you mean, 'not that I'm not worth it?'"

"Oh, you know I'm teasing you. What is it you like to say? 'Sometimes you have to laugh or you'll cry.'"

"Yeah, yeah. It's just like you to use my own words against me. So, how did things go with Lucy?"

She smiled at JW. "Oh, she had a wonderful time in Vegas. I won't give you the 'what happens in Vegas stays in Vegas excuse,' but some things should stay between just us girls."

"You know, if I used that excuse, it wouldn't stand up. You wouldn't let me get away with that."

"Nope."

"OK. Fine. At least tell me how Lucy feels about the program and Ben's future involvement."

"Oh, we had that all worked out before we left Long Beach. Do you remember the party you abandoned me at? You know, the barbeque?"

"How could I forget? I spent hours getting those ribs ready for the smoker."

"Oh, and they were incredible. Too bad you weren't here to enjoy them with us."

"What in God's name are you talking about? Could you just please say what you have to say?"

"Well, sure I can if you would just sit back, be quiet, and listen for a minute. And you might want to be careful about taking the Lord's name in vain. You and Ben will need all the help you can get."

"Wait, what? Will you quit screwing with me?"

"Just giving back what you have been giving me all these years."

"That's not right. I just drove in from Vegas. I'm exhausted."

"Oh, poor JW."

JW stood as if to leave and glared at Bonnie.

"Sit down, JW; I've had my fun."

JW returned to his seat and continued to stare.

"Lucy and I were having a long talk before you guys left. I just about had her convinced, and boom, you guys had to run off."

Sensing JW was about to interrupt, she pointed at him and pulled her fingers across her lips in a zipping motion.

"I know you guys got the call you've been waiting for. But here is something you and Ben are terrible at—understanding how the ones left behind feel. I know you guys get all excited and want to run off and do your duty while the rest of us sit at home and worry. It doesn't take much; we just need a couple of quick words before you leave."

JW nodded his understanding but didn't say anything as he had been instructed to keep quiet. Bonnie also nodded, indicating they had reached a silent agreement.

"OK, we went through all that because I had her pretty much sold when you two ran out the door; I was back to square one. That feeling of being abandoned is what she had when Ben was doing this the last time. But then she didn't have a friend she could talk to about it. A friend she can call in the middle of the night and voice her frustrations and loneliness. Because, frankly, you two guys suck at sharing your feelings or listening."

"Is it my turn to talk now?"

Bonnie nodded.

"I don't know about Ben because guys don't share their feelings with other guys. I guess maybe some do, but I know I don't. You can call that a failing if you want, but I simply view it as how I am. There are things I am good at, and others, not so much. I wish I could be everything you want me to be, but I can only be me."

"Oh, JW, you know I love you just the way you are. Let me try a different way to explain this. You started this project, but as it has grown, you needed someone to take point and do the things you hate to do. Those are also things I like to do. While you enjoy taking the dogs and having them find bad guys, I enjoy the idea of putting together the organization and making it support what you're doing."

"And I appreciate the hell out of that. You know I do. Without you, this whole thing never gets past the idea stage."

"Yep, I know. Somehow, through this program's metamorphosis, I ended up in charge. If you're OK with that, I am too. You asked me to help get Lucy involved, and I almost had her. Now, bringing her to Vegas was huge. I wish I had thought of it sooner and had her come with me when I flew over. At that point, I was just not thinking clearly.

"Once she arrived at the Ultimo, made it to the nice suite, had a few good meals with first-class service, she started to come back. I'm having a hard time putting this into words for you. When you and Ben find a suspect, it's a big deal to you. Well, it's a big deal for us too. But while you two high-five and move on, we like something a little nicer. Maybe we get dressed up and go out to celebrate, or we have a nice barbeque where we can all decompress."

"OK, I follow where you are going with all this, but can we get back to where Lucy stands?"

"Right about now, she is having this same conversation with Ben."

"Oh, poor Ben. I hope he is OK."

"Very funny, JW. I believe she is sold on this. But, and this is something you might want to share with Ben, she will need a little more positive reinforcement now and then. The whole point of this conversation is that, although women are alike in some ways, we are all different. Lucy is wired a little differently than me. She needs more encouragement and reward than I do. I think she is on board with Big Dogs. Still, as the head of this organization, I am asking you, the head of operations, to please talk with Ben and share some of this conversation with him. If he wants to run with the Big Dogs, he will have to pay more attention to Lucy's needs."

"I am sure there must have been a way we could have gotten to this point without all this drama."

"Arrrggghhh," Bonnie exclaimed, banging her head on the table and spilling some of her coffee. "Oops, that wasn't supposed to happen."

They were both interrupted by JW's phone ringing. "Ah, saved by the bell."

Bonnie scowled at him, and JW smiled back as he answered, "JW North."

"Lieutenant North, this is Mary from the Comm Center. If you are available, we have a callout on a homicide."

JW paused and ran through a few things in his head. He had just fed the dogs, but that was almost an hour ago. By the time he arrived and was briefed and collected scent, enough time would have passed that he would not need to worry about torsion. Torsion, or gastric dilation-volvulus, was a serious problem in large, narrow-chested dogs. It was caused by, among many things, exercise or other vigorous activity, often after eating. As a result, a dog's stomach literally flips inside the abdomen, pinching off each end. This causes serious problems that could lead to death. JW remembered from his early days of training to give the dog at least an hour of quiet time per cup of food after feeding.

"Yeah, we're good. Give me a few minutes and I'll log on and put myself on the call."

6

JW drove the Tahoe to an alley on the west side of Long Beach. Ares was already asleep in the back. Addy remained at home with Bonnie. As he left, she had been sitting by the front door, asking to go, giving him the sad dog stare. To JW, the German Shepherd had mastered this look of sadness and abandonment. It was in their genetic makeup. Her brown-eyed gaze could crush the heart of even the most hardened dog handler. She was not happy when the door closed in front of her and she let JW know with a series of loud barks. He hoped she wouldn't wake the neighbors; it was, after all, the middle of the night.

When he arrived at the scene, he saw that Ben was already there, talking with the detectives. *How the hell does he always beat me to these things?* As JW got out of his Tahoe, he recognized the detectives as his old friend, Alex Brennan, and his partner Andrew Jones.

"Hey guys, thanks for the call," JW said with a smile.

Brennan said, "Well, you did good things for us last time, and now, with the big deal in Las Vegas, how could we not call?"

"Still, thanks. So, what do we have?"

Brennan picked up with a briefing of the details as he knew them. "We have a victim down this alley," nodding to the right down a dark alley. "Single gunshot wound to the chest. He's been there for a little while, but we'll wait for the coroner to give us a time of death estimate. She's down there now doing her work with our lab tech and will call us when you guys can do your thing."

JW, Ben, and the two detectives chatted, catching up on life and what had happened while they were out of town. Occasionally, their eyes were drawn to the alley by camera strobe flashes. Finally, Ben went to the Tahoe and retrieved the Scent Transfer Unit (STU). The STU was a battery-operated vacuum unit designed to collect human scent on a sterile pad that could then be used to start a dog on a trail. The unit they were currently using was an improved, ruggedized model developed by the government as part of the original Human Scent Detection and Trailing Project.

Finally, the group heard a voice from the alley. "OK, guys. Come on in."

JW led the group down the alley and, upon seeing the coroner, asked, "OK to collect scent? We won't touch the body." JW had learned from dealing with coroners previously that they were very protective of the contamination of the victim. Rightly so. He leaned in and looked at the victim. He didn't need to do this as part of his job; call it professional curiosity. Unfortunately, the site was nearly dark. The only lighting came from two patrol officers' flashlights constantly moving, casting shadows here and there.

The victim had been dumped mid-alley along a wall. Unfortunately for the victim, the dump site was in a large black widow's nest. JW thought the victim must have been there for a while since he was already covered in webs and spiders. *What the hell is this, Halloween?* The victim's eyes were open, gazing off into nothingness. JW noticed the victim was wearing contact lenses, and they were drying out. The contacts were lifting off the victim's eyes. It created an extra layer of spookiness to an already eerie site. *I guess the victim doesn't really care about where they dumped him but cleaning up this mess is gonna suck for the coroner.*

Ben collected several scent pads, two of which were given to the patrol officers to be placed into evidence. Next, JW went to get Ares and fitted his harness on him. By the time he returned, Ben was ready. Brennan asked JW, "Hey, you mind if we tag along and watch this time?"

"No problem. It's the middle of the night, so I'm not anticipating much traffic. A quick question, though. Any idea who this guy is?"

"Yeah, I asked a gang unit to come by and see if they knew him. Local drug dealer. His name is, or was, Abraham Rodriguez; street name 'Spider."

JW looked down at the body, again noting all the black widows crawling over the victim. "Ironic."

JW put Ares on the tracking lead and let him take a good sniff of the pad that Ben gave him. He then gave the trailing command, "Geo-say," and Ares immediately pulled to their left. Ares was pulling hard, so JW applied resistance to slow him down. The detectives didn't look like they were ready to run this morning. *He's pulling hard, fresh scent.* As they reached the end of the alley, they turned left. JW looked down and could see what appeared to be new tire tracks in some dirt where the alley transitioned to the street. He pointed this out to Brennan who nodded in recognition.

"I'll ask the lab to photograph those." He paused and used his radio to call and tell the lab tech what they'd found and where it was.

The trail continued along the streets, with Ares pulling strongly the entire way, making several turns without difficulty. They were traveling northbound, mid-block when Ares stopped near a parked car. He sniffed it for a few moments and then sat, giving his alert that the trail was complete. JW praised Ares and patted his side. Ben contacted dispatch on his radio to run the plate of the car.

"King Nine Nine, I have a plate to run: two Frank Adam Nora one two three."

The dispatcher immediately replied, "King Nine Nine, that vehicle is Ten Twenty-Nine Victor. Are you code four?"

Ben, recognizing the radio code for a stolen vehicle, immediately drew his sidearm and, using his light, cleared the vehicle's interior.

"King Nine Nine, the vehicle appears abandoned. Code four for now," he replied, indicating that no further assistance was necessary.

Ben turned to JW and said, "I have an idea. See if you can restart Ares." JW smiled, realizing where Ben was going with his idea.

JW again scented Ares on the scent pad and tried to start him. Ares worked up the street in both directions, back and forth, but kept returning to the car. JW encouraged him to try several times, but finally, Ares just stood and looked at him. Then, he turned to Ben and said, "Negative. We've got nothing beyond here."

Detective Brennan said, "OK, JW, I think I understood everything until we arrived. Care to explain what's happening?"

"Sure thing. Of course, this is conjecture on my part, but here's what I think. We started the trail at the victim. I believe he was dumped in the alley by our suspect using this stolen car. If you look in the trunk, you will probably find a lot of physical evidence. After dumping our victim, they drove out of the alley and abandoned this stolen car because they didn't want to get caught in a rollin' stolen. Then, the suspect was picked up in another vehicle and left the area. If he had walked away, Ares would have continued after the restart. We were doing a car trail, and I can tell you, those are tough. Sometimes the scent just doesn't come out so the dog can follow." Looking at the stolen car, JW pointed to the driver's open window. "The window is down. Lots of scent coming out due to the air movement."

Brennan nodded. "Wow, JW. You would have made a pretty good detective, if you were a little smarter, that is."

The group laughed, and Brennan added, "I think you're right, though. What you said makes complete sense."

"Sorry we couldn't find you a suspect, though."

"Sometimes it's the big time, sometimes it's small, and others you get nothing at all. Nothing ventured, nothing gained. We'll ask patrol to do some 'knock and talks' on the block and see if anyone saw something. Who knows? Maybe we get lucky. I'll need you to file a follow-up report on the trail."

"No problem, I'll get the case number from dispatch and file the report online. Is first thing in the morning OK?"

"That should be fine. I'll email you and let you know if we get anything from our investigation."

With that, JW and Ben said their thanks and started walking back to their cars. Ben smiled and said, "Well, it wasn't a big find, but I think we will see more of that as we do this more often. We got lucky and had a bunch of apprehensions early. When I did this ten years ago, there were many dead ends like this one."

"I hear you. Like Brennan said, 'Nothing ventured, nothing gained.' We gotta take the good with the bad."

"I'm just glad that wasn't a real long trail."

"Why?"

"I'm still beat from Vegas, man. I should have had a patrol officer follow in the Tahoe. I'm not on top of my game. I'm just happy we don't have a long walk back."

"Exercise is good for the soul, Ben."

"Says the man who knows it's not that far back to the cars."

"Oh, by the way, Bonnie asked me to share some stuff with you about feelings."

Ben slowly turned to JW, an incredulous look on his face. "You? Feelings?"

"That's exactly what I said!" JW then provided a condensed version of his conversation with Bonnie earlier in the evening.

Once JW finished, Ben said, "Huh. Well, on that note, Lucy and I did have a talk when I got home. I believe we can make a commitment to Big Dogs. We are both all in."

"That's great news! Welcome to the team, not that you weren't on it already. Do you want me to talk to the chief and see if he will continue to let you train? Then, we need to reach out to Vohne Liche Kennels about getting another dog. How long until you retire? Sheesh, we gotta get in gear here; there's not much time."

Realizing that JW was getting spun up with excitement, Ben said, "Easy, big boy. How about we sit down for a four-person family dinner in a couple days and we can put together another solid argument for the chief?"

"Good idea, Ben." They continued to their cars with a bit of extra spring in their steps. "You want to stop on the way home and grab a bite to eat?"

7

JW woke after the rest of the house. Bonnie tiptoed about, fixing breakfast for the dogs, and trying to keep them quiet. Unfortunately, Ares and Addy had other ideas. The dogs became frantic at the sound of the first piece of kibble striking stainless steel. There was little unusual about their whining and quick movements. This was a twice-daily ritual and the dogs were not to be denied. *Feed me… feed me… feed me…* Bonnie continued to shush the dogs, but her efforts only made it worse.

"You know, I appreciate you trying to do this quietly, but the truth is, eating is the only thing they like more than running a trail. Your attempts to quiet them are winding them up more," JW said.

"Oh my God, you startled me!"

"What? You were expecting someone else?"

"No."

"Sorry, I wasn't trying to. With all the noise, a herd of elephants could have snuck up on you. Speaking of elephants, where did you hide my coffee cup this morning?"

"After I washed it, I put it in the kitchen cabinet where it belongs."

"Wait, you washed it? I thought we talked about this. It takes a while to get the buildup of coffee exactly right. There is a science to this and washing my mug keeps setting me back."

Bonnie scowled at JW. "Shut up, get your coffee, and go sit down in the dining room while I finish feeding these dogs. If I don't get them fed soon, one of them is gonna stroke out. You must have had a good night because you sure are being a pain in the butt."

JW laughed to himself and made his coffee in the cup-at-a-time brewer. *I wonder if there is a way to speed these things up.* Once done, he stumbled and sat at the table, waiting for Bonnie. *Ah...coffee good.* He picked up the paper and scanned the sports page. "Hey, Bonnie, there is an article here about COVID-19 and possibly canceling the NCAA basketball playoffs. What is COVID-19 and why is it messing with sports?"

She called out from the kitchen, "That's the virus that is all over the news. I can't get a clear picture because the so-called experts can't seem to agree on how bad it is. It is getting serious, though. There's talk about shutting the country down. I think I read the president closed travel out of China. They believe that is where it came from."

Bonnie came into the room with her own cup of coffee. "OK, I can tell you are busting at the seams to tell me about what happened, so go ahead."

"Weird deal. Body dump on the westside, guy was shot, local gangbanger. His body was covered with black widow spiders."

"Yuck, they didn't kill him, did they?"

"Nah, lead poisoning. We ran a short trail that ended up at a stolen car. I'm hoping Alex Brennan can get something from that."

"Alex was the detective? He's good. If there is anything there, he'll find it. That sounds like a nice trail, but somehow, I think there has to be more."

"Well, Ben and I had to walk back to the cars, so we talked. I think all your work on Lucy sold her. Ben committed to being the second handler last night."

"Really? That's great. Now, he just has to continue to work with her. He can't leave her behind like last time."

"I know; I told him what we talked about. But, Bonnie, you're just gonna have to accept that not everyone can be JW North. We are not all models of perfect husbandhood. It is a lofty goal that many aspire to, but a difficult mountain to climb."

"OK, I no longer need to worry about what I want for breakfast."

Ignoring her comment, JW continued, "Ben suggested we have a group get-together in a couple days so we can all sit down and brainstorm the whole thing. I want to get started before he retires, but that will need the chief's approval."

"Wow! You go, Ben. I only wish you were as easy to train as he is."

JW opened his iPad and scanned his email. *Still nothing from the FBI. Is Gaurdia expecting me to call her? After all, she is the reason we were in Vegas. She has her sources and knows what is going on. So why the hell hasn't she called?* JW felt like the guy who went on a first date with a hot chick and never heard from her again. This was not making him happy.

There was an email from Alex Brennan, which JW opened:

JW, thanks for coming out last night. Another great trail. After you left, we talked to the neighbors around where that car was parked. We found one guy who was up due to tiny bladder syndrome. He saw the first car drive up; a guy got out and then climbed into a van. There was a distinctive paint job on the van. I got ahold of the gang detectives, and one of them recognized the description. We are currently putting together a warrant on the van and its owner. We hope if we get him, then we can get whoever dumped the victim. Anyway, great work. Put together a complete follow-up; your testimony will be critical in this case.

AB

JW grabbed his coffee and went outside to log onto the computer in his Tahoe. It was linked to the police department report writing system. He quickly wrote his report and found Bonnie waiting when he went back inside.

"I decided in your absence that you are taking me out to breakfast. I was thinking of that nice place in Seal Beach by the ocean. I could use some crashing waves for a little peace. I think things are going to get really busy soon."

Bonnie and JW sat outside at a table with an ocean view. Bonnie had a faraway look in her eyes. JW quickly ordered coffee and scanned the menu. Their peace was interrupted by the ringing of his phone. Since they were the only ones outside at the moment, JW didn't feel guilty about disturbing others. He looked at his phone and said to Bonnie, "Dr. Gaurdia, finally."

"Good morning, Doctor. How are things at the FBI?"

"Hi, JW. It's not morning here anymore, but things are going well. How is Adeliene? Is she recovering from her injuries?"

"Addy is doing well, thanks for asking. Unfortunately, it'll be a few weeks, maybe a month, before she can work again."

"And how is your lovely wife, Bonnie?"

"She's right here with me; she appears well."

"Oh, could I talk with her, please?"

JW passed the phone to Bonnie and listened to one side of the conversation. It appeared Dr. Gaurdia was doing most of the talking as Bonnie merely answered with the occasional OK. Finally, she passed the phone back to him.

"JW, I know you have probably been waiting for my call. It has been rather hectic here, but I have had a chance to read the reports on your activities in Las Vegas. Very exciting. But I need to ask, was it necessary to kill the suspect?"

"Whaaaat?"

"I understand you were shot and all, but did you have to kill him?"

At this moment, JW was about as confused as he could get. *What the hell is wrong with this woman?*

"Actually, Doctor, I didn't shoot your suspect. The Las Vegas Metro SWAT team shot the suspect after he shot one of their officers. I'm certain they felt completely justified in the shooting."

"Oh, I understand all that. It was a good shooting. What I am trying to explain to you is how important it is that I am able to interview these killers. It is invaluable to our understanding of their behavior."

"What I am trying to explain to you, Doctor, is that if a suspect shoots at me, I will defend myself and shoot back."

"Oh, I completely understand your need to defend yourself. Of course, I don't expect you to get injured just so I can have a little chat with a murderer. But if you can possibly bring them in alive, it would be greatly appreciated."

JW sat back in his chair and stared at his phone. *What the hell? What planet am I on?* He was more than a little irritated and said, "Doctor, I'm sure you didn't call just to critique my law enforcement techniques. What can I do for you?"

"Oh, good. Back to business. I'm sure you were anxious to hear from me, but I have been busy here. COVID has complicated things as simple as travel. I wanted to make sure I had everything arranged before I called. After Las Vegas, I briefed the director on your accomplishments, and he was very impressed. I have arranged for a meeting with him here in Washington, DC, followed by a full briefing at our facility in Quantico.

JW listened to Dr. Gaurdia lay things out for him. Her voice was controlled, placing emphasis in all the right places. To him, it sounded more like a sales pitch than an invitation. He wondered if she had rehearsed this conversation and how many times. He decided to create a little turmoil for her and see how she handled it.

"Dr. Gaurdia, I need to interject something here. Things have changed in the local environment. That is certainly something we can discuss during my visit. Still, I think we need to include Ben Kellum in any discussions."

JW listened for a few moments, waiting for her to pick up the conversation. Then, finally, she said, "I have some time now if you would like to tell me what has changed."

He knew she hated surprises and imagined everything in her life was highly organized, with a calendar entry for every moment in her day.

"That's not necessary, Doctor. Although it is significant, I believe it can wait until we are there to discuss it face to face."

He was still a bit pissed at her earlier comments but didn't want to push her too hard. He didn't know her well enough to drive her up to the edge.

After another pause, JW closed his eyes and could see her face. Lauralynn Gaurdia was tall, thin, and athletic with brown hair that she usually pulled back into a ponytail. She was somewhat attractive in a plain way. She certainly didn't do herself any favors in terms of her looks. She was driven and probably didn't even think about the image she projected to others. She was thoroughly professional in a forced, stilted way. He imagined a look of confusion on her face as she tried to think of a way to regain control of the conversation.

When she finally started talking again, it seemed more natural. That was good, as the other Dr. Gaurdia sounded like a used car salesman. This one seemed more relaxed, and he could hear her passion for her work.

"Transportation for you and Ben have been arranged. If you can both be ready by next Tuesday, I will have a military jet at Joint Forces Training Base - Los Alamitos bring you here. Then, when you land at Joint Base Andrews, we will have a car waiting to bring you to FBI Headquarters for your meeting."

"That sounds great. I need to talk with Ben and see if it works for him."

"I understand completely. Can you let me know as soon as possible if, for some reason, that doesn't work for you and Ben?"

JW laughed to himself. "Certainly, I will talk to you soon," and he ended the call.

Bonnie looked at him expectantly. "Well, I could tell that was the FBI, and they want you to go back to DC, but what was the rest of that?"

"Honey, all I can say is that Dr. Lauralynn Gaurdia is friggin' weird."

"Oh, that! All I can say is you two are made for one another."

Lauralynn Gaurdia sat at her desk, staring at the phone, thinking something was amiss. She had anticipated a higher level of excitement from JW. Instead, she was nonplussed, feeling like a kid on Christmas morning, opening a gift, expecting a toy, and getting clothes. *Something was bothering JW. I wonder what it is.*

JW called Ben Kellum as soon as he was home from breakfast.

"Ben, grab Lucy and get your butt over here, ASAP. We got the call from the FBI. They want us in DC next Tuesday. We have a lot of work to do."

He was in the dining room with Bonnie. They had paperwork spread out on the table, each organizing their thoughts in preparation for the power meeting with the Kellums.

"Ben, you wouldn't have believed it. She was upset that the suspect in Vegas was killed because she wanted to talk to him."

"I told you she was different. She doesn't think like a street cop because she has spent almost all her time in staff roles. Trust me, she is brilliant and, believe it or not, you and she have very similar goals. You want to trail all the serial killers in the world to eliminate the threat they present. She wants to understand them, to make it easier to find them. You're working toward the same thing, with different approaches."

JW considered this for a moment. "Ben, sometimes you're smarter than it seems."

"OK, I know somewhere in that veiled insult, there actually was a compliment. So, I'm going to take that and ignore the rest. How are we going to deal with this?"

"Based upon our conversations, I called Chief of Staff Javon Hudson and scheduled a meeting with Chief Estrada for Monday morning. I think we need his buy-in before we talk to the FBI. At the same time, we need to be ready for our visit to DC. I think I have an idea of what they will offer, but I'm not sure after my last chat with Dr. Gaurdia. I want to make sure we maintain a certain level of independence, so I think we show the FBI that we are prepared to carry this on our own. We will accept reimbursement for expenses and an hourly rate for staff. We also need to make sure we build in support staff." This last comment was directed at Bonnie, who was reviewing their financial reports with Lucy.

"We also need to include reimbursement for training time," added Ben.

Bonnie nodded in acknowledgment of both comments. "How much support staff are you thinking, JW?" And then to Ben, "I have some ideas on how we can do that because you're right."

JW started, "Either one or two per team. That will be the team leader/handler's call. I think we need to have our own internal backups. We can't expect our back-ups to always be available; plus, if we cross-train them, we have another handler."

"There you go again with your backups," said Ben with a smile.

"How many times have you ever seen me get caught short, Ben?"

"Never. I'm still trying to figure out how you let yourself get shot."

Being reminded of the Shadow never made JW happy, but he knew Ben was screwing with him and said with a smile, "To that, Ben Kellum, I can only say 'fuck you.' Now can we get to work?"

8

The Truck Stop Killer waited. He had stopped the night before at a large truck stop outside Albuquerque, New Mexico. The place was perfect for his needs. There were a lot of drivers coming and going and several Jezebels here that would meet the needs of the Lord. He arrived late and had crashed in the sleeper in the back. He woke early, and now he sat in the driver's seat, reading his bible. Occasionally, he would look up and scan the lot. There were trucks and trailers as far as he could see. It was unfortunate that it would be hours before the sun went down. He didn't want to invite anyone into his sleeper during the day—the chance of being seen and remembered was too great. So, he waited.

A few hours later, he heard a knock on his door. He looked down and saw a young girl, maybe not even eighteen. Hansen wasn't ready yet, so he opened the door just a bit and asked, "Aren't you a little young to be out here?"

She was surprised by his question. She had been expecting, 'How much for head?' or something similar. Her answer was simple.

"A girl's gotta eat."

He didn't think she would use any money he gave her for food, more likely drugs.

"No thanks," he said and closed the door. She seemed new at this. He knew she wouldn't have any trouble finding business at another truck.

Floyd went inside the diner to get something to eat as the sun went down. It was not very busy; the number of drivers seemed down from normal as everyone worked through how to deal with COVID. After eating dinner, he went back to his truck and waited. It didn't take long. This woman was older and had a sharper edge to her. She looked like she had been working the streets for a while and showed the signs of a hard life. He flashed his running lights and she quickly changed direction and walked toward him. As if mocking an old makeup commercial, the closer she got, the worse she looked. He thought she looked diseased. He was glad he had no intention of having any form of sex with her. He believed that he would be doing her a favor by killing her.

As she approached, he opened his door partway. She asked, "Hey baby, you lookin' for some action?"

"Might be."

"You ain't the police, are you?" She was good at reading people and didn't get a cop vibe from him. The question was more habit than anything suspicious.

"Police, nah. Just lookin' for a good time."

"You lookin' for a good time, huh? Well, I'm you're girl. You name it, I'm good at it. What you want, baby?"

"Just head. How much?"

"Twenty-five dollars for head."

He climbed down from the truck and said, "Twenty-five, huh? That sounds good. Follow me."

She was amazed at his size as he got down to the ground. He was tall and thick, and although he did not appear muscular, he radiated strength. His face was weathered, his hair dark with some gray, and he had a thick, large beard. She saw he was leading her to the entrance to the sleeper and said, "We don't have to go there, baby."

"I like my privacy." He climbed in, and she followed. Once inside, she moved past him and he closed the door. The inside of the sleeper was neat. She hadn't expected that. She turned to face Hansen and came face to face with the Truck Stop Killer. She looked into his eyes and saw nothing. There was no emotion in his eyes. No expression on his face. She realized she had made a mistake. She had heard the other girls talking about a trucker who killed prostitutes and knew this was him.

"No, no, no! I need to get out of here. I didn't do nothin' and you don't want to try and kill me, motherfucker!"

He moved toward her to try and get her under control. The sleeper was insulated but not soundproof. There was too much risk of being discovered if she didn't shut up. As he reached for her throat with both hands, she moved to the side and slashed his face with her fingernails. He could feel blood begin to trickle down his cheek. Hansen took a wild swing at her, but again she dodged and he missed. Her movement left her unbalanced and exposed. He stepped forward into her side. She again tried to move out of the way, but this time he was faster. His elbow connected with the side of her head and she dropped.

He opened a drawer and took out a handkerchief that he used to wipe the blood from his cheek. He applied some pressure and waited for a few minutes. He watched the whore closely in case she woke up or was faking it. He doubted that—he had hit her hard. He wouldn't be surprised if he'd killed her. Finally, the bleeding stopped and he bound her hands and feet and taped her mouth shut.

He sat and watched for a while before leaving. He didn't see anyone paying any attention to his rig. He drove away from the truck stop, this time keeping his trailer attached. He would not be coming back here. He didn't want to take a chance in case someone had heard the whore. He drove for almost an hour, watching his mirrors for anything unusual. Seeing nothing, he turned off at a highway exit, far from any signs of life. He drove for another hour until he reached an abandoned farm set well back from the road. He sensed there were no homes for miles in any direction.

It was dark and quiet as he dragged her from his truck. He was angry. This bitch had hurt him. He believed the Lord's will was for him to remove whores from the earth, but he tried to do it as painlessly as possible. This whore was vile and she had his DNA under her fingernails. She would need to be cleansed. Cleansed with fire.

He pulled her, feet first, across the dirt next to the barn. He paid no attention as her head hit rocks and holes along the way. Finally, he reached a large elm tree with a tire swing slowly swaying in the wind. He used a piece of rope, tied it to her ankles, and hoisted her above the ground. Now she swung gently in the cool night breeze. He removed the tape from her mouth, thinking, *Perhaps her cries will ease some of my pain.*

The Truck Stop Killer ambled around the lot. He was in no hurry now. The whore had awakened from her slumber and was crying for help. No matter, no one who cared could hear her. There was only him. He was gathering wood scraps and piling them beneath her. As he did so, he hummed, "Fire, da da da…da da…da…" She could tell what he had in mind and stopped cursing him. Now, she was pleading for her life. When she saw that had no effect, she began praying out loud to God.

"That's right, whore, you pray to the Lord. You have brought a blight upon the land and now you will be cleansed. You are foul and vile, a servant of Satan. Therefore, I will send you back to hell from whence you came."

She became increasingly frantic, shaking her head and begging him, "You don't have to do this."

He wondered why she would say this. *But, of course, I have to do this; the Lord has commanded me. Well, you can't fix stupid.*

When he finished collecting wood, he returned to his truck and brought out a one-gallon can of gasoline. If anyone ever asked him why he had it, he knew there wasn't a good answer. His truck ran on diesel, but this was better for setting fires. He poured the contents on the wood and on her hanging body. She started to cry, tears streaming from her eyes. Since she was hanging upside down, the tears fell across her forehead onto the wood. *You can't cry enough to stop the hellfire, whore.* He pulled a box of matches from his pocket, removed one wooden stick match, and struck it against the box. The match ignited, the flame shedding light upon her face. Her eyes fixed on the flame. She hoped it burned down to his finger, forcing him to throw it away. Without a word, he dropped it, and the gas quickly caught fire. There was a loud whoosh and the flames shot into the night sky. The entire lot was illuminated as the flames crawled up her body and into the tree. It, too, caught fire. The night was filled with her screams of agony. Her body bucked and twisted, fighting to escape the hungry flames.

Hansen turned away from her with a little smile on his face. He climbed back into his truck and slowly drove away. TSK looked in his mirror and saw her swinging back and forth. He believed she was dead because she stopped screaming. The fire was spreading and soon the barn would catch and be consumed. The Lord had promised Armageddon and the Truck Stop Killer had delivered it here to her. As he turned onto the road from the farm, he looked and saw the entire night sky was on fire. "Fire, da da da… da da…da…"

9

Ben and JW sat quietly in the Gulfstream jet on their way to Washington, D.C. The meeting yesterday with Long Beach Chief of Police Estrada had gone well. Their program had been cast in a positive light due to the trail's success in Las Vegas. The chief even seemed to ignore that JW and Addy had almost been killed because the media was putting a positive spin on its coverage. The Fox News reporter JW had spoken with during the press conference was especially complimentary, bordering on gushing. As a result, Ben was going to be allowed to continue to work two half-days a week to prepare to become the second handler for Big Dogs. They would need to contact Vohne Liche Kennels about getting another dog, but that could wait until after the FBI meeting.

They weren't the only occupants on the aircraft. There were a couple of high-ranking Air Force officers along with their aides. After landing at Joint Base Andrews, they got off the jet and Ben asked, "Did you see the Air Force brass? You could tell they were wondering who we were and why we were on their plane."

JW looked around and then spotted a man waving at them from a black Tahoe not too far away.

"We'll just let them wonder. They will recognize us on TV one day and say, 'Hey, remember when we saw those guys on the flight to DC?'"

"Are you JW North and Ben Kellum? I'm Special Agent Matt Blair," the driver introduced himself as they approached. "I'll take you to FBI headquarters."

"Excellent, Special Agent." As they loaded their bags into the SUV, JW asked, "Who did you piss off to get stuck driving us?"

Blair looked confused for a second, then replied, "Oh, no. This isn't bad duty. I just graduated from the academy and am temporarily assigned to Dr. Gaurdia's unit. She's brilliant and it's very exciting working with her."

JW and Ben smirked at each other. *Poor kid.*

Blair said, "We've got some time before your meeting, so Dr. Gaurdia suggested I show you some of the local landmarks."

On the way to 935 Pennsylvania Avenue NW, Special Agent Blair narrated a small tour of Washington, DC. Both Ben and JW had been there before. Still, they politely listened as Blair talked about Arlington Cemetery on the way to the Memorial Bridge and across the Potomac River. He stopped in front of the distinctive building and put on his flashers. He turned to JW and Ben and said, "Go in the main entrance. They're expecting you. Ask them to call me when you're done, and I'll pick you up right here." JW nodded and thanked him. They got out and looked around as the Tahoe pulled away.

"I'm not complaining, but didn't that feel like a bit much to you?"

Ben nodded and said, "Yeah, we're definitely getting the full-on sales pitch. I'm not sure what to make of all this. I guess we just roll with it."

"I guess we just go in and see if it is a cookbook."

"Say what? Is that another obscure movie reference?"

"TV, not a movie. *Twilight Zone, 'To Serve Man.'*"

"Oh, of course. How could I miss that one?"

"Sheesh, Ben, lighten up. We're supposed to be enjoying this, after all."

Ben laughed. "I'll feel better when I know it's not a cookbook."

"There you go, now you're getting in the spirit."

JW paused outside the J. Edgar Hoover Building, looking up at the massive structure. He thought of all the times he had worked with the FBI over the years and attended the FBI National Academy in Quantico, and then he yawned. In a city of magnificent architecture, this building served as an example of how to underwhelm. JW felt bad; he knew this was the home of the premier law enforcement agency in the United States and certainly one of the best in the world. It was probably to the architect's benefit that J. Edgar Hoover didn't live long enough to see the finished building.

Ben looked at JW and wondered what he was thinking. "What's up, JW? We goin' inside?"

"Yeah, I'm just looking at this building and wondering what the inspiration was: a maximum-security prison or a cinder block? I'm sorry, and please don't say anything to Lauralynn, but I don't know if I have ever been this unimpressed."

"Maybe it's nicer inside."

"I don't know. I'm sorry, I'm being a buzzkill. We should be excited and happy. I just feel that looking at this," JW pointed toward the front of the building, "it just sucks the happy right out of me."

They walked into the lobby and immediately ran into Dr. Gaurdia. "Gentlemen, did you spend too much time looking at the sights? I was going to give you a quick tour of the building, but we are meeting with the director in five minutes. I signed you in. Here, put these badges on."

As they followed instructions, she ushered them across the lobby, through a metal detector, and into an elevator. As they ascended, she said, "You guys look nice; thanks for getting dressed up."

JW said, "We were going to wear Levi's and polo shirts, but this felt more appropriate."

"JW," she replied, "I love your sense of humor. But please don't do that with the director. I'm not sure he would understand you."

Ben laughed, "I'm not sure I understand him most of the time."

Dr. Gaurdia looked like she wanted to hit the stop button on the elevator and slap them both.

"Please, gentlemen, this project is too important for your sophomoric humor. You both need to put on your professional faces and act with proper decorum."

JW made a mental note to joke with Ben about this later. It was all he could do to keep from laughing out loud. As the elevator slowly climbed, he wondered what was on TV tonight.

As the elevator's doors opened on the seventh floor, JW instantly became nervous. He had been hiding behind humor to deal with the stress. The last year flashed before his eyes and he realized how much the next few moments of this day could mean to them. If they botched the meeting, it was over. His plans for a national human scent and mantrailing team would fall apart. The weight of the meeting now fell heavily on his shoulders, and he began to sweat. He glanced at Ben, who looked a bit pale to him. *Well, at least I'm not the only one having an anxiety attack.*

Lauralynn walked them down "Mahogany Row," so named because the entrance doors from the corridor have a mahogany veneer, unlike the others at FBIHQ. They walked past a set of massive doors, clearly the main entrance to the director's office. They continued down the hallway, passing a large conference room, obviously too large for a meeting of this scale. Finally, she opened the door to a much smaller conference room. It could easily hold over a dozen people. There was coffee at a small table off to the side. Dr. Gaurdia gestured to it and said, "Go ahead and help yourself. I will go see if the director is ready to begin."

JW and Ben each filled a mug with coffee and looked at each other. "You nervous?"

"Oh yeah," said JW, nodding his head. "It hit me when the elevator doors opened."

Before they could say another word, the door to the conference room opened and Alexander Murphy, Director of the FBI, entered the room. He was of medium height, slim, and in good shape, even though he was nearly ten years older than JW.

"Lieutenant North, Officer Kellum, thank you so much for traveling across the country to meet with me."

As Dr. Gaurdia began to close the door, another man pushed into the room. He glared at Lauralynn with contempt and anger.

"Oh, I'm sorry, Avery. I didn't know you were coming to this meeting," Lauralynn said without a trace of genuine regret.

Clearly, these two do not like one another, thought JW.

The director began with introductions. "Of course, you know Dr. Gaurdia very well by now, and this other gentleman is Special Agent Avery Abbott. He is on temporary assignment to my staff."

Avery looked Ben and JW over like they were bugs under a microscope. That he felt superior to them was apparent.

JW looked back at him, giving him a firm "Don't fuck with me" look. It didn't appear to change his attitude, and JW considered asking the director if he could step outside for a moment while he cleaned the floor with this obnoxious piece of crap. Here, in front of him, was the living embodiment of what the average police officer hated about the FBI: obnoxious, egotistical, and arrogant. He looked at the director, considered what he had heard about the man, and then wondered why this prick was working directly for him. JW thought of all the highly professional FBI agents he had worked with over the years and sighed. *They probably didn't like this guy either. Maybe he will just sit there and keep his mouth shut. Nah, not likely.*

Dr. Gaurdia spent the next half hour briefing the director on what Ben and JW had built over the past year. She went into detail about the training and the trails run in the field, culminating with the search in Las Vegas. You could tell by listening to her that Lauralynn was very proud of what they had accomplished. He wondered if she hadn't been there with them through the whole thing for a moment.

Finally, she finished and turned to the director, waiting to see if he had any comments or questions. He looked at JW and said, "Lieutenant North, I would like to compliment you on what you have achieved. I know that programs of this type have been attempted before, but with nowhere near the level of accomplishment that you two have attained. This program could genuinely be a game changer for law enforcement—a powerful tool in helping eradicate serial criminals throughout our great country.

"As you know, this nation comprises numerous law enforcement agencies. They go from exceptionally large to small operations. Each tends to the needs of their local citizens, and most do so in an outstanding manner. However, crime occurs at the local level. Because of that, the most potent crime-fighting force available sits on the sidelines, waiting to be asked to join the fight. Law enforcement is over a million strong yet has difficulty talking to one another. I am sure you know, but we do not intervene with local jurisdictions unless requested. Now, I am not a proponent of a national police force. It would be unable to respond to those local needs as our brethren do.

"So, how do we better serve the citizens of America yet maintain cooperative relations with other agencies? We are not going to impose ourselves on other departments. Still, we will be more aggressive in seeking their requests for our assistance. We track crime information in this country in many ways. Every agency is required to report crime statistics and provide us with basic information on select fields of data related to violent crime. This is useful but limited for a real, deep dive analysis. Dr. Gaurdia, in cooperation with a brilliant computer scientist from the Massachusetts Institute of Technology, developed a new computer system. It not only ties many disparate systems together but allows them to help possibly identify serially related crimes. I don't want to steal her thunder as I know she has a detailed presentation for you two tomorrow at her headquarters in Quantico."

Special Agent Abbott then interrupted the director. "Sir, I have a question for Mr. North, if I may?"

The director looked slightly annoyed at him for breaking his train of thought but said, "Go ahead, Special Agent Abbott."

"Thank you, sir. Mr. North, I have a concern," he said, his words dripping with arrogance. "My research indicates that search teams like yours often have overstated qualifications. Are you aware of the number of instances where a criminal case has been corrupted by the improper actions of these so-called scent experts? What can you tell me about the case in Hollins, Colorado?"

The air was immediately sucked out of the room. Dr. Gaurdia looked shocked by the question and the manner in which it was delivered. The director turned to Abbott as if to respond, but JW said, "I would be happy to address his concerns, sir.

"Before I discuss Hollins, let me first say that human scent detection and mantrailing is not a perfect process. Significant scientific evidence has been established through controlled testing and proven that it works with a high degree of reliability. However, the courts have ruled that scent evidence and identification cannot stand independently. It requires further substantiation to establish the high degree of confidence necessary for something like a search warrant.

Therefore, our program is not a silver bullet. Instead, it is one more tool in the crime-fighting toolbox.

"As for Hollins, that was a missing person case, which eventually was found to be a homicide. The local police had hit a dead end and were looking for any way to advance their case. A local search and rescue dog handler offered her services and she was able to identify a suspect. Unfortunately, it was the wrong suspect. The handler and her dog were not trained using any reputable program and without any knowledgeable supervision. She got lucky, found a child in another missing person case, and then proceeded to exaggerate her results to anyone who would listen to her. This was unfortunate and certainly damaging to the efforts of reputable search dog teams."

Before JW could continue, Abbott interrupted him. "Who gets to say whether a team is reliable? How do we, the FBI, know that your team is trained to the reliability level you claim? How do we know your actions will not damage our reputation?"

JW looked at the director, who appeared ashen, the blood draining from his face. JW didn't know whether this was from anger or embarrassment, but he knew one thing for sure. If some jackass like Abbott would be able to give him orders, he was not interested. He considered all their work and the prospect of dealing with this dipshit for the next couple of years and carefully chose his next few words.

"Special Agent Abbott, no single national authority exists with guidelines on scent dog qualifications. Some have tried, but none is recognized as the standard. That is one of the things that the original scent dog program worked to establish. That would be the program Long Beach ran ten years ago and the FBI was closely involved in that. As to whether my team is qualified, I would be happy to give you complete copies of all my dogs' training records, but I am not sure if you are intelligent enough to understand them. As to damaging your reputation, I have been in law enforcement for over thirty years. I have always worked to develop and maintain a professional reputation. As for the FBI, I think they should start with you if they were concerned about their reputation."

"Gentlemen, I think we should take a short break." The director could see things were spiraling out of control and needed to cut this off before it came to blows. The director rose and turned to leave the room. "Lauralynn, would you please see to the needs of our guests?" He motioned for Abbott to follow.

Dr. Gaurdia, looking upset, mumbled an excuse and left Ben and JW alone in the conference room.

"Coming on a bit strong there, JW?"

"Yeah, I'm sorry, Ben. That idiot righteously pissed me off. I was ready to drag him down to the gym and go a few rounds. But now that I've had time to think, I don't think any of that was about us. He and Lauralynn have their own private war and he was using us as leverage to score points with the director. I gotta be honest here; I don't want to be part of their team if it means being subjugated by an ass like Abbott."

"You would give up all we worked for because of an hour with that jackass?"

"Not because of him directly, but because of what he stands for. I hope to God the director realizes what is going on here because I do not want to work for a guy like that. I find it hard enough to tolerate Dr. Gaurdia, let alone that contemptuous sycophant. But if that is the kind of guy that Murphy surrounds himself with, it does not portend well for us in the future. He would sell us out in a heartbeat if something went a bit sideways."

"Still, after all the work we have put in, all the sacrifices, would you give this up?"

"I hope I don't have to. I hope I am wrong about what just happened. Worst case for us, we go home and do this on a more local level. Mind you, that is not what I want. But I feel strongly that we have to assert a degree of independence. If we sell our souls to these guys, I am not sure where that leads, but I don't think either of us would like it."

Director Murphy looked out his office window at the skyline of Washington, DC. He sighed, *Abbott's family is well connected, but this is unacceptable.* Abbott was standing behind him, waiting for him to speak. Finally, Abbott couldn't stand the silence. "Sir, I don't believe we can trust North to represent this agency. Did you see how angry he became in there? He's just too volatile."

"Special Agent Abbott, before you speak—ever—you should consider the potential ramifications to your career. And perhaps think about why Lieutenant North became so emotional. Maybe it was because you forgot who you are and thought you could speak for the FBI. Do you actually think that, before I would bring outsiders here, I wouldn't thoroughly vet them? That I wouldn't have someone besides Dr. Gaurdia examine their past? That perhaps I would get another opinion from someone that I respect? Special Agent Abbott, I do not attend meetings like that expecting to learn anything new. I go in to get a feel for the person's character and confirm what I already know."

"Sir, if I could…"

The director was getting more heated now; he was trying to help this young man, but he wouldn't let him. "No, you may not. You should not speak. I am finding it is not your strong suit."

Abbott was silenced by the director's tone and words. He merely nodded.

"When I look at a man like Lieutenant North, I see a man full of pride and determination. He would die before dishonoring himself or any organization he is associated with." Director Murphy paused; he found his words tiring and needed a moment to refocus. He considered Abbott and made a decision. "Special Agent Abbott, would you like to know what I see when I look at you? I would advise you to be careful how you answer. You may not like what I have to say."

Severely chastised, Abbott nodded and said, "I would, sir."

"Very well, Avery. I know you came to the FBI because you didn't want to be like the rest of your family, living off an inheritance earned generations ago. You sought to make your own place in the world, even against your father's wishes." Abbott looked at the director, wondering how much the man knew about him.

"Oh, I know your father. A good man who certainly deserved better from you. He and I have talked on several occasions about his favorite subject, you. Your father cares a great deal about you and has given me his approval to take the steps necessary to assist you in your quest to become your own man. I wish I could assign you to spend some time with North. I believe he could teach you a great deal about values."

"Believe it or not, sir, I think I would like that."

"Well, I don't think that would be a good idea, seeing as you didn't start off very well with him. I don't know how your father would feel about you being found in a roadside ditch with a bullet in your brain. Lieutenant North is an outstanding shot, Abbott. I believe if I had let that meeting go on one minute longer, you would have found that out. And I would have lost an important crime-fighting tool—him. Oh, you're right; North can be a bull in a China closet. I just don't see that as a problem, as long as he breaks the right things."

The blood from Abbott's face drained. Although he wanted to say something, he couldn't find any words he deemed appropriate. He looked at the director and considered his earlier comments. *Perhaps, this is one of those times to just shut up.*

"Mr. Abbott, you have allowed your personal animosity toward Dr. Gaurdia, your unchecked ego, and your incessant desire to self-promote, even at the cost to others, to cloud your judgment. You have done yourself no favors today. Therefore, I have decided your fate: I am sending you to Wyoming. Now, before you start complaining, I am not doing this as punishment." The director paused a moment to look into Abbott's eyes; he wondered if this gamble would work.

"No complaints, sir," said Abbott.

"Very well. If you are wondering why I chose Wyoming, the answer is simple. A very old friend of mine is assigned there. He chooses to stay there because he loves it. It is a beautiful place and perhaps you will learn to love the outdoors while you are there. If you show promise, my friend may teach you how to fly fish. It's a challenging sport requiring great patience and finesse, both things you need to learn. My friend there is an interesting man. He doesn't really like supervision much. He is kind of independent and headstrong. But he has a good heart and I believe he can help you find your way. I would be careful, though, Mr. Abbott. He does have a bit of a temper and is quick to violence. There is a lot of lonely, abandoned country and many places where a person might go in and not come out. I know because my friend once showed me one of them."

10

JW and Ben sat quietly. They had been alone a while now, waiting for someone to return. Ben had visions of Director Murphy, Gaurdia, and Abbott arguing about how to kick them out of the building. JW and Abbott had really gone after one another, and he worried about how the FBI would view such a display. Finally, Dr. Gaurdia returned to the conference room, quietly walked over to the refreshment table, and made herself a cup of tea.

"Well, that was certainly interesting, wasn't it, gentlemen?"

JW responded, "Sorry, Lauralynn. I know you worked hard for today, and I kind of came into the room and lit off a block of C-4 explosives."

"You have nothing to be sorry about, JW. Abbott was totally out of line. I am surprised the director let that go on for as long as he did."

"I believe he was taking a measure of both Abbott and me. Hopefully, it doesn't sour him on your idea."

"Hopefully."

Dr. Gaurdia, her shoulders slumped, looked deflated. JW hadn't realized his actions could have such a direct effect on her. He felt bad. Based on her earlier actions and words, he should have realized how important this was to her. Not to mention Ben, who'd had to work hard on the project and his wife, Lucy, to gain her acceptance. It was time to stop being such a selfish bastard. He wondered what he needed to do to repair any damage he had done.

Director Murphy re-entered the room, and everyone stood in recognition of his position. He motioned for them to sit and then did so himself. The Director paused, not for drama but to collect his thoughts. Finally, he said, "My apologies. That includes you too, Doctor. Special Agent Abbott overstepped his position and was out of line in his aggressive questioning of you, Lieutenant. Not to make excuses, but he is young and needs more experience before working in a position like this. That is my error, and I hope everyone here can forgive me."

JW decided this was his time to say, "Sir, that's not necessary. I wasn't prepared for that line of questioning and didn't handle it well."

The director laughed, "I was beginning to worry that I would see a display of your marksmanship abilities."

"No, sir, I wouldn't have shot him. Perhaps beat him to a pulp, though."

Everyone laughed, and the conversation returned to the question at hand. "Lieutenant North, my original plan was to lay out a complete offer for your services at this point. Unfortunately, that idea seems to have stalled, and I believe we all could use some time for reflection. I have learned not to ask questions if I am unsure of the answer. I worry that perhaps this meeting may have soured you on working for us."

JW started to say something, but the director cut him off. "Not necessary at this time, Lieutenant."

"Sir, if I may," and immediately JW regretted using the same words as Abbott, "what I meant to say was, I was not going to speak to the subject of the meeting, but rather to make a small announcement." The director nodded, and JW continued, "I wanted to inform you that if you make me an offer, you will be making Officer Ben Kellum an offer as well. Ben has decided that, when he retires from the Long

Beach Police Department next year, he will become the second member of the Big Dogs Human Scent Detection and Mantrailing Team."

Lauralynn quietly kicked him under the table, her form of payback for a surprise. She hated surprises. He turned to her with a look that said, "What? I thought you'd like it." He raised his eyebrows at her and thought, *You mess with the bull, you get the horns.*

Director Murphy said, "Well, that is good news. One of my few questions was about your ability to replicate your results. So, you believe you can recreate the success of your first two dogs?"

"Director, we believe we have a solid training and certification regimen. The first key for us is to acquire a high-quality dog. We will use the same importer that we did with Ares and Addy. Hopefully, the breeder in Germany will have another dog of similar prospects or know of one. He is very well connected there, and I believe our success will serve as a motivator for others to provide dogs."

"Very well. And thank you, Officer Kellum. Here is what I propose: you two will go to Quantico, enjoy academy life, and tomorrow you will get the full briefing from Dr. Gaurdia and her team. Then, tomorrow evening, I will take the three of you and Lauralynn's number two, Special Agent LeClair, out to dinner at The Globe and Laurel."

Lauralynn said, "I think Rick would love to have a good steak."

JW knew the Globe and Laurel was a fantastic steak house near the main gate of the Marine Corps Base at Quantico. They served great food and grilled a delicious steak. He nodded enthusiastically and said, "That would be perfect, sir."

"Being a former Marine, I thought you would approve. OK then, Dr. Gaurdia, if you would walk them down to the front of the building, I will have one of my staff contact their driver. And Doctor, please come back after you drop them off. We have some things to discuss."

Ten minutes later, Lauralynn stood before the director's desk. He had neither offered her a seat nor addressed her. He was letting her stew and wonder what his following words would be. Finally, he asked, "Dr. Gaurdia, you do realize your ownership in what almost derailed that meeting?"

"Sir?"

"OK, let me be more direct. Do you understand that your petty grievances with Special Agent Abbott almost cost the FBI the use of a valuable asset and personally embarrassed me?"

Gaurdia had not realized that the director was aware of the anger between her and Abbott. "Sir, I accept responsibility. I did not understand the depth of his anger toward me."

The director slowly took a deep breath and let it out. "As far as Abbott is concerned, he is going to Wyoming. Lauralynn, you have little understanding of human interactions. This is a severe flaw in your character and you need to work on it. If you ever aspire to any form of a leadership position in this organization, you will need to learn to lead and not undermine those around you. You are in the place you are now, in charge of this project, because of your brilliance.

"To be honest, Special Agent LeClair carries the leadership duties within your group. I asked him to. If your involvement were not so important to this project, I would be shipping you off to Wyoming for a dose of humility. I would recommend you spend some time around Lieutenant North. He has been a leader in the Marines and at the Long

Beach Police Department. He is certainly not my idea of perfection; hmm, perhaps we should send him to Wyoming too. No, there's only so much room there."

The drive to Quantico went quietly. Special Agent Blair drove them on a back route; he told them the main highways were clogged with traffic. Ben was admiring the countryside when JW asked, "You been to Quantico before, Ben?"

"No, when I was in DC before, they stuck me in a hotel in the suburbs. I've heard so much about the place I'm anxious to finally see it."

"I was there when I was in the Marines, at The Basic School, which isn't far from the FBI Academy. We used to go over to the theater and watch movies. That was before 9/11; it was easier to get into the place then. Everything was much more secure when I returned for the National Academy. The base is beautiful—so unlike the Marine Corps to be here. They usually locate their bases in the most desolate, miserable places on earth. It makes for excellent training because the places we go and fight are just as bad or worse."

They drove through one of the gates to the base, Blair using his credentials to gain access for them all. Marine Corps Base Quantico was huge but seemed even larger because there were trees everywhere. They turned off the main road and into the area reserved for the FBI Academy. JW pointed out the massive crime lab building off to the left, and then they passed through the woods and into a large open parking lot with a group of buildings across. As they parked, Blair said, "Good news, gentlemen, they have reserved rooms for you in Jefferson Hall."

Ben looked at JW for clarification. "Jefferson is that nice tall building to the right. It has single rooms with their own bath. The rest of the housing here is two to a room and four to a bathroom, so we will be living in luxury. We must be important."

Blair escorted them inside and got them checked in. They went to their rooms, cleaned up, and returned downstairs, dressed casually in tan cargo pants and polo shirts. This was standard dress for the academy; however, JW and Ben each wore newly minted Big Dogs polo shirts. Blair gave them a quick tour, showing them the cafeteria, store, bar, and gym. The buildings were all connected with glass tunnels. JW joked to Ben that when he was there, they called them "Habitrails."

At the end of the tour, Blair looked at his watch and said, "Unless you want to go out into town, you may want to head over to the cafeteria."

JW nodded and said, "Don't worry, Ben, the food here is excellent. Blair, would you like to join us, or do you have someplace to be?"

"Really? That would be great."

JW sighed, "Blair, relax. I'm JW; this is Ben. We're just regular guys. There's nothing special about us; it's all about the dogs."

"I don't know about you, JW, but I *am* special," said Ben. "Lucy tells me so all the time."

"Oh, you're special, all right."

After dinner, JW and Ben said goodnight to Blair and went to their rooms to phone their wives. After finishing their calls, they sat down and chatted, strategizing for the next day before calling it a night.

The Shadow drove through the small towns outside Bowling Green. His new job as an automotive parts deliveryman was perfect. Numerous small repair shops in the surrounding area had business agreements with his firm. They would phone in orders during the day and he would drive through the night making deliveries to them. He was given keys to each shop to allow him to drop off the parts inside. The position was perfect. He now had a perfectly legitimate excuse to wander the streets of these various towns to make his deliveries. If he wandered off the main routes to do some victim shopping and was stopped by the police, it was easy to explain away. "Oh, I'm sorry. I was going to such and such auto repair shop to drop off parts and trying to find a shortcut. I guess I got turned around and lost."

The story was perfect; it had worked once already. He delivered to over fifty repair shops and couldn't be expected to remember where they all were. The Shadow had explored enough to feel comfortable with the area. He had stalked several women—potential victims—here. There were just so many of them from which to choose. The old saying "a kid in a candy store" came to mind. If that was true, the Shadow had a sweet tooth.

Tonight would be his first kill since the woman he had killed in Wyoming. He had been patient; he had planned to perfection. But the pressure within him had built to the point that he was ready to explode. And explode he would. The Shadow had decided this time would be much more spectacular than any of his previous attacks. He knew he wanted to do things differently. He didn't want to be tied to the Long Beach attacks and the shooting. That would create too much focus and interest in him. This time, he was going to be a savage. No more Mr. Nice Guy.

The Shadow parked his delivery truck a few blocks away, behind a business. There were other vehicles in the lot, so it was unlikely it would be noticed. He walked from the lot into the neighborhood, acting as if he was out for his evening walk. It was late, so no one was out to see him. If he was stopped, he had a story prepared that he was working overnight and went for a walk to help him wake up. He didn't know if it would work, but it was better than being unprepared.

His target this evening was a young, single woman. She lived a few blocks from where he was parked. The houses here were a little farther apart and he believed he could approach the rear of his date's home unnoticed by her neighbors. She worked at a local bank, but he wasn't sure what she did there. He also didn't know her name; it was more difficult here to do the deep dive backgrounds he was used to. No matter, he could use some quiet time with her to ask a few questions before the fun started.

The house behind hers was up for sale. It was perfect since there would be one less potential witness to worry about. As he started to cut through the lot of the home for sale, he noticed the lights were on inside. There was movement. *Had the place been sold already?* It was very late for anyone to be up in this working-class neighborhood. He peeked through the window.

He recognized her; she matched the picture on the "for sale" sign. *Did she buy the place?* As he watched the woman, she moved some furniture around. *Staging?* He silently went back out front and noted that the sale sign now included a message that there would be an open house in the morning. The real estate agent's name was May Everly. He returned to her; she moved with grace, even as she was doing menial chores. He liked the look of her. She was even better than the target he had planned to take tonight. *This would be perfect!* Certainly, no one was coming here until tomorrow. She was his all night long, with no interruptions.

He moved to the back door and discovered she had left it unlocked. He went inside and crept down the hallway to the dining room, where she was arranging fruit on a table. She sensed him there and turned, startled. He said, "Sorry, I didn't mean to surprise you. I saw the sign and wondered if I could look at the house?"

His comment confused her for a moment. He moved slowly toward the kitchen behind her, and she realized, *It's almost one in the morning. No one visits an open house at one a.m.*

"I'm sorry, I'm not ready yet. You'll have to come back later."

It was then she saw the surgical gloves on his hands, and she panicked.

He looked at her face, seeing the fear set in as she understood. His anger began to rise as he recalled his hatred for a girl just like this from his past. Before she could say another word or scream, he stepped toward her, swung, and hit her head with his hand. She fell as if poleaxed. He dragged her to one of the bedrooms and discovered a bed as part of the staging. *That was very considerate of you, May.* He pulled her clothes off and tossed them into the corner. He pulled her onto the bed and started to ask her questions, but she was still unconscious. *Oh well, a little less fun for me, but time is tight.*

He raped her repeatedly. He exorcised the hatred he felt for her and those like her and released it upon her being. He beat her body and kicked her ribs until he felt something crack. He left her face alone; he didn't want to blemish that. May was fortunate that she would never recover consciousness. She would never know how the Shadow had violated her and his ultimate plans. Finally, exhausted, he left the home by the back door. The bedroom looked like a slaughterhouse, with blood everywhere. The Shadow smiled at the thought of the present he had left for the police whenever they came.

A young couple, anxious to see the house, arrived precisely at ten a.m. that morning. They were excited at the prospect of finally owning their first house. They had seen the listing online, but there was nothing like the real thing. The young woman knocked on the door, but there was no answer. Finally, she told her husband, "I'm sure it's OK if we go in." She looked at her watch and said, "The sign says ten…" She checked the door, "and the door is unlocked." She went inside, calling, "Hello, we're here for the open house. Hello." Her husband stayed on the porch for a moment, admiring the neighborhood. *This place is perfect. I hope the seller will negotiate as it is just above our price range.* He was jarred out of his revelry when he heard his wife scream. And then she screamed some more. He ran into the house, wondering what she had found. She was at the entrance to the dining room and pointed over her shoulder. She stopped screaming at the sight of him, seemingly calmed a bit. Her husband looked over her shoulder and saw a woman's head in a bowl on the table. Her eyes pleaded to him silently. "What in all that's holy...?" was all he could say.

He grabbed his wife by the wrist and pulled her toward the front door. At the same time, he pulled his phone from a holster on his belt and dialed 911. The police arrived less than five minutes later. *Good response time,* he thought. The officer went inside and immediately returned, vomiting into the bushes by the front door. As a second officer arrived, the first called dispatch on his radio and advised, "This is a confirmed homicide. I need you to get Chief Johnson and some detectives out here. This place is a mess."

By the time the day was through, every on-duty officer, plus several who had been called in, were at the scene. The county sheriff responded but quickly departed in favor of state investigators. It wasn't until much later in the day that the coroner was called. As everything was finally wrapping up early the next morning, the chief talked with the lead state investigator on the front lawn. The sun was already warming the day and he was sweating. Finally, the chief said, "Best we can figure, the victim was killed overnight. She was here setting up for an open house and most likely surprised by her killer. The neighbors we interviewed said they didn't hear anything."

"Makes sense. I've spoken with my people and they say there are no signs of a struggle. Course, looking at that bedroom, how the hell could you tell? I'd like to run something by you if I may?"

"Sure thing, whatever you think is best. We're not equipped to deal with something like this."

"Looking at this scene," he said, pointing to the house, "it could be a former boyfriend or something. It's a mess, but the killer could have staged it to look like something bigger. But I don't get that feeling. This feels like more, and I don't know what it is, to be honest. I was thinking of giving the FBI a call, show them what we've got. I've always wanted to work with them and see how they do things. This might be my only chance. There's something more here; I don't think this is the end. This is the start."

"If that's what you think is best, you go ahead. I have no issues with the FBI coming in on this. Helps shift some of the focus off me. I don't need the city council crawling up my ass on this."

"OK then, I'll have my folks pack it up and send everything to Quantico. I always wanted to talk to a real live profiler." He looked at the for-sale sign and said, "Open house, huh. I wonder if they got any offers."

The house would not sell for a very long time.

11

JW and Ben both woke early and decided to go for a run. JW took Ben out on a long loop that ran by Lunga Reservoir. The place was beautiful, even with a chill in the morning air. Back at the academy, they sprinted around the track before finishing. The run seemed to erase all the negative vibes from the day before. After a quick shower, they met outside their rooms and went to breakfast. The dining hall was full of young, energetic FBI agents. JW looked at Ben and asked, "Do you remember ever being that young?"

While waiting on an omelet, Ben said, "Nope," then scanned the other offerings. JW went for speed, gathered his meal, and sat at an empty table, away from the other students. Next, he searched for a cup of coffee, and when he returned, a group of four student agents was standing at the table.

"May we join you, sir?"

"Sure thing. The more, the merrier. Just save one seat for my associate."

JW knew a question was coming, and it didn't take long. "Sir, I'm sorry to interrupt your meal, but could I ask a quick question?"

JW nodded while he continued chewing. He also noted Ben was laughing as he walked up to the table.

"Are you the officers involved in the shootout in Las Vegas? We were all wondering why you were here. Not that there is anything wrong with you being here, but we're curious."

JW smiled. "That's a great question; I think my partner, Ben, could give you a better answer." He laughed as he watched the four heads, once focused on him, swivel toward Ben, who had just taken a mouthful of food.

"Yes, we were involved in the Las Vegas incident. But we can't talk about it because it's still being investigated. I'm sure you understand."

Smooth Ben, very smooth, but you won't get off that easily.

"Certainly, we talked about statements in our media class. But could you explain how the dogs follow the suspects' scent?" All the students leaned forward, even further toward Ben as JW laughed inside.

About fifteen minutes later, Ben finished his presentation, and the students said, "Thank you, sir. That was great. We need to run to class now."

JW had finished his meal and was enjoying a cup of coffee. Ben looked at his tray and said, "I only got one bite. You could have chimed in, JW."

"Nah, you were doing great. I didn't want to ruin your momentum."

Dr. Gaurdia chose that moment to text them. JW and Ben's phones chirped with the message: "I will meet you in the lobby in five minutes."

Lauralynn greeted them in the lobby and said, "Nice shirts, guys. Let's walk over to my unit." She walked them across the parking lot and down a path into the woods. They came into a large opening and faced a somewhat blocky, indistinct structure. "I know it's not much, but it's home."

They entered through the main doors. Inside the lobby area was a large reception desk. Dr. Gaurdia picked up the narrative, "This is where our duty officer sits. Generally, during business hours it is an FBI police officer, but after hours we usually have a recently graduated agent here. So,

JW, when they call you in the middle of the night, be gentle. We'll give you a proper tour later, but for now, let's go to my office."

Lauralynn's office was on the first floor. Her window provided a nice view of the woods behind the building. Ben asked about a restroom and left to find it. Lauralynn told JW to have a seat while she went to get coffee for them. JW sat in the chair and looked around the room. There were several plaques and awards scattered about. His eyes were drawn to a bookcase on one side of the room. The shelves were nearly full of books about behavioral psychology and serial killers. In the middle of the display was an old, weathered doll. It was on a stand covered with a glass globe. He looked at it and wondered.

She came back into the room and noticed JW's focus. He looked over his shoulder at her and his eyes asked about it. She answered, "That belonged to my cousin. We lived in this beautiful little town in Iowa—Bellam. For an eight-year-old girl, it was perfect. She and I were best friends; we had our whole lives planned out. She was going to be a librarian; she loved books. I was going to be a doctor. One day, we played hide and seek in the woods, but I couldn't find her and she never came back. I looked for hours and finally went home with tears streaming down my face. Ultimately, my parents called the police and they searched. They didn't find her for days; it was horrible when they did. She had been raped and killed and left in the woods for the animals. I kept her doll and it has served as my inspiration every day since then.

"I'm sorry, Doctor. I knew a little about this, but I didn't understand the depth of your pain."

"My pain is nothing compared to that of my cousin. I swore on her grave that I would find her killer. But, of course, that was a long time ago. I suspect her murderer has died by now. Still, I wonder. What would I do if he were in front of me right now? What would I ask him? Or would I simply shoot him in cold blood? Maybe it's best if I don't find out."

JW looked at her carefully. Because he felt the same way about the Shadow, he could relate to her pain. Her heartache permeated the room, and he found he wanted to help her. "I tell you what, Doctor, you help me find him, and I will handle the rest."

She looked at him and measured his sincerity. Finally, she nodded and said, "Deal. Thank you. And please call me Lauralynn, at least when it's just us."

JW felt something change in the room and between them, "Deal."

"JW, may I ask you a favor?" He nodded, and she continued, "The director told me something yesterday, and I believe I need your help."

This came as a bit of a surprise to JW, who merely said, "Go ahead."

"The director confided in me that he has concerns about my interpersonal skills and leadership ability. He told me yesterday's blow-up at the meeting was as much my fault as Special Agent Abbott's. He told me I should look to you as an example."

This caught JW entirely off guard. He certainly had not expected this. "Why do you think he said that?"

"Well, he knows I respect you and what you have accomplished. He has been thoroughly briefed about your career. I believe he sees you as a good leader, but also, and I quote, 'a bit of bull in a China closet.'"

JW laughed and said, "Well, he is half right." JW then got serious, "Lauralynn, I would be happy to help you. I have some excellent books I can recommend. But one thing, sometimes the things I say may be a bit hurtful to you. I will try to not do that, but I don't think you realize how the things you say and do are received. It may surprise you, so you have to promise me you will listen first before you argue."

"The director said he would send me to Wyoming and have someone leave me in the wilderness. I think this might be a better alternative."

"OK, before Ben gets back, let's try something."

She nodded, seeming almost excited, "Sure."

"After the Las Vegas shootout, when you called, the first thing you asked about was Addy. Not me, but Addy. Actually, you didn't ask about me at all."

"But I love your dogs, JW, especially Addy."

"I understand that. I love the dogs too. I tend to prefer dogs to people. But, when talking to a person, it might be best to ask about them first, even if you don't care."

"But I do care about you. I'm just not sure I'm following your train of thought."

He paused and thought for a moment, "OK, here is an idea. If we are talking and I say, 'Aardvark,' I want you to stop and think of a lonely, desolate place in Wyoming, far from anywhere. Then think about what you are saying and how you could say it better."

Still clearly perplexed, Lauralynn said, "Okaaay."

Ben walked in, looked at the two of them, and asked, "Did I interrupt something?"

Both replied, "No," very quickly.

"Alright, before we meet the group, I want to give you an idea of where we fit into the FBI organization." Dr. Gaurdia explained, "The FBI has an alphabet soup of acronyms for various groups dedicated to solving all types of violent crimes. Many of these initiatives took place during the '80s and '90s. I don't want to get into what came first and which one does the best job. We all try to work together to solve problems, just like the director said yesterday. Things are constantly being modified to meet the ever-changing needs of crime fighting.

"So, overarching is the Critical Incident Response Group. It was developed to integrate tactics and support to facilitate a comprehensive rapid response. Within that is the National Center for the Analysis of Violent Crime. This group includes the various behavioral analysis units, from terrorism to adult crime, to crimes against children and the Violent Criminal Apprehension Program, also known as ViCAP, to Research and Instruction. We are a subset of CIRG that combines both operational and investigative elements. Our unit is currently being evaluated to determine its effectiveness and viability as a long-term aid in solving serial crime. I understand this may be a lot to take in. But the bottom line is you work with my team and me.

"As you may know, before I came to the FBI, when I was in school finishing my second Ph.D., I wrote my thesis on computer modeling of serial killers. In simple terms, it involved using a supercomputer to analyze crime data to determine whether crimes were related to one another through an analysis of their elements. This is part of what a profiler does, but now we are trying to do this on a massive scale, with the ability to search the entire country. Of course, that was not possible at that time; my thesis was entirely theoretical.

"After my paper was published, I was contacted by Dr. Stefan Fischer, a brilliant computer scientist. A friend had shown him my paper, and he immediately began assembling the systems necessary to make it happen in his mind. He will provide a briefing on it during our upcoming meeting."

JW laughed, "I hope we can understand what he says."

"Oh, don't worry. I'll be there to translate, if necessary."

JW and Ben turned to one another and immediately knew what the other was thinking. *We're screwed.*

They moved to a conference room on the second floor of the building. There weren't as many people present as JW expected. Lauralynn saw JW's look and anticipated his question, "These are the section heads from my group. I didn't want to bring everyone in and overwhelm you. You will meet many more people as we go through the day."

JW nodded and found a seat near the coffee pot. Ben sat on one side and Special Agent LeClair on the other. Lauralynn took her spot at the head of the table and said, "OK, everyone, if we can all take a seat and get started." Lauralynn quickly introduced JW and Ben to the group, then asked that the representatives introduce themselves and explain what their group does.

"Special Agent Rick LeClair. I am second in command here. I'm also responsible for the tactical elements when we are in that role."

JW wondered about his words but decided that could wait until later.

"Stefan Fischer, I lead the computer team and am responsible for the care and feeding of 'Frankenstein'— that's what we call the supercomputer."

"Cecelia Mercado, I am the lead for our forensics team."

The last woman turned to JW and Ben and said, "Hello, gentlemen. I'm Louise Gallagher; everyone here calls me Lou. I'm the lead for the profiler team."

Doctor Gaurdia then picked up the presentation, "As you can see, we have representatives from all the major criminology disciplines. Each works with their own group but is also involved with the other teams. Let me explain: Dr. Fischer has developed a powerful computer program that allows us to evaluate data from several criminal databases. We use this to identify potential candidates for serial criminals. A team of members from each group evaluates all the available crime report information related to an incident—reports, photos, witnesses, forensics, everything. They do this individually and then meet as a group.

"The group does two things. First, they break down the data on hand to clarify the language to help identify method of operation, victimology, and signature. In simplest terms, method of operation, or MO, is the how of the crime. Victimology relates to the specifics of the victim. We are finding that some serial killers tend to choose victims of similar characteristics. We believe they do this subconsciously, which, of course, makes it more useful for us. Finally, signature is different from MO. It is similar in that we tend to see it regularly, but it is not essential to committing the crime. Signature is more personal and is what the unknown subject, or unsub, does for his own reasons: things like staging or keeping a personal item from the victim.

"The second thing the group does is to evaluate the crime data to determine whether crimes are related. The computer will help us identify a cluster of crimes and tell us with a degree of confidence if they are related. This allows us to focus on our work, reach out to local law enforcement, and offer assistance. In the early stages, local agencies may have difficulty identifying a serial case."

Dr. Fischer interjected, "Most of the time, this step is unnecessary as Frankenstein will tell us by a degree of confidence if the crimes are related. Dr. Gaurdia prefers to have us work together to identify things the computer may not have recognized. It has impressive capabilities but does not match the human mind…yet. I have to say, these meetings can get rather heated with members arguing their positions. The greatest value comes from working with other members and understanding each person's specialty better. I personally find the meetings stimulating and believe we have forged an impressive team, bonded together in one goal, to remove this scourge from society."

Another true believer, thought JW.

"I am sure some of you are wondering why Lieutenant North and Officer Kellum are here," said Lauralynn. "They are, of course, the officers who trailed the suspect in Las Vegas. You were all briefed on that incident. Our 'little' unit does a great job of identifying patterns and potential serials. We respond at the request of local agencies, but then we reach a bit of a roadblock. We reduce the size of the haystack we are looking for the needle in, but that haystack can still be quite large. Using their scent detection dogs, these two can help us identify suspects so we can focus our attention and all the law enforcement tools on them."

Dr. Fischer stated, "We have a little demonstration for you. If you look at the large display, I will show you how this works." The screen changed to a map of the United States with many red dots. "Each dot on the map represents what we have classified as a related killing. These are the work of Unsub 17-11. He is our most prolific active serial killer, or at least we believe so. We classify them by year and number. To help clarify them, we often will assign a moniker. Here, we chose the name given by the media, the 'Truck Stop Killer.'"

I've heard of that serial killer, thought JW. He sat back in his chair and focused on every word said, digesting the presentation and realizing he could be a part of something big. *I am in a room full of people I know very little about and have difficulty relating to, yet I have never felt so at home. Everyone here is a believer.*

"There are twenty-four dots on the screen, covering mostly the eastern and southeastern United States. These represent the killings that we have a high degree of confidence are related." The screen changed, with several green dots added. "Here are another twenty-two that we are less confident in but believe may be related. Just like your work, Lieutenant, we can never say things with absolute certainty. So let me make a small adjustment."

JW noticed the dots on the screen were now doing the wave, from north to south and east to west.

"This visual reinforces our belief that these are all related. The wave is set to the estimated time of occurrence, which in our line of work is not one hundred percent accurate. Here is another visual that Dr. Gaurdia asked me to prepare specifically for you, Lieutenant North." The screen changed, and now there were only two dots, one on the west coast and one in the upper mid-west.

"This is a small sample; however, we have linked these two crimes using forensics." Dr. Fischer highlighted the dot in the middle of the country. "This was a rape and murder that occurred in a rest stop near Rawlings, Wyoming. An observant officer at the scene found a used condom in a trash can at the scene. We obtained DNA that was identified as the victim and an unsub. Frankenstein linked that unknown DNA to another crime in Long Beach, California. That was the incident where you were shot, Lieutenant. The murder in Wyoming occurred a few weeks after you were injured. We related these two incidents with several rapes in Long Beach and labeled this as Unsub 19-2. I can say with a high degree of confidence that Unsub 19-2 is 'the Shadow.'"

JW felt his body tense. He looked at the screen and then at Dr. Fischer. "Where did he go?"

"That we do not know—yet. Frankenstein is unable to project due to the limited data. Conjecture says he continued east, but where he stopped was not identified. Believe me, we are looking. Once we identify an unsub, we never stop looking."

JW nodded, thinking, *Nice job, Lauralynn. This presentation was designed specifically to bring me on board. She probably thought Ben would just follow me without question. She's probably right.*

The group took a break, with the section leaders returning to their areas to prepare for a tour by JW and Ben. As the group broke up, Ben walked up to JW, excitement in his eyes. "JW, we have got to get in on this! This is absolutely insane."

"I assume you are using 'insane' in a good way."

"Oh, yeah. And don't try to bullshit me. You want in. I saw you when Dr. Fischer started talking about the Shadow."

JW nodded and smiled, "Yep."

After their break, Lauralynn escorted JW and Ben through the building. Each section leader explained in detail what their group did. The entire staff showed great pride in what they were doing. Dedication. When they paused outside a large room, JW said, "Doctor, this place is fantastic, but I have a quick question."

"That's what we're here for," Lauralynn replied.

"This building is incredible. It's like its own free-standing crime-fighting facility. But I haven't seen much of the crime labs and other facilities I expected."

"Good question. This building was designed by my section heads and me. When we put it together, we decided not to recreate the capabilities of the entire FBI. We have all those things you mentioned and more here at the Academy. We have miniature versions of some of them here so we don't have to leave whenever we need something. There is some duplication, but only to maintain our efficiency. Our team members have full authorization to use any resource here in Quantico. Of course, we try to do that, so we do not alienate anyone."

"Huh," was all he could manage. *I believe I may have underestimated Dr. Gaurdia.* "Doctor, do you have naked pictures of the director?"

Lauralynn had a look of total confusion on her face. Finally, Ben decided he would step forward and clarify for her. "What JW is asking is—your section represents a substantial commitment from the director. How did you get his buy-in for all of this?"

Her face cleared, "Oh, that makes more sense." She gave JW an annoyed look as she said, "Why didn't you just ask that?"

She then spoke to the two of them. "The director's reasons are his own. He is a believer like the rest of us. Maybe one day he will share them with you, as he has with me. You should never doubt his enthusiasm for this project but understand that, without results, we will be shut down."

JW got a few minutes to chat with SA LeClair and asked, "Rick, you said you were in charge of your section if you went operational. What did you mean?"

"When we deploy, I usually take a team of three or four. My people are cross-trained in forensics, things like photography, evidence collection, and the like. When we first get there, we assist with the lab work. We gear up and go from there if we get a lead and need door kickers. We find it's better than just showing up in SWAT gear; it's less intrusive."

"That makes sense. What do you do here while you're waiting to deploy?"

LeClair smiled, "We work on team tactics and, of course, a lot of shooting. I know you're a gun guy, so if we get some downtime I'll take you to the range, and we can play with the Hostage Rescue Team's toys."

JW and Ben finished the tour with a few hours of free time. Instead of sitting in their rooms, they used the time to hike to one of the picnic areas around Lunga Lake. JW found that being in nature settled him and allowed him to clear his head.

Reaching the picnic area, which consisted of several picnic tables and a large dumpster, they each grabbed a seat and looked out at the lake. Ben said, "There is much more to this than I imagined."

"Yeah. I didn't think the team would have a lead on the Shadow."

"You won't like this, but I think you need to put that aside. We're making a decision that will affect the rest of our lives, our family's lives. The Shadow represents just one small part of that."

"You're right. It's hard to let him go, though. OK, let's flip it around. Is there a good reason not to sign up?"

"You mentioned something the other day about not being owned by the Feds. That concerns me too. I think the people we met today are great, but what if that changes tomorrow? What if we get another ass like Abbott?"

"Well, a little bird whispered in my ear that Abbott is on his way to Wyoming. I feel a little bad about that. After all, he is a young man trying to find his way in the world. I guess the director reassigned him there. He has a friend there that he sends personality reclamation projects to."

"Let's hope we never have to run a trail in Wyoming."

The group sat at a large table in an isolated area of the Globe and Laurel restaurant. The director was regaling them with stories from throughout his career. It was far more colorful than JW imagined and included a short Wyoming tour.

The food was as good as he remembered and he genuinely enjoyed the company.

The director motioned for everyone to be quiet. "I hate to ruin a good time with business, but I did promise to have a presentation for you. I needed to discuss some things with Dr. Gaurdia and Special Agent LeClair, who are very passionate about your participation. I must admit, the idea of you two running down serial killers is very exciting.

"Before I proceed, I would like some input from you two. Are you interested?"

"I can't fully speak for Ben, but we talked about it," said JW. "We are extremely interested in what you have to say, sir."

"Very well then, here is what we," indicating the group, "are offering you. We believe you two bring a unique opportunity to the FBI. We have a powerful tool that we have developed, but the ability to close the deal and bring the suspect to heel seems beyond our grasp on occasion. To use a football analogy, we want Big Dogs to help bring the team across the goal line. As we see it, there is a place for you on the team; the question is, to what extent?

"Having spoken with the leadership component of my team, I would be interested in hearing your thoughts on how we could optimize your team within ours."

JW took this as his cue. "Sir, first of all, thank you for the opportunity to come to DC and Virginia and learn how this all works. I believe both Ben and I were aware of the role that Dr. Gaurdia's organization plays. However, we did not know the extent of its resources or the quality of the people working here. That said, it would be an honor for Big Dogs to contribute in whatever way you think is best. If you are asking our opinion, Ben and I have discussed this and we are of like minds; we believe a full-time role would be an overreach. Your needs will always be cyclic, with periods where we would be wholly inactive. We think your mission would best be served by us working in an on-call capacity.

"We would require some form of federal law enforcement status to be able to work throughout the country in support of your needs. My wife and I are currently in the process of researching a new location for our headquarters. We believe we cannot support the needs of the Big Dogs organization from a small house in the middle of a residential area. Ben will remain in the Southern California area and manage his own team. I will be relocating to an as-yet-unknown location with enough space to maintain more dogs and provide an area where we can train new teams. I see each of us needing a support team with one or two members. Even when we are working for the FBI, there will be occasions when we are independent and without Special Agent LeClair's resources. Additionally, if those support members could meet Rick's standards, we could provide support to him if needed."

"Thank you, Lieutenant North."

"Sir?"

"I was faced with a dilemma. I was concerned that, should we offer you the plan you just so effectively laid out, you would not be interested in a part-time offer. However, it seems we are all in agreement and we should move on to the dessert menu."

Everyone laughed, and the director continued, "I'll have my office draw up a contract to explain what I am about to say in detail. We are prepared to offer you federal law enforcement status as US Marshals. We will pay for you and approved support members to travel to and from investigation sites, including an hourly rate starting when you receive the first call and expenses. We will pay for a level of maintenance training for your program staff and dogs. Obviously, we will cover any injuries that occur in an on-duty status, dogs or staff. Questions?"

"One thing, sir. We will be very popular, especially when the word of our successes gets out. I believe we will need some assistance from the FBI in controlling access. If not, we will be chasing every lost child in the United States.

However, there is a flip side to that as well. We can help generate some goodwill by running the occasional trail to assist local law enforcement. I believe finding a lost child is significant; we just may need some help determining when that is appropriate. I know what I just said may not be very clear."

"Sir, if I may," interjected Lauralynn, "I believe I understand exactly what JW is saying." She looked directly into his eyes with understanding. "And it is hard. My team receives calls from people who have lost a child. We can't tell if it is a serial killer's victim or a runaway. It is a family reaching out to you as the one hope of getting their child back and it is hard to say no. But, as JW stated, they can't be everywhere at once. There must be priorities, and there will be pain associated with the guilt of saying no."

The director paused for a moment, considering the question before him, "A bit of a conundrum. I see why this was troubling you, Lieutenant. Here is my thought: if you are in your home state, you are free to answer requests as you see fit. Dr. Gaurdia will help you develop a protocol for response for both the FBI and local agencies requesting your help. Gentlemen, you may carry the US Marshal badge, but you are representing the FBI. As I have with Dr. Gaurdia, I would remind you that we are in the business of helping others. You have not chosen the quiet life. You should be prepared to be very busy.

"Now, if there is nothing else, Dr. Gaurdia will serve as my point for any further details. Let me be clear, Lieutenant North, if there is something you need, you will get it. Now, I am thinking the chocolate mousse and a coffee will be the perfect cap for the evening."

12

JW, Bonnie, Ben, and Lucy sat around the fire pit in the backyard of the North residence.

They had spent the last hour going over the DC trip in detail. As they concluded their briefing, Bonnie declared it was time for a toast. Bonnie and Lucy chose champagne, Ben a beer, and JW his favorite tequila. When everyone had a drink in hand, Bonnie said, "A toast to Big Dogs and their future success."

Ares and Addy, who had settled in after receiving the required attention from their guests, now decided they should be included in the toast. "Sorry, you two, only water for you," said JW. After everyone had sampled their drinks, JW continued, "I have to say, that was an impressive display by the FBI. They really rolled out the red carpet for us. Ben, did you learn anything from our visit?"

"Well, for one thing, beware the man who picks the chocolate mousse over the butter cake with ice cream and caramel sauce."

Everyone laughed, but JW steered the discussion back on course, "That's not quite what I meant, and by the way, I had the mousse and it was excellent."

"OK." Then assuming a pretentious level of seriousness, Ben said, "What stood out to me was the universal message from everyone of how badly they wanted us on the team."

"Yep, that's it, but I felt that the director was the driving force behind this entire thing. I think he sees it as his legacy and, of course, he wants that legacy to be a huge success."

Ben said, "Are you saying we should have asked for more?"

"No, I think he gave us everything we were asking for anyway. And he is sincere when he says, 'if something comes up, we will get what we need.' Now, let's focus. First, you two start laying out what the Kellums will need in terms of support to get started on their satellite program. Next, Ben and I will reach out to Vohne Liche Kennels, Axel, and Josef in Germany to see about another dog. For budget purposes, I think we should anticipate a full price this time. We can't go through life expecting the discount we received the last time. Then we need to determine how to bring that dog along and maintain Ares, plus decide how long we will sideline Addy before we start working her again."

Bonnie chimed in, "Addy is not going to like being left behind."

"She can come along, just not work for a while."

"I doubt she will understand that either," added Bonnie.

Their discussion over, Ben and Lucy left at ten p.m., and JW went to bed. He was exhausted from the trip, the time change, and the stress. He needed some rest. Unfortunately, the witching hour came at zero three hundred hours with his phone's not-so-gentle chirp. JW stood; he found he became more alert if he stood up and clicked the phone, "North here."

A cheery voice came over the speaker, "Hey LT, this is Janie in the comm center. There was a rumor that you were back in town, so I thought I would call and welcome you back."

JW recognized the voice of Janie McCall, dispatch supervisor. "Hi Janie, it's good to be back. How can I help you?"

"Well, first, I heard a rumor you may be leaving us. Can you provide any details for the rumor mill?"

JW understood rumors ran rampant in any large organization. People were naturally curious about things and public safety, perhaps more so than the average person. He gave Janie a tidbit to raise her status as an information broker. "We're finding things a bit small here, and I think we will relocate to someplace larger. Ben will still be around and will have a trailing dog soon too."

"LT, you know I'm gonna be sorry to see you go, but I wish you the best of luck with everything. Thanks for the scoop. I'm not sure what we're gonna do, though. When you're in town, we have a weekly lottery to see how many days it will be before you get a callout. You're a hot commodity, you know."

"Well, I'm sorry to ruin the fun, but Ben will be around for you to bet on. So, assuming you're phoning at three a.m. to call me out, who won?"

"You're talking to the lucky girl right here, LT. My guess was less than twelve hours after you came home."

"So, Janie, what did you win?"

"Sorry, sir, that information is classified. You know, the 'Top Gun' thing."

"Well, I wouldn't want to violate any national security laws. What do you have, and where am I going?"

"Assault with a deadly weapon; possible homicide. The victim is at St. Mary's hospital in critical condition. The Command post is at Pacific Coast Highway and Atlantic. Officer Kellum has already logged on. Can I show you en route?"

"Ten-Four. I will be rolling in ten."

JW walked up to the command post and saw Ben talking with the watch commander, Lieutenant Melissa Livingstone. Ben turned and walked to JW, saying, "We got a shooting that occurred in the empty lot next door. The victim was hanging out with about ten of his friends when the suspect walked up and shot him. Eight witnesses; remarkably, no one saw a thing. I have collected a scent pad from a hat that was dropped at the scene when the suspect ran off. We do have a witness from across the street who saw an unknown subject run across Pacific Coast Highway immediately after hearing the shots. We think that is our suspect.

"If you want to chat with the watch commander, I can get Ares ready and meet you in five minutes."

"Sounds good."

JW walked to the watch commander to catch up with another old friend. He told her their plans and asked for a couple of patrol officers to run the trail with them. Usually, considering the violent nature of the crime, JW would have wanted a parade led by the SWAT team. However, he did not believe the trail would lead to a suspect in this case. He fully expected the suspect to have fled the area in a vehicle or to do so as soon as he got word of the search team. It would have been nice to have the helicopter to provide an eye in the sky, but they were gone for the night.

Randall Flynn ran away from the scene. He had received a phone call that a rival gang member, Richard "Big Richie" Hayes, was hangin' on his turf; that could not be allowed to happen. Randall lived at his father's home. His mother had passed years ago. The Flynns were well known in Long Beach—they were involved with drugs, prostitutes, and gangs. His father served as the head of the family's criminal activities, and Randall knew he should talk with him about what he had in mind before he went out. Unfortunately, 'Daddy' was asleep. The price for waking him would be worse than anything bad that might happen due to his plan.

He didn't want to drive down and shoot Big Richie, that fat motherfucker. Cars were easy to describe whereas, if he walked, he was just one more gangbanger in the hood. So, he walked, taking his time. Before he left, he took a big hit of methamphetamine to give him a little extra courage. He had a nine-millimeter pistol tucked into his waistband to deal with this motherfucker. *Trespasser. What the fuck is he doing on my turf?* As he traveled across Pacific Coast Highway, he looked into the lot where he had been told Hayes was. And there he was. Flynn walked up, pulled the gun from his waistband, and shot him. Flynn didn't say a word, just shot Big Richie twice in the chest. As he turned to leave, he bumped into one of the group there, knocking his hat off.

Flynn looked him in the eye and said, "You don't know me and you didn't see me or you're dead like that motherfucker."

The drugs had him amped up. Flynn panicked and ran off, leaving his hat where it had fallen. It didn't matter; nothing was in it to lead back to him. He jogged back across Pacific Coast Highway and disappeared into the neighborhood.

JW and Ben quickly briefed their assigned cover officers. Unfortunately, they didn't have time to teach a class to the officers, so they went with the basics: don't watch the dog, keep your eyes moving around you; look for someone running away or paying too much attention to them. The two officers, Eric Orozco and Jenna McClure, listened patiently and acknowledged their orders. Neither felt overly comfortable with what they were about to do, but neither wanted to admit it. To do so was a sign of weakness.

JW scented Ares on the hat and gave the trail command, "Geo-say." A pair of black and whites blocked traffic so they could jog across Pacific Coast Highway. PCH was heavily traveled, even in the middle of the night. However, the group made it across safely and began to trail down the north sidewalk, moving east.

Donnie Harrison was one of the officers providing traffic control. He was an old friend and knew JW had a habit of getting into trouble at every opportunity, so he figured he would hang around just in case.

The trail went on for several blocks with only a few turns. Ares was strong on the trail and JW could tell it was fresh by the way he was pulling. He told Ben to advise the command post of their location and to let them know they believed the suspect had not transitioned to a vehicle yet. As the trail continued, JW noted that it was a cool night with no wind. He thought the trail they were following was not only fresh but also dead on. Since they were on asphalt and concrete, JW would not have been surprised if the trail had blown several feet from where the suspect walked. He stopped, knelt down, and praised Ares. "Ben, you notice anything strange about this trail?"

"You mean the feeling like a thousand eyes are on us, or how damn quiet it is?"

Their cover officers grew anxious at what they were describing. JW knew they were not as experienced as some officers. The overnight "graveyard" shift was composed of two types: senior officers who were there because they wanted to be and very junior officers who had no choice. These two were competent but not yet tuned into the street.

They moved away from the middle of the road, next to cars and trees that provided cover.

"You notice how our suspect keeps going from the sidewalk to the street and back again?"

"Yeah," Ben said, "I was wondering about that. Oh, shit!"

"Uh-huh, he's not going for a car. He's going out into the street and looking back to check if anyone is coming."

"He's staying on foot because he's local."

JW keyed the microphone, "King Nine Nine to the command post."

He heard the watch commander respond, "King Nine Nine, Edward Twenty-Nine, go ahead."

"King Nine Nine, we believe our suspect may have remained on foot rather than leave the area in a vehicle. Can you find a couple more units to send this way, just in case?"

At this point, the radio dispatcher cut in, "King Nine Nine and Edward Twenty-Nine, I have two units that are paralleling the search team and no other units available at this time in the area."

"Edward Twenty-Nine, check with the other areas and see if any units are available."

Before the dispatcher, Cynthia Hewitt, could reply, several units from North and East got on the radio and advised they were en route. JW relaxed a bit, knowing help was on the way. In the communications center, the tension had turned up several notches. Dispatcher Hewitt looked at her GPS map and thought, *What kind of trouble have you gotten yourself into this time, LT?* The dispatch supervisor, who had just talked to JW a few hours ago, was also worried. She and the dispatcher exchanged looks. Hewitt thought, *The last time I worked with the LT, he was shot. Please God, not again.*

Randall Flynn was jogging now, his fear of the police growing. He was cranked up on the meth and his heart was pounding. After the shooting, he heard numerous police and fire sirens driving to the scene. Within minutes, black and white cars were cruising the neighborhood, hunting him. Twice he had ducked between some houses to keep from being spotted. Now, almost three-quarters of a mile and an hour from the shooting, things had quieted. Still, there was the fear of being followed. He kept looking back but saw nothing—yet. Finally, he reached into his waistband and the feel of his nine-millimeter comforted him. Flynn started walking again. He was close to home now.

"Well, Ben, as I see it, we can sit here and wait for someone to shoot at us, or we can start trailing again and find the guy who will shoot at us. So what's your poison?"

"Gee, when you put it that way, I just can't decide. Neither option sounds particularly attractive."

"Well, since I've been shot, I can tell you it sucks a lot."

"Here's my thought. If we're gonna get shot, I would rather we were hunting than sitting here waiting. We've got lots of help coming."

"Ares, geo-say."

It was dead quiet in the communications center. It was the middle of the night, there were not a lot of calls and all the units were now on either the shooting or other calls for service. There was no radio traffic, just dead air. Hewitt looked at her mapping software, watching the assisting units driving to the LT's location slowly move across the map. *Come on, you guys, I can feel it; the shit is gonna hit the fan.*

Randall Flynn was finally home. But, of course, he forgot his keys when he left and was now locked out. His paranoia that someone was following him was reaching a peak. He needed to get inside, somewhere safe. Maybe another hit of meth to calm him down. He lightly knocked on the door and whispered, "Hey, Daddy, let me in. The door is locked."

From inside, he heard a deep, growling voice, "Who the fuck is at my door in the middle of the night. Whoever it is, I'm gonna shoot the motherfucker."

"Daddy, it's Randall; let me in," he whispered.

"Randall, what you doin' out there? You got a key; let your own self in. Oh, I bet you left your key here again, didn't you, you dumb motherfucker. Well, get your brother to let you in."

Randall considered this for a moment. His brother Michael was asleep upstairs in his bedroom. "Crazy Mike's" room was in the front of the house. Randall was on the covered porch with a balcony directly above him. He looked up and wondered if he could wake Mike without rousing the entire neighborhood. But then there was the problem of what would happen when Crazy Mike woke up. If Randall was considered violent, then Mike was crazy—he made Randall look like an honor student. The only thing Crazy

Mike liked better than his guns was shooting them. He slept with an AK-47 by his bed.

From inside, he heard his daddy yell, "Michael, wake the fuck up and let your dumbass brother in; he forgot his key again." He could hear movement inside the house. Soon, hopefully, he would be safe inside. He looked over his shoulder, and this time he saw them. There were several police officers in the street about half a block away, with a dog leading the way. "Motherfucker." He reached into his waistband and drew his nine-millimeter; it still felt warm from the earlier shooting. He ducked down behind a heavy wooden railing and watched. The dog was getting closer. Randall Flynn knew he would die; it was only a question of how many he could take with him.

He saw the officers getting closer and stood up, raising his pistol. It was dark and he couldn't see his sights, so he just pointed. He yelled, "Die motherfuckin' police!" and pulled the trigger. Nothing happened. In his drug-addled state, he forgot to take the safety off. He flicked the switch on the side of the slide and began pulling the trigger rapidly.

JW and his team continued up the street, following Ares. The dog was still pulling hard and JW felt like they were close now. Then he heard something from a house to their right. There wasn't much light, but he could see someone on the porch. He heard a voice yell, "Die motherfuckin' police!" and then nothing.

Ben reacted first and yelled, "Cover!" Both Ben and JW moved toward the suspect. The only cover between the house and them was a low stone wall bordering the front yard. It wasn't much, but it was better than nothing. Just as they reached the wall, the night lit up with pistol fire. The pistol rounds weren't that loud, but the suspect made up for it by sending many of them their way.

JW could see the rounds skipping off the ground just behind them. They were safe for the moment, as long as the suspect didn't move. The suspect stopped shooting, and JW thought, *Reloading?* JW raised a bit, leading with his own Springfield Armory Operator, and spotted the suspect on the porch. As he aimed to fire, the suspect ducked behind a railing. His .45 barked and a round sailed over the suspect's head, where he had just been.

JW didn't bother using the radio to tell everyone they needed help. They weren't that far from the command post—they would be able to hear the gunshots. As if on cue, he listened to the watch commander on the radio, "Edward Twenty-Nine, I hear multiple shots fired from the search team's area. Send all available units to the call now!" The watch commander didn't say the radio code "999" for officer needs help, emergency, but her words had the same effect. All over the city, units stopped their actions and started driving to help. The quiet of the early morning was soon disturbed by sirens from every direction.

In the comm center, Dispatcher Hewitt took a deep breath. *Oh shit! Here we go again.* A small stress tear leaked from her right eye. *Not again!* She took another deep breath, wiped her cheek, and said, "Suck it up, girl; they need you the most now."

Crazy Mike woke to his father yelling at him to get up. He wasn't sure why, it was early, but if the old man called, you came. As Mike stood, he heard his brother's voice below and gunshots. He grabbed his AK-47 rifle and chambered a deadly 7.62 x 39 round. He climbed onto the balcony and saw shadows moving quickly in the street. "Fuckin Randall got the motherfuckin' police hoppin." He then began shooting at the shadows.

Right after the suspect began firing his pistol again, JW heard another sound, even more deadly. It was the loud boom of a rifle; he could tell it was a large caliber from the years he had spent shooting on rifle ranges. From the rapid-fire, he also knew it was semi-automatic. He knew they were completely exposed now. The rifle could easily penetrate his bullet-resistant vest as if it weren't even there. He also knew the rifle rounds might come through the wall. He pulled in tight against the wall, holding Ares to his chest. He realized the bullet would likely go right through him and the dog if he was shot. No matter, this felt reassuring to both him and Ares. Ares gave him a look that said, *What did you get me into this time?* Ben was nearby, also hiding behind the wall. It would be suicide to raise their heads. Now there were multiple suspects, and they had fire superiority over them. The loud report of the AK was disorienting and demoralizing. JW knew it would get ugly if they didn't get help soon.

Officer Donnie Harrison's instinct to stick around had been dead on. He'd thought that JW would find a way to get in trouble. Usually, Donnie was a training officer, but he was on his own tonight. He heard the gunshots to the east and thought, *Oh hell, there it is.* He listened to the radio traffic about the shooting. *Yeah, I know there's shooting; I'm here. It would have been nice to have some help tonight.* He turned the headlights off on his black and white. *No need to advertise that I'm here.* He drove into an intersection just south of where the shooting was. He could see officers behind cars and a low wall and shots being fired in their direction from a dark house.

He stopped and got out, thankful the interior lights on police cars were disabled. He went to the car's trunk, retrieved his AR-15 rifle, and loaded a round into the chamber. It was too long of a shot for a pistol; he needed the ability to reach out and touch someone. He moved to the side of the car and then to the front, where he would have some protection from the gunfire by the engine block. He aimed the rifle over the hood of his car, looking through the telescopic sight at the bright red dot in the center. He could see someone on the balcony, armed with a rifle, shooting at the officers below. Donnie placed the red dot in the middle of his chest and squeezed. The 53-grain VMAX bullet launched from the barrel at over 3,200 feet per second.

JW continued to crouch behind the wall, keeping Ares in tight. To raise his head was death; to stay here was likely death. The bullets came from the house in a continuous roar. *Don't these guys ever have to reload?* Bullets sprayed the sidewalk and the street all around him. Finally, he heard a cry, "I'm hit," from behind a car. Then he heard the other officer's voice, "I got him." JW was getting frantic. He hated being this exposed. He wished he had a military-style armored vest with a helmet. He was tired of being shot at and feeling stark naked to the bullets. *Note to self: investigate better body armor ASAP.*

JW heard another shot, this time from down the street. *Another shooter? Oh, come on, as if this isn't bad enough!* He looked and saw a black and white. *The cavalry has arrived.* He heard a loud thump on the other side of the wall. *One down, one to go.* The remaining suspect shouted, "You shot my brother, you motherfuckers." Tiring of his passive role in all this, JW stood to his full height and looked over the wall, partially exposed. He could see the suspect coming down from the porch, but his attention was up the street. The suspect turned toward him and raised his pistol. Before the suspect could fire, JW raised the Operator and shot him twice in the chest. The suspect stopped and collapsed immediately. JW was sure he was dead, but he wasn't going to leave cover to go check on him. Not until more help got here.

Within three minutes, ten black and whites joined them. They formed a tight perimeter on the house and waited. Finally, the watch commander called SWAT; they weren't sure if any more suspects were inside, but why take chances. Besides, SWAT guys needed work too. While they waited, JW heard a voice from inside the house, "You motherfuckers shot my sons, don't shoot me too." As he was known on the street, Daddy Flynn stepped into the waiting arms of two patrol officers. He was handcuffed and taken away for questioning.

JW kept looking down the street, wondering who had saved them. He couldn't make out the officer's face, but he could see him sitting on the hood of his police car, his rifle unloaded next to him. Then, as the morning sky lightened, he finally saw that it was Donnie Harrison; they waved to each other.

JW turned to Ben and said, "Hey Ben, I think I found you a cover officer after you get your dog trained. Donnie ran with me on the certification trail, so he has a basic understanding."

Ben looked at him with a small smile, simply happy to be alive, "Dog, what dog? I don't know nothin' about those trailing dogs, except their handlers are always getting shot at."

JW and Ben both laughed and then went silent. They weren't supposed to talk to one another until after their interviews with the detectives. He asked about the officer who had been shot, Orozco. McClure, her hands covered in his blood, said, "He got shot in the calf. I didn't have anything to dress the wound, so I just used my hands to help control the bleeding. There was a lot of blood," she said, looking at her hands, "but the paramedics said he would be OK."

"You did good, McClure. That was quick thinking under fire. I'm proud of you."

"Thank you, sir. But I didn't even shoot at the suspect."

"Neither did I, until the very end. It would have been suicide to raise your head up. Besides, you were taking care of Orozco. And don't call me 'sir,' my name is 'JW.'" He looked into her eyes and saw the adrenaline had worn off; the shock of the incident was setting in. He called to a passing officer, "Could you do me a favor? The three of us could really use a cup of coffee. Can you see if they have anything at the command post?"

"Sure thing, LT, I'm on it."

Another officer told JW that two neighbors who lived across the street from the shooting were injured by suspect bullets that went through their walls. Police officers and paramedics evacuated these victims from their homes. They lifted them over their back fences to take them to the hospital. JW then remembered the shooting in Vegas. He needed to call home and tell Bonnie what had happened before she got up and heard it on the news. It was bad enough getting shot at; he didn't need an ass chewing from his wife to top it off.

"Ben, call your wife. Tell her you're OK. Don't talk about the shooting." He then dialed home.

Bonnie North was asleep when her phone rang. *Uh oh, this can't be good. Well, at least the chief isn't knocking at the door.* She saw the call was from JW. *Oh, no! Ares? Ben?* She looked at Addy, who was still asleep on the bed. *At least I know you're safe.* She answered the call, "JW, please don't tell me you got shot again."

"Not this time, Baby. There was a shooting, though. One of the cover officers was hit. That's about all I can say right now. Policy, you know. Turn the news on. I can see a bunch of their vans down the street. I'm sure they can tell you more than I know."

"OK, but you're not hurt, and neither is Ares or Ben?"

"Nope, we're all OK. It'll be a while before I'm home, though."

"I understand. I love you."

"Love you too. See you soon."

People who watch police shows on television don't get a realistic perspective of the job. They see officers involved in a shooting and then they are back on the street an hour later. It doesn't happen that way. This was a complex crime scene with a lot of evidence and statements to be taken. It would be dark again by the time JW and Ben returned to their families.

13

JW sat in his backyard, staring at the small waterfall in the corner. When they moved, he needed to ensure that he had two things: a fire pit and a water feature. They had a calming effect and he certainly could use some of that in his life. Ares and Addy were asleep nearby, sunbathing and working on their tans. It was quiet; Bonnie had gone into the office of her "real" job to give notice of her resignation. She had enjoyed working there, but she was taking on a much bigger job as the CEO of Big Dogs. It was time for her to move on.

JW let his mind wander as it usually did at times like this. As he sat there, something occurred to him. He had unfinished business. He needed to meet with Susan Patterson, the Shadow's other victim, on the night he had shot JW. He had beaten her brutally, almost killing her. Only the arrival of JW at the scene had saved her.

JW felt a kinship with her even though he had never met her. He didn't know how she recovered from the incident, but he knew he needed to talk with her to get a few things off his chest. He hoped that talking with him would be helpful for her too.

JW's daydream was disturbed by the ringing of his phone. "Hello, Lieutenant. How are you and your dogs?"

"We're doing OK. How are you, Doctor?"

"I'm fine. I'm here at the office and just finished reading the reports on your latest escapade. I was wondering, is it possible for you to run a trail and not get involved in a shooting?"

"Aardvark, Doctor," giving her the code word that she was being insensitive.

"What? I asked about you like you said."

"Yes," he said, encouraging her.

"Was it the question about the shooting? Is it too soon?"

"More your choice of words. We need to work on how you phrase things."

"OK, that's not entirely what this call is about. I'm shipping some things to you overnight; they'll be there in the morning. Ben will receive a similar package. It includes your US Marshal credentials, a new iPhone with secure calling and texting features, and a contract for you to review. I suggest you go over the contract completely with an attorney before signing. I didn't see anything unexpected, but it is easier to make changes before you sign than after."

"Well, that is certainly exciting news. Thank you for getting this handled so quickly."

"That's the director. He seems to have taken a liking to you. Although he is a bit worried about your propensity to be on the wrong end of a gun."

"Aardvark, Doctor. Aardvark."

"OK, too soon," she said matter-of-factly. Please call me after you've had a chance to review the contents of the package and we can discuss in more detail how this will all work."

JW called the detectives who handled the Susan Patterson case and asked if they would reach out to her and ask if he could visit. He was surprised that not only was she OK with meeting him, but she was available that day. He cleaned up, put on a fresh uniform, and then drove to her home. When he arrived, he looked down the street to where he had been shot. It seemed so much closer from her porch. He knocked and a woman answered. "Susan?"

"No," she answered, "I'm Leslie, her sister. You must be Lieutenant North."

JW wasn't sure, but he sensed a coolness in her attitude. He wondered if she blamed him for what happened to Susan. He knew he blamed himself.

"Follow me. Susan is in the sunroom in the back. I stay with her now; she doesn't like being alone."

JW followed and entered the sunroom behind Leslie. As he did, Susan Patterson stood to meet him. He looked at her and saw that most of her injuries had healed, leaving some light scarring. However, her face seemed a little misshapen, probably from the Shadow striking her face repeatedly. He became aware he was staring and said, "I'm sorry."

"It's OK, Lieutenant. It happens every time. I've grown used to it. Would you like some coffee? Leslie, could you please get the lieutenant some coffee?" Leslie left them and Susan said, "Please, sit. May I call you by your first name? I feel we have a bit of a kinship, you and me. It feels awkward calling you by your title."

"Yes, please call me 'JW.' And I agree, we are connected now."

"JW, is that your Christian name or a nickname?"

He didn't usually tell people the story of his name. For some reason, because of their bond, it felt OK to do so. "My father loved John Wayne. He thought he embodied what it meant to be a man. He idolized him as I idolized my father. He named me JW to set a goal in my life. He wanted me to always be like the Duke, even though he didn't believe I could. It's like that Johnny Cash song, 'A boy named Sue.' I'm a bit sensitive about being just 'JW,' as if he didn't feel I would live up to the full name.

"Anyway, we would watch all those old John Wayne movies every time one of them was on. It got to the point that I hated them all, but I got over that and love to watch them now. I hated my dad for a while, too, for not believing in me, but as I grew up, I understood. He wanted me to be the best, which has driven me all my life."

"Did you always want to be a police officer?"

"No, I wanted to be a Marine at first, like my dad. I went to college and was an officer in the Marine Corps for a while, but I wanted to settle down. I hated the thought of moving every three years."

"So, you became a police officer?"

"Yes, I was a good cop for over thirty years. Unfortunately, my last night on the job was when you were attacked and I was shot."

"Oh…"

"I came here today to tell you I'm sorry."

"Really, why?"

"I feel like I failed you."

"How so?"

"I came to help you, but I ended up needing help. I might have kept you from getting hurt if I had been more aware."

"You know, I wasn't what I would call pretty before the attack. But now, I will always look a little different. You haven't seen me walk, but I'm still learning how to do that again. That attack changed my life, but none of that is your fault, JW. The Shadow did this to me, not you. You did your best and almost died as a result. Now, I read you are working with the FBI and chasing people like the Shadow. Can you tell me about that?"

JW told her of his last year's work and what he was doing with Big Dogs and the FBI. Then he decided to tell her about his dream. He had no idea why he was being so open with her.

"When I was shot, I died for a few minutes. The doctors told me that later. I had a dream that I was in a meadow with dogs everywhere. I met a man there and we talked. He told me I was coming back here; I had work to do. My wife, Bonnie, is deeply religious. She has tied a lot of significance to the dream. She thinks I went to heaven for a few minutes. I'm not sure, but I know that since I woke up I have been driven to work with dogs and get to where I am today."

"That is an incredible story. Thank you so much for sharing that with me. I could tell it wasn't easy. But you don't have to worry; I won't be judgmental of you, and your story will stay with me. Do you think you will ever find the Shadow?"

"I don't know, but I sure hope so."

"Can I ask a favor of you?"

"Of course, name it."

"Could you bring your dogs by some time? I love dogs."

"You got it; there's nothin' like a dog."

The time came for JW to leave. Susan was tiring and Leslie told him she needed some rest. As JW stood to leave, she reached out and hugged him.

"Thank you for coming today. I believe it was very helpful. Oh, and if you ever find him, please kill him for me."

He looked at her hard, deep into her eyes. He could feel her pain; it was his now. He nodded and turned to leave.

"I look forward to meeting your dogs."

JW returned home to find Bonnie reviewing Big Dogs financials in her office. Adding Ben to the team would mean even higher costs, but, fortunately, it appeared the FBI was going to cover some expenses. The good news was they had ample funds due to Bonnie's family inheritance. They also had a wealthy friend/benefactor in Las Vegas who had offered to assist if needed.

Bonnie heard JW digging around in the kitchen, so she called out, "In the cabinet with the other coffee cups."

"Why do you feel the need to always hide my favorite cup? And do you want a cup? We need to chat; I want to tell you about my meeting."

"Yes, on coffee, no on hiding. It's called putting things away, something you and the dogs have an issue with."

JW looked out into the living room. A dozen dog toys were scattered about. There wasn't a dog in sight. They were apparently doing their second favorite thing—sleeping in the yard. Finally, they met in the dining/family meeting room. JW filled her in on his meeting with Susan.

"She sounds like a very nice woman. I would like to meet her someday."

"She wants to meet the dogs, so you can go with me when I go back."

"I'm surprised. You shared a lot with her; more than you do with most people."

"I know. I guess we have a bond due to our mutual experience with the Shadow." JW didn't tell her about Susan's request that he kill the Shadow.

"So, how do you feel about the meeting?"

"I don't know. I'm glad I did it. Susan's a nice lady who didn't deserve what happened to her. I'm not sure how I feel yet. I think I need to sort it out."

"Sounds like you need a round of golf with Mark."

Mark Powers was another good friend of JW's. He was retired now but had been the Rangemaster at LBPD and was responsible for the department adopting the Springfield Armory Operator, the pistol JW continued to carry when on duty. They both shot together on the department's pistol team. Mark was a great golfer and had volunteered to help JW work through his issues while they played golf. Bonnie wanted him to see a therapist, but real cops didn't talk to counselors, so they had compromised with JW talking to Mark. It was better than nothing.

"That would be great; I hope I can fit something in. Things are going crazy right now with getting Ben his dog and everything else."

"All the more reason you should play golf with Mark. Call him, now."

JW set a tee time with Mark for the next week. A couple of their other golf buddies were going to play too. He would let Mark handle the details.

Seeing him off the phone, Bonnie said, "I forgot, Ben called. He's on his way over. You two need to call Vohne Liche Kennels and set up a time to look at a dog."

"Kurt found a dog already?" They had just called him two weeks ago and asked about a dog for Ben.

"Apparently. Ben didn't give me any details. Of course, I'm just the CEO, so I don't need any information."

"To borrow your favorite phrase, 'Quit your whining.'"

"We'll see who whines when you arrive at Vohne Liche without the corporate checkbook."

"Honey, have I told you how nice you look today?"

"Quit your sucking up, JW. You don't do it very well and it will not make up for that comment. Now, when Ben gets here, you two need to decide when you are going so I can get to work on plane tickets, hotel reservations, and a rental car. Also, find out if Ben wants to drive the dog home if it works out."

"You're not coming on this trip?"

"As much fun as it was last time having you step all over my feet and call it dancing, I am so busy right now, I can't afford the time. I am considering recruiting Lucy as a full-time assistant, but I'm unsure how she would feel about working for me."

"Well, Ben and I will be gone for a few days; perfect time for you two to work out the details."

"What about the shooting?"

JW looked at Bonnie with a question in his eyes, "What about it?"

"Aren't you supposed to see a department psychologist?"

"Oh, I did that. She's a nice lady and all. We talked; she knows she can't fix me, so she just wanted to make sure I wasn't completely crazy."

"How did she miss that?"

"Ouch, that's gonna leave a bruise."

"Look, I'm not trying to beat you up here."

"I know; it's a team sport, no fun alone."

"JW, how can you go through all you've been through in the last couple of years and not be bothered by it?"

"Look, Honey, I feel OK. I don't drink to excess or need drugs to act normal. I don't have bad dreams or yell at my wife. I'm just not sure what it is you want me to be. I'm happy; my wife supports me in an incredible venture." With that, he raised his hands in a questioning gesture and said, "Look, I feel bad about taking a human life. But you must admit he and his brother were doing their best to kill Ben, me, and Ares."

"I'm sorry. I'm not sure what I'm trying to get at. It just seems like this is all so normal to you and it isn't to me. I think I'll go to church tonight and pray about it. Maybe I can make some sense of it all."

"That sounds like a good idea."

"You know, you could do with some time in church too."

JW smiled and said, "I knew that was coming. If you want me to go to church, I will. But you know that's not where I go to talk to God. Besides, when was the last time you had the structural integrity of the building checked? I wouldn't want the roof to fall in. People could get hurt."

The return trip to Vohne Liche Kennels went as smoothly as the first. Ben and JW had no trouble navigating Chicago's O'Hare airport and getting to their rental car. This time they left Los Angeles earlier and went out to see Kurt Steigerwald before checking into their hotel and calling it a night.

Kurt, the owner of Vohne Liche Kennels, greeted them warmly as he had the last time they were there. He was a bull of a man with large arms and a barrel chest, but with a smile that would light up a room. He was one of those people who, once he met you, if he liked you, you were a friend for life. "Hey guys, I didn't expect you back so soon. I've been following your escapades online. Wow, you really know how to find trouble." They spent a few minutes catching up on life before getting down to business.

"I spoke with Axel and he is very impressed with what you two have accomplished. Nice job in Vegas, by the way. Josef was upset about Addy getting hurt, but Axel explained that sometimes those things happen in police work. It is a hard fact of the life you guys have chosen. Anyway, he sent a letter along with the dog they found for you, Ben." He handed Ben a handwritten letter and said to JW, "Here, these are his papers. I know you speak some German, so you'll get more out of them than Ben."

Ben opened the letter and began to read:

Mr. Ben Kellum,

Greetings to you and Mr. North. I congratulate you on your successes with Ares and Adeliene. Of course, I was confident it would go like this, but achievement must be acknowledged. I am a bit surprised by the timing of your most recent request; I had not expected you to need another dog so soon. Mr. Steigerwald explained you are going to search for killers also. Because of this, I am happy to help.

Normally, your request would not be too difficult to fill. I would simply reach out to Josef and see what is available. He, like me, supports your work and is happy to help. However, Mr. North's wish that the dog is suitable for breeding with Adeliene does complicate matters. Germans take the breeding of their dogs very seriously. The national club, the S.V., determines who can be bred to whom. If a member were to go against that, they would be removed from the membership. Finding a dog that could meet your needs, plus be approved for Adeliene, is no small task.

Josef found the answer. He and another breeder, Wolfgang Reichenau, have been friendly rivals for years. They are two of the top breeders in Germany. They are specifically focused on tracking and the other aspects of Schutzhund. Each has wanted to breed into the other's lineage, but they have been reluctant due to their competitive natures.

Josef felt it would be best if I approached Wolfgang as an intermediary. So I went to see him and explained the situation. I told him about what you two were doing and showed him some Internet articles about your work. He was impressed and congratulated Josef on breeding such fine dogs. I then told him about JW's desire to breed to Adeliene. This brought a small smile to Wolfgang. It was then I knew we had him.

The dog I am presenting to you is "Zeus." He is from outstanding German lines and has excellent obedience, tracking, and man work scores. He has one minor flaw—he is a long-coated German Shepherd. Roughly ten percent of German Shepherd puppies are born with long coats. It is a recessive gene, but it does show from time to time. At one time, a long coated could not compete in conformation. Now, these restrictions are lessened, but there are still the old prejudices. Personally, I believe he is a beautiful dog. His scores are impressive, and I think from what Mr. Steigerwald has told me, he will be a good match for you.

The arrangement is similar to the last one, $5,000 to cover the cost of raising and training Zeus...with one condition. After the mating with Adeliene, both Wolfgang *and Josef want to have a pick from the litter, preferably not long coats. There are no guarantees in this world, but Zeus is as close as they get. He is a very social dog but can be intimidating until you get used to him.*

I wish you the best of luck with Zeus. You would be a fool not to take him.

Godspeed,
Axel Schmidt

JW had read through the German paperwork for Zeus and finished reading the letter over Ben's shoulder, urging him to hurry up and finish.

"Kurt, if this dog is as good as his scores, Axel is magic. So how does he get these guys to give up these good dogs?"

Kurt nodded, "Axel and I talked about this. Germans love to train their dogs and love them to death, but they aren't nearly as attached to them as we are. In this case, Wolfgang saw a less desirable dog to some Germans because of his coat. You should accept that you will never get the German's best dogs. But what they will sell is usually better than what we need. You'll only get their best dogs if you're willing to spend a lot of money, which in this case is not practical. What do you say we go look at this dog? I'm gonna warn you, he is scary looking. If you were to use this dog for patrol work, you would never have to worry about him biting a suspect. One look at him and the toughest felon will give up."

JW and Ben exchanged glances. "What the hell have you gotten me into now, JW?"

When they arrived at the kennel and first saw Zeus, JW's and Ben's mouths dropped open. Zeus had a beautiful long coat, alright. He was almost black, with deep red fur below his chest and belly and behind his ears. His coat was thick and long.

JW said, "Oh my God! He looks like a werewolf. You were right when you said he was scary looking."

Kurt opened the gate to the kennel and Zeus walked into the room like he owned it. He looked at everyone and approached Ben with his tail wagging.

"Go ahead and pet him, Ben. If he bites you, I'll put you down with a silver bullet," JW said, laughing.

Kurt smiled and said, "What, Ben? You don't like him?"

"Like him? I don't think I have a choice." Zeus was leaning heavily into Ben while being petted. "I think if I stop petting him, I'm done for. Actually, he is so friendly, I wonder if he will bite."

Kurt took this as a personal challenge, "OK, Ben. You go outside. There is a full bite suit hanging in the shade. Put that on and go out about twenty-five yards. When I release him, you do the courage test. We'll see if he bites or not."

When JW and Kurt came out, Ben was ready, "Hey Kurt, I was only kidding."

"Really?" Kurt replied, "Let me know if he bites properly."

Ben watched as Kurt pointed him out to Zeus. The dog began barking and then let loose something that sounded like a howl. *Oh shit, he is a werewolf. I'm a dead man*, thought Ben. When Kurt released Zeus, the dog moved quickly to full speed. Ben remembered the German courage test and turned to run a few paces. When he turned back toward Zeus, he was already there. Ben raised one arm as if to strike and was hit by the shepherd at full speed. Zeus caught his arm and continued his momentum, carrying Ben with him. Ben was pulled off his feet and thrown to the ground, hitting his head and causing him to see stars. Zeus continued gripping Ben's arm and began pulling him across the field. The bite pressure was unreal, more brutal than anything he had ever felt.

JW and Kurt walked up to Ben, and Kurt asked, "How's that bite pressure, Ben?"

"OK, I'm impressed. Please give Zeus the release command."

Kurt said, "Aus," the German release command and Zeus dropped off the bite. He sat and began barking at Ben. There was no doubt he would reengage if Ben did something dumb. Kurt put the leash back on and told Ben to go inside, take the suit off, and then come back out. Zeus continued his guard and bark routine while Ben walked away.

When Ben returned, Kurt released Zeus, who trotted back to Ben, wagging his tail. Kurt said, "Don't worry; he recovers quickly and does not hold a grudge." In a few moments, Zeus again leaned on Ben, getting petted.

"OK, I admit it. I was wrong, but my arm will be covered with bruises."

Kurt smiled, "Never question the master."

They put Zeus through the same testing process they had for Ares a year before. This time Ben was the handler and JW was the cover officer. Kurt, always happy to get a few jibes in, said, "JW, notice how much smoother Ben is than you were?"

"He might be smoother than me, but I'm better looking."

"That's not what your wife says," added Ben with a smile.

Zeus seemed to be the only one taking the testing seriously. Kurt gave him a nice leather harness, like the ones Ares and Addy used, and a tracking lead.

"There is a longer one in the office, but I think you'll use this one most of the time."

After getting Zeus ready to trail, Kurt gave him a scent pad. Ben scented Zeus and started him on the trail. Ben was smart enough to get a heavy-duty pair of gloves before starting.

Although each dog had their own style and cues, the results were as impressive as Ares'. At the conclusion, Zeus the Werewolf, as JW called him, passed every test with flying colors. Ben laughed but disagreed with the title. JW said, "Ben, what else are we going to call him? His owner's name was Wolfgang?" Then, recalling a line from the movie "Young Frankenstein," JW said, "Werewolf? There wolf," and pointed at Zeus. Everyone busted up laughing.

It had been a long day. But, like the first time, there was so much excitement in the air with the new dog that no one realized how late it was until the sun went down. Kurt turned to JW and Ben and said, "I don't feel like I need to ask this, but do you want this dog, Ben?"

Ben looked to JW, "What do you think? I mean, you're paying for him, and you want to breed him. I feel like you should have some say."

"I'm no expert, so I'll have to trust Axel and Josef as far as the breeding goes. It seems like more than a fair deal, and I understand why each would want a puppy from the litter." He looked at Kurt and asked, "Do you think the SV will have a problem with the breeding?"

Kurt scrunched up his face and said, "I have no idea how the Germans think, but I did get a call from Josef last week. He is highly respected in the dog world there. Apparently, the Germans are also aware of what you are doing and are interested in how their dogs are viewed here, so they will allow a breeding of this pair. Of course, you two will have to join the German National Shepherd Club, but I think it will be OK. I believe the SV wants to continue the good press for their dogs and is interested in how the breeding will come out. These two lines have never been bred before, and this circumstance creates an opportunity for them to get to see the result. If it goes bad, they'll just blame the stupid Americans."

JW smiled, "Why can't things ever be easy?"

Kurt laughed, "Sorry, brother, you didn't pick that life."

"I say we go with this. The dog tests fantastic and looks great. Although I do feel like a bit of a pimp on the breeding part," said Ben.

JW and Kurt broke into song, "It's hard out here for a pimp."

Ben scowled, "Please don't ever do that again. I thought Zeus's howl was scary, but that was horrifying."

Kurt replied, "That hurts, Ben. OK, same deal as last time. We'll meet for dinner at seven at 'Bob's Place.' We'll keep Zeus and you can pick him up in the morning."

14

The Shadow was cruising. He had a short delivery list tonight and finished early. On nights like this, he liked driving in the countryside to get a better feel for his hunting grounds. He was challenged by the rural atmosphere and had some difficulty acclimatizing himself. He felt like a kid on his first camping trip in the wilderness. Every sound made him jump, and it was hard for him to concentrate. The more he traveled these backroads, especially at night, the more comfortable he would be. He wanted to make friends with the darkness here. It had served him well in the past.

Of course, his cruising led to being lost. But, thanks to the GPS on the dash, he was heading back to the highway. Soon he would be driving home. As he made another turn in the woods, he spotted a hitchhiker walking on the side of the road. He could see it was a female, but not much else because she was wearing a huge backpack. He pulled alongside her and asked, "Are you looking for a lift?"

A teenager, about 16 years old, turned to face him. She had long brown hair and he immediately felt a stirring inside. She said, "Well, I got kind of turned around and could use a ride back to the main highway."

"No problem. I was a bit turned around myself. I do deliveries overnight and thought I was on a shortcut back to the highway. What's your name?"

She looked down at his truck and read "Collins Auto Parts Delivery" on the door. This seemed to calm her fears, and she replied, "Amber, and thanks, I appreciate it."

He got out to help her put the backpack into the truck's bed. As he finished, he turned and said, "Aren't you too young to be out this late?"

He could tell she was irritated by his question when she said, "I've been on my own for a couple years. I can take care of myself."

He pulled a length of heavy pipe from the truck's bed and swung at her, striking her on the top of the head and dropping her instantly. "We'll see about that." He pulled her into the woods, quickly bound her arms and legs, and taped her mouth shut. He then ran back to his truck, drove up the road, and pulled into a turnout. The vehicle went so far that it could not be seen from the road.

When he returned to her, she had regained consciousness but was disoriented. He rolled her over quickly, pulled down her pants, and raped her from behind. When he finished, he slit her throat as if it were nothing. To him, it was nothing. Her life meant nothing; she was merely a vessel for his anger. He smiled and went to work on her body with the knife.

An hour later, he returned to his truck but hesitated. He considered where he had left the girl and his work staging her body. He was concerned that coyotes or something would come along and ruin it before she could be discovered. He reached into the back of his truck, grabbed a roll of baling wire, and began walking back. He wasn't worried, it was late, and no one would be on this back road.

Fifteen minutes later, he was back at this truck. He drove off, back toward the highway. At one point, the road was adjacent to the Barren River. He stopped, took the backpack from his truck, and tossed it into the river. It was heavy enough that it would sink and probably never be found.

In the morning, a local farmer, James Jefferson III—Jimmy Jeff to his friends—was driving into town. He wasn't happy. His tractor had broken down this morning and he needed to go into town for a part. He thought *This trip will ruin my schedule and put me way behind.* He had no idea how right he was. He was driving a little fast on these roads for his old pickup truck, but he wanted to get the tractor fixed. Also, he wanted to finish his work in order to watch *Wheel of Fortune* tonight.

He slowed to clear a sharp turn in the road and then began accelerating. His eyes were drawn to a road sign. *Funny, it ain't Halloween.* He slammed on his brakes, and the truck skidded to a stop, pulling to the right and almost putting him in a ditch. He took a closer look at the sign and thought, *That looks real!* He was looking at a human arm, the hand pointing into the woods. It was attached to the signpost with baling wire. He reached with his right hand and touched it, pulling it back when he felt how cold and soft it was. He sniffed the air and thought, *Rotting flesh.* He looked into the woods in the direction the hand was pointing and said, "Nope, I want nothing to do with that." He reached into his pocket for his phone and called 911.

Deputy Sheriff Artur Zyma arrived in twenty minutes. The call he received was unknown trouble. Zyma hated unknown trouble calls; as the name said, you never knew what you were getting into. He had an excellent record and worked hard to keep it that way. Zyma knew if he was ever going to make detective, he would need to work hard to show he was capable. His parents had immigrated from Ukraine before he was born and had always encouraged him to love this country and to work hard.

He got out of his car and took a notebook from his back pocket. He asked Jefferson for his identification to get everything he needed for his report. Jefferson looked at him oddly and motioned with his eyes to the sign. Until this moment, Zyma had not noticed the arm and asked with a strong accent, "What the hell is that?"

Jefferson said, "I'm not positive, but it looks like an arm, maybe a woman's arm?"

"It sure looks like a woman's arm."

"Yup."

"Where's the rest of her?"

Jefferson raised his eyebrows and shook his head slowly, then turned his eyes to look toward the woods.

Zyma said, "It's pointing. Do you think that's on purpose?"

"Maybe?"

"I guess I'll take a walk in the woods and see what I can find. My back-up will be here any minute; tell him where I went." Zyma unholstered his duty pistol and began walking in the direction indicated by the arm. He scanned the ground carefully as he walked; the Deputy had seen booby traps while in the Army. It wasn't long before Jefferson could no longer see him.

Jefferson could hear him pushing through the brush, and then he heard, "Oh my God!" He could hear Zyma talking, but he couldn't understand him. *Was he speaking a foreign language?* His curiosity overcame reason and he followed the deputy. The woods were thick here, with young and old trees growing closely together. The trees threw shadows, and the wind blew through, making everything move. It was as if the forest was alive. He stopped after pushing through the brush and coming to an open area. He had found something that was not alive.

Blood was all over the ground and trees and in the center was a woman, well, most of a woman. Her arms, legs, and head were hacked off her torso. Her body was arranged as

Michelangelo's Vitruvian Man, in a spread-eagle position. But, of course, it was not the Vitruvian Man; it was a woman with one arm missing.

Zyma, aware that Jefferson was with him now, said, "I'm not sure what this is, but I know it's bigger than I can handle. I'm calling this in. We need to back out of here, using the same path we came on. Try not to disturb anything at all. This might be connected to that case with the real estate woman." Everyone knew about that case; it was all over the newspaper. You didn't have a murder like that and not have it be the subject of every conversation in the area.

The pair returned to the road to wait for the rest of the police units to arrive. Jefferson turned to Zyma and said, "I heard you talking in there, but I couldn't understand what you were saying. Was that a foreign language?"

"Yes, my family is Ukrainian, and my mama is Orthodox Christian. What you heard was a prayer for the departed. When I was young, I considered being a priest. I wanted to help people. But then I went into the Army, and afterward, I came here. Now, maybe I think I should have become a priest."

Since this crime was in the county jurisdiction, Sheriff Reed was in charge. He immediately made the connection to the earlier homicide and called Chief Johnson. When Johnson arrived, Sheriff Reed greeted him with a firm handshake and grim eyes. "Bill, we got a murder that looks similar to the one you guys had a while back."

"The real estate agent? John, that can't be good at all. One was bad enough, but if we got a serial killer on our hands, we've got real trouble. Did you call the Department of Criminal Investigation yet? I did it right away."

"Yeah, I did. Didn't want to, but I think you're right. And if we are right about this being serial, we need someone to help coordinate all the local jurisdictions. Otherwise, things will slip through the cracks or take longer to solve, and more innocents will die."

"Chief, has anyone looked to see if there are others like this in the area that haven't been connected yet?"

"I believe the Department of Criminal Investigation did a search, but they didn't find anything yet. We have several missing women in the area, but so far, nothing to connect them. I talked to a guy from the DCI when they were here. He asked me about calling in the FBI. I said I was OK with it, but I never heard anything from them. Maybe we need to make a call to them directly? Do you mind if I take a look at your scene?"

"Sure thing. Let me take you in; we have a path marked where there doesn't appear to be any evidence."

Chief Johnson had to turn his head when he reached the scene. "Well, whoever our killer is, he is getting worse. This is similar to ours, but there is a lot more mutilation. On ours, he decapitated the victim but left the other limbs intact. She was a real estate agent. Any idea who your victim is?"

"Nope. She looks young though; it might be a runaway. We haven't done prints yet. We're waiting for the coroner to arrive."

"Yeah, ours was older than yours. One thing the murders have in common, though, they both had long, straight brown hair."

Sheriff Reed said, "That's interesting. I wonder if that's a coincidence or something our suspect seeks out."

Chief Johnson said, "Well, that's what those profilers at the FBI are good at. We can let them decide."

JW and Ben were on the long drive home in the rental van. The good news is this time Bonnie was able to arrange for them to drop the van off in Long Beach. The bad news is it rained the entire way. Zeus was not much on going out into the rain, but it was sometimes necessary. The van was inundated with wet dog smell and so were they. JW could see another cleaning charge in their future. They stopped at a department store on the second day and picked up a load of towels to dry Zeus off. Ben had discovered the joy of the long-coat shepherd; the need to brush their coat regularly. In this case, it meant daily; this did help Ben and Zeus to bond, though.

On the second day, while Ben was towel shopping, JW called Bill Lombard to order another Tahoe K9 police vehicle. This one would be for Ben. Lombard was a police vehicle specialist with Chevrolet. They had worked together on acquiring JW's vehicle over a year ago.

"Hello, Bill, how is everything at Chevy?"

"Everything is great, Mr. North; I hope your Tahoe still meets your needs. I'd be happy to put you in a new one if you wore that one out already."

"Well, that's why I'm calling, Bill. I need another one."

"Oh, no, did you have an accident? I hope everyone is OK."

"No, Bill, no accident. We're adding another member to the team, and he needs his own Tahoe."

"Oh, that's great! I guess that means your program is going well. I read about you in Las Vegas. I was a little worried; that sounded like a scary deal."

"We're all good, Bill. Thanks for asking."

"OK, so do you want the same package as the last one?"

"Yep, same exact thing."

"OK, give me some time to put this together for you. Of course, I will need another letter authorizing this."

"No problem. I'll give the FBI a call and have them send it."

"The FBI, huh? You've moved up in the world."

"Some might say that."

"Well, alright then. If it is OK with you, I will send this in today. Nothing has changed, and I know you guys in law enforcement are always in a hurry."

"That would be great. But to be honest, this dog became available very quickly, and I should have done this a couple of weeks ago."

"No problem, JW. I'll see if I can get this one done in a rush. Since this is the same as the last one, I think we can shave a couple weeks off for you. Oh, what are the names of the officer and his dog?"

"Ben Kellum and Zeus. Why?"

"That would be a surprise."

Floyd Hansen was stopped at the Meteor Crater rest area on Interstate 40 near Winslow, Arizona. He had been here for over a day, waiting for a promised job in Flagstaff, Arizona. The life of an independent trucker was like this on occasion. Sit and wait for a call. There was no work here for his 'calling' either. The rest stop landscape was open, with many rock formations and high desert scrub brush. Not much to see or do here. He unhooked and drove west to look at the crater.

He gazed upon what he saw as a massive hole in the ground but marveled at a God who could create such things. He questioned why but knew those answers were not available to him. He also wondered why a God who was this powerful couldn't get rid of his own hooker infestation. Then he thought better of that. What would he have in life if not for the Lord's work? He hadn't been able to do much with that. Lately, the pickings were slim in number and too popular with the other drivers for him to get near them. He wasn't worried; the Lord would provide.

His satellite phone chirped as he sat in his truck and marveled at his place in the universe. He answered quickly, thinking that it might be work.

"Yep, I'm near Winslow.

"No, I could certainly break free for that.

"Prescott, I know where that is. I can be there later today.

"OK, see you then."

The big diesel rumbled as he started it and then roared as he accelerated out of the rest area and drove west. *Well, I guess I won't get to see that statue on the corner in Winslow from that Eagles' song.*

15

Hansen rode into Prescott, Arizona, in an Uber rideshare vehicle. He didn't want to find parking for his tractor-trailer rig in the central part of town, especially on the weekend. TSK had parked his rig off to the side of the road, facing north and out of town. He wanted to be able to leave in a hurry, if necessary. He marveled at a city that still maintained its small-town feel, even though it had over forty thousand residents. Floyd had been here years ago and the town had grown quite a bit.

The downtown area looked familiar enough, though. There was an arts and crafts fair in the town square surrounding the Yavapai County Courthouse. Prescott was twice the territorial capital (1864-1866, 1877-1888) during the early days of Arizona. The old west feel permeated the place, and you could tell the people who lived here loved their country. There were flags everywhere and people wearing hats and shirts supporting that ideal.

Floyd wandered around the courthouse square. There were booths scattered throughout with people selling their wares. He paused next to a bronze statue of a cowboy lying down next to his horse. He thought about how, all over the country, people were trying to tear down their history, yet here it was celebrated. He heard his satellite phone chirp and stepped off to the side.

"Yeah, I'm here now."

"Tomorrow?"

"OK, how 'bout I meet you up north. The town is busy now, some kind of craft fair. Unfortunately, traffic is a nightmare, and there are too many people."

"OK, see you then."

With nothing to do today, he continued to wander. He stopped at a food booth and grabbed a quick bite to eat. He saw lots of things that caught his interest, but with only a truck, he had no place to display them. *Maybe one day after my work is done.*

Floyd finally grew tired, having covered the area more than once. He contacted Uber and requested a ride back to his truck. The same driver arrived and soon he was back in his rig. But before he drove off, he decided to get out and relieve himself. He climbed down the hill next to the highway and searched for a protected spot.

Hayden Jerome stood at the back of her mom's car, stretching. She was out for her daily run, but this time her mom drove her north of town to run the trails by Willow Lake. Hayden was fourteen years old and had a thin runner's body. She was the star of her school's cross-country team and needed to increase her training to maintain her standing. They were parked near a dog park; she could hear the dogs in the background barking. As she finished her stretch, she told her mom, "I'm off; I'll see you in about an hour." Her mother nodded and went back to her book. Hayden put in her earbuds, turned on music on her iPhone, and started to jog. She ran the trails with an easy gait. The girl loved it when she could get away and run in nature. She passed an occasional hiker on the trail, but otherwise, it was deserted.

The Truck Stop Killer stood in the brush, having finished relieving himself. He was watching some ducks on the lake, captivated by the beauty of nature. Floyd Hansen was near a trail and had seen a hiker earlier, but now he was alone. Then, off to his right, he spotted a jogger. She was wearing very tight and, to him, obscenely revealing jogging shorts and a sports bra. *Jezebel.* He hadn't come to Prescott to search for whores, but when the Lord provided…

He stumbled from the brush, acting as if he were hurt. The girl stopped, removed her earbuds, and asked, "Are you OK, mister?"

"I parked by the road and my dog took off down here chasing a rabbit. I was looking for her and I twisted my ankle. I can't find her, and I'm worried the coyotes will get her."

Hayden considered this for a moment and decided she had time. She would just cut her run short. Her mom would worry if she was late. "I can help you look. Which way did she go?"

The TSK pointed into the brush and started to turn back as if in search of his make-believe dog. She passed him quickly because he was still faking a limp. As she looked for the dog, she asked, "What's the dog's name?" She was answered with a hard blow to the back of her head. Her last memory was of the ground rushing up to her face. Hayden hit hard, and the landing knocked her iPhone out of the holder on her arm. The TSK picked her up easily and carried her off into the brush. The day was ending; soon it would be dark and then he could move.

At the same time the Truck Stop Killer's rig was driving away, Hayden's mother, Julie, sat waiting in her car, worrying. It was dark now and Hayden was not back. She used the locator app on her iPad and could see where her daughter's phone was. Hayden had been stationary for a long time, which scared her even more. It was too far to walk, and she didn't even have a flashlight in her car. Finally, it was time to call the police.

The first officer to arrive on the scene, Wil Royston, listened to her story and looked at her phone. He was familiar with the area and knew there was a parking area off the highway near the phone. Before leaving, the officer decided to call in some more officers and a sergeant. He told Mrs. Jerome to stay there in case her daughter returned.

After arriving at the parking area, Royston stopped and, using his headlights, saw what looked like fresh tire tracks in the loose earth. He decided to stay out of the area just in case. As he was putting up crime scene tape, Sergeant Marilou Branson arrived. This took a load off his shoulders; he had handled many missing person cases that turned out to be nothing, but this one felt real.

Sergeant Branson listened as Officer Royston briefed her. She looked at the tire tracks but couldn't decide if they were related. She contacted dispatch and asked for additional officers, one of which she wanted to go where Mrs. Jerome was waiting.

She sent Royston to see if he could find the girl's phone. As he climbed down the hill, he spotted footprints in the soil. They were big and deep. "Hey Sergeant, I've got fresh footprints coming up this hill toward where you are."

He continued to search but decided to just follow the tracks on the ground. It wasn't difficult, and he soon found what he was looking for. Tucked under some brush was a cell phone. He decided to leave it there in case the crime lab wanted to photograph it where he found it. Officer Royston called Sergeant Branson on his radio and advised her that he had located the phone.

Sergeant Marilou Branson had a daughter at home. She knew what it was like to worry about her when she came home late. But, in her twenty-two years of law enforcement experience, she had never felt like she did right now. This wasn't a runaway or a girl who met up with a boyfriend; this felt like something much worse. She pulled out her cell phone and notified her lieutenant, who told her to call the chief at home. After completing that call, she put out a statewide Amber Alert.

Prescott Police Chief Doyle Booth soon arrived at the scene. He had been the chief for six years, having come from the Arizona Department of Public Safety, or DPS, to take the job. Booth, who had been in law enforcement for over thirty years, was tall and lean, his face weathered by years of exposure to the Arizona sun. After listening to Sergeant Branson, he decided he agreed. Then something came to him, "Marilou, do you have that flyer from the FBI? It came out a couple weeks ago?"

When she realized what he was asking, Sergeant Branson looked at the chief and the blood drained from her face.

"Yes, sir. It's in my car."

She retrieved the flyer advising of a serial killer who was believed to be working west and might be in the Arizona area. She handed the document to Chief Booth, who quickly scanned it. While he was reading, Branson took a call from dispatch. An Uber driver had called dispatch in response to an Amber Alert he heard on the radio. He told them he had picked up a large male white from a tractor-trailer on the north side of town. The alert said the girl was missing from the general area of where the truck was parked. Dispatch was sending an officer there now to get a complete report.

Sergeant Branson told the chief about the call, and Booth asked, "Do those look like dually truck tire tracks to you, Sergeant? They sure do to me." He looked at the flyer and then dialed the phone number at the bottom.

The Truck Stop Killer was waiting. He had driven north and then turned off the highway onto a dirt road. TSK knew no one lived up this road because he owned the land. It had been purchased years ago when he was in the area for the first time. He thought then it would be an excellent place to live; now, he would use the privacy it offered to deal with this girl.

As he pulled her from the sleeper unit and dragged her across the ground, he noticed a cross hanging from a thin chain around her neck. *Why would a whore wear this symbol of belief?* He decided to wait to kill her. But he wasn't in a hurry as usual. He would have to stay in the area until tomorrow, anyway. *Perhaps she can be saved.*

He made a small fire while he waited. It took some time, but the girl finally stirred. The TSK wasn't concerned that she would run off; he had trussed her up in anticipation of her upcoming cleansing. He wasn't worried that she would start yelling; no one was around for miles. He walked over to where she was lying and looked down, curious. He didn't usually talk to the whores he killed. He didn't want his soul soiled by their words.

She slowly shook her head and asked, "What happened? Why does my head hurt?" When she realized her hands and feet were bound by zip ties, she panicked and started twisting, trying to get free.

"Quit that. You aren't gonna get free of those; they're industrial strength. And don't bother calling for help. We're far from town; no one will hear you."

She stopped wriggling and asked, "Why did you do this? What do you want?"

He laughed, "Whores always seem to think I want something."

She was shocked by his words. "I'm not a whore."

"I see by the cross you wear you must have some faith. But tell me why Jesus died on the cross only to have you wear that symbol with almost nothing else. Why do you display your body like this if you are not a whore?"

"I go to church; I believe in God. This is my running outfit. It's what I wear when I work out. I am NOT a whore!"

He looked at her for a long time without saying a word. Then, finally, he turned back to the fire. He could hear her mumbling in the background, "I'm not a whore." He wasn't sure what to do with this girl. It troubled him because everything had always been so straightforward.

"JW, it's Lauralynn. Are you awake?"

"Yep. What's up, Doc?"

"The duty desk just transferred a call to me from the chief of police in Prescott, Arizona. He believes they have had an abduction by the Truck Stop Killer."

"Abduction? I thought that guy just kidnapped and killed them?"

"He does, but this one is different. It's a teenage girl. She was taken while she was out running in the woods. They have a description, and everything else matches. Do you know where Prescott is?"

"No, I don't. But I'm sure I can find it on the GPS. So, are we doing a callout?"

"Yes, of course. This guy is the big fish. I am scrambling my team, but it will take some time. My people say Prescott is only six hours driving time from you. However, we won't be there for at least ten. Can you and Ben respond and serve as the advance team? Do what you can to start our process, and we'll be there to take over ASAP."

"OK, I'm gonna get off the phone and get started. We'll call you when we get on the road. I need to call Ben."

"OK. This is the real deal, JW. I can feel it."

"I'm on it."

JW and Ben were on the road about thirty minutes later. They left Long Beach, and JW asked Ben to call the Comm Center and tell them they were going to Arizona to assist the FBI. He knew he didn't need to do this, but if Long Beach called them for a trail, he wanted someone to know they were out of town. As JW drove, Ben went through a stack of research that Bonnie had printed on Prescott and the surrounding area. Then, Ben showed him a photograph of a statue of a military man on horseback. "That's kind of cool, huh?"

"Yeah, I like it, but I need less travelogue and more on how to find the bad guy."

Lauralynn sent them an email with updated information on the Truck Stop Killer. They had seen a lot of this while they were in Quantico, but there were a few new developments. The TSK had been a busy boy.

There had been a few more murders since their visit back east. TSK was cutting a bloody path across the country, from the southeast to the southwest. Now he had taken an innocent. It was late, and they made good time leaving the LA area. Once they were outside the city limits and on Interstate 10, JW opened up the truck and took the speed close to ninety miles per hour.

The team didn't have the CHP escort they'd had when they went to Las Vegas, but he figured if they were stopped, the US Marshal's credentials would keep them from being delayed for very long. Traffic was light. Somewhere east of Palm Springs, JW's phone rang. Ben accepted the call over the vehicle's speakers.

"JW, Lauralynn. We will be leaving for the airport soon. I arranged an Arizona DPS escort for you into Prescott. After you cross the border, they will meet you at the first rest area."

Just as advertised, JW and Ben crossed the California/ Arizona border and stopped at a rest area within ten minutes. Two Arizona DPS SUVs were there waiting for them. JW and Ben got out, quickly introduced themselves, and ran into the restroom. They came back out and then gave Ares a quick break. They were back on the road within five minutes, eastbound on I-10. They got off the interstate within thirty minutes and began a northeasterly route on State Route 60. They passed through several small towns; their residents had long ago gone to sleep. The red and blue strobes of the cars reflected off the buildings, casting a ghostly glow.

As they passed through another town, Ben said, "Hey, look, we're in Hope." Then, within moments, he continued, "and now we're out. Did you see that sign on the way out?"

"I'm concentrating on the road; what did it say?"

"It said, 'You're Now Beyond Hope.'"

JW laughed and said, "Buddy, we've been beyond hope for a long time."

They continued on highway 60 for almost an hour and then turned onto State Highway 71. As they drove, Ben read through some preliminary information they had received via email about the crime in Prescott.

"Looks like a fourteen-year-old girl was out running. Her mom was waiting for her to return, but she never did. So she called the local PD, and they ran a track on the girl's cell phone, which they found in the bushes. They got some more info from an Uber driver that leads them to believe a truck driver is involved who matches the basic description they have of TSK."

"So, we're not certain the suspect is TSK, or the girl is a victim?"

"Nothing is certain. I bet that girl's mom thinks she was abducted."

"I see you're looking at Google Earth on the computer. What can you tell me about the area?"

"Where the girl was last seen is near a lake. A lot of trails in the area. Lots of small trees and scrub. I don't know if we're looking at some kind of a rural trail, but if TSK took her, I'm thinking a car trail."

"OK, we can do that. Any idea if local law enforcement knows we're coming or what we do?"

"I have to suspect they know we're coming, or we wouldn't have the escort."

"Good point. As far as the rest goes, we'll find out when we get there. Damn, Ben, I wish Addy was well enough to come. We might be trailing for a long time."

"Yeah, either Addy or I wish I could've brought Zeus. I would love to get him on a real trail."

"The werewolf? He's not even certified yet. Besides, these are small-town people; we don't want to scare them to death before we even start," JW said with a smile.

"Funny guy. You know he'll certify. I don't think it will take as long as Ares. I got a lot of experience working with you to certify Ares and Addy. I think Zeus is as good, so I believe we'll get him certified even faster."

"I agree, but for now, we're shorthanded. We need to think of a way to try to use Ares carefully and get the most out of him."

"I have an idea, but let's get there, and then we can work out our strategy."

The caravan continued northeast until they passed through the small town of Congress, where they turned north onto State Highway 89. JW said, "I wonder why they're taking us this way. I looked on a map, and it seemed easier to go through Phoenix."

"I was curious about that, too, so I checked on the computer. This route is more direct and saves us almost ninety minutes compared to going through Phoenix."

"OK, that makes sense, unless they just wanted to give us a scenic tour of Arizona."

"I'm thinking not. You may not have noticed, but it is dark out. I haven't seen anything except blacktop since we left Long Beach."

"Not for long, my friend," said JW, pointing to the lightening eastern horizon. After Congress, they began climbing a steep hill with many switchbacks. Ben could look out on the desert floor as the dawn's light made it more visible.

He said, "I never thought of the desert as a beautiful place, but this view is incredible."

"I wish I could take a look, but I'm busy trying to keep us from going over the side."

At the top, they entered the small town of Yarnell. It was beginning to show some signs of life, and a local sheriff's vehicle was stopped by the side of the road. A deputy sheriff stood and watched them go by.

"Yarnell. Why do I know that name?"

"I recall the name; that's where that crew of firefighters was killed a few years back."

"Weren't they from Prescott?"

"Yep, the Granite Mountain Hotshots. It was a huge deal, the most firefighters killed in one incident in a long time. They made a movie about it."

"I saw it. *Only the Brave*. Incredibly sad how those guys died."

In less than an hour, they were in Prescott. The last part of the drive was over ten miles of switchbacks. There were several impromptu memorials along the way. JW said, "Boy, I hope those are not a sign of things to come."

As they drove into town, a Prescott Police Department vehicle joined them. The convoy didn't stop; they just followed the SUV through town. A few minutes later, they stopped at what was a massive command-post operation. Ben said, "Go check-in and I'll dig out the vests and get Ares ready."

When JW walked up, he was greeted by Prescott Police Chief Doyle Booth and Yavapai County Sheriff Jeanne Gregory.

"I'm JW North with the FBI task force. My partner, Ben Kellum, is prepping the dog at the Tahoe. What can you tell me?"

Chief Booth gave JW a complete summary of everything that had occurred before their arrival. Sheriff Gregory added, "I'm here because the chief requested that we activate our search and rescue team. If you can follow a track on the suspect, I suspect we will be in my jurisdiction real soon."

JW gave them a quick summary of what they could do and how Ares would trail, finishing with, "We were in Southern California, so we're the first team members here. My last update had the team from Quantico arriving at your airport in about two hours. Unfortunately, they won't have vehicles, so an FBI team from Phoenix is coming up to provide support."

JW looked the two over but paid more attention to the chief as it was his case. "Chief, what would you like us to do?"

"This trailing thing you do, can you do that from where we found Hayden's phone?"

"We can certainly give it a try. Just remember, nothing is guaranteed."

The sheriff added, "I've seen a lot of search and rescue dogs, Doyle, some good, some bad. These guys are the ones who found that killer in Las Vegas. I normally don't put a lot of faith in these types of things, but if it means getting that girl back, I recommend we give it a shot."

JW thought, *Well, that wasn't the strongest endorsement I've ever received, but what the heck.*

Ben walked up to the group with Ares on a leash. After quick introductions, JW asked, "Where are we going?"

Chief Booth started to lead them down the side of the hill, pointing out a line of yellow tape, "We've got some footprints over there. If this trailing thing works, you will probably come back there."

Before they could leave, a woman walked up to the group. Chief Booth said, "This is Julie Jerome, Hayden's mom. These gentlemen are here from the FBI to see if they can help us find Hayden."

The woman looked them over with tired eyes. She gazed at Ares and asked, "Are you gonna use the dog? I have some of Hayden's clothes in my car."

Ben went with her to retrieve a scent article. When they returned, she said to JW, "Your friend told me how this is supposed to work. Is your dog friendly?"

"Yes, ma'am."

Mrs. Jerome bent down, looked Ares in the eyes, and said, "Please go find my girl and bring her home to me. She's all I've got."

The group left her at the command post and walked down the hill and into the brush. They went about a hundred yards to find an officer waiting for them.

"I found the phone right there," he said, pointing out a crime scene number under a bush.

Ben removed a sweatshirt from an evidence bag and gave it to JW, who scented Ares on it. JW returned it to Ben and then said, "Geo-say." Ares put his nose down to the ground and began casting about for scent. He started to work away from the direction they thought the trail would go. JW let him work, and Ares turned and began working back toward the road.

JW tried to stay off to the side to avoid contaminating any evidence. When they returned to the road, Ares again began casting and then turned toward where there were deep tire tracks in the dirt. He pulled hard and they were off. Ben had arranged for several law enforcement vehicles to provide an escort. One officer was asked to drive their Tahoe and follow along. Both the chief and sheriff got into one car and followed the group.

After a mile, JW called for a stop. The chief approached and asked, "What's wrong? The dog was doing so well. Did he lose the scent?"

"No, it's not that. Once we get out of town, how far to the next town?"

"Probably a few miles. There's Chino Valley, then Paulden and a few other small towns, all the way up to Ash Fork and Interstate 40, which is about fifty miles or more."

"OK, there's no way any dog can run a trail that long. So here's how we think we should do this. We'll load up in cars and continue on this road. Once we reach a turnoff, intersection, or any place where our suspect could get off, we'll get out and see where Ares takes us. Then we load back up and continue until we do it again. Hopefully, this guy gets off the road at some point before he gets to the interstate. His past MO has been to take them someplace that is not too far away."

"What does he do with them once he gets there?" asked the sheriff.

JW replied, "He kills them. I won't get into details, but it's not pretty."

The chief said, "OK, I like your plan. Let's not stand around here talking about it."

The trail continued until they reached a closed gate in a long barbed-wire fence. There was no sign that a vehicle had turned here, but JW didn't want to take any chances. He got Ares out and they quickly determined the trail continued north. This continued with the same pattern for miles until they reached Chino Valley. There were several roads entering from the side and many places to turn off. JW decided to just run the trail all the way through the town.

The sun was clearing the eastern horizon, and the clouds in the sky were lit up as if the heavens were on fire. JW looked to his right and said, "Wow, incredible sunrise over there, Ben. It's almost beautiful enough to make you forget why we are out here."

Finally, after going through the town, they got a bit of a break and rode for a few minutes. Ben and JW gulped down water and caught their breath.

"Ben, I don't know what is going on, but this trail is kicking my ass. I can't catch my breath."

"Well, the elevation back in Prescott is over 5,000 feet. It could be that."

"Maybe we should start packing oxygen?"

"Nah, suck it up, buttercup," Ben replied, smiling.

JW started to respond when he noticed a sign off to the side of the road that read, "Gunsite." Distracted from his earlier train of thought, he said, "Gunsite? Huh, I knew it was in Arizona but didn't realize it was here."

"Gunsite, what's that?"

"Firearms training facility. I'll tell you about it sometime when we're not chasing serial killers across the desert in the early morning hours."

The trail had been grueling so far, lasting well over two hours. Ares still looked fresh, but JW and Ben showed some signs of fatigue. They worked through a small town named Paulden, and JW wondered if TSK had simply gotten on the road and kept going. They stopped at several turn-offs after Paulden to see where the scent went, but the trail continued north.

Dr. Gaurdia called the search team to let them know her team was on the ground at Prescott airport. She told JW, "We just landed and are organizing our gear."

JW replied, "We went by the airport over an hour ago; it looked like a nice place. We are on a trail north of there. The trail still seems fresh; Ares is pulling hard. If my recommendation means anything, send your technical people to the command post. You and LeClair load up the shooters and head this way, just in case."

"That sounds like a good idea. But, JW, this is not a 'Go ahead, make my day' moment. Please do not shoot the suspect unless absolutely necessary."

"Lauralynn, was that a movie reference?"

The line went dead, and JW said, "Ben, Lauralynn made a movie reference!"

"Yeah, I heard. I also heard her tell you not to shoot the bad guy."

"Ben, when have I ever shot anyone who didn't need it?"

They continued following the road for over a mile. There weren't many openings, so the team traveled in the Tahoe, which allowed everyone to catch their breath. Finally, there was an opening on the left side of the road. JW stopped the Tahoe and got Ares out once again. The dog restarted quickly and then crossed the roadway toward a secured gate. Ares jumped onto the gate and looked at JW, who looked down, raised his chin, and motioned with his eyes for Ben to look. The dirt in front of the gate showed fresh large truck tire tracks that continued up the road and out of sight.

JW turned to meet the chief and sheriff walking toward them. He pointed to the ground, and Chief Booth stooped and examined the tracks carefully. He said, "I'm no expert, but those look a lot like the tracks we saw back at the scene."

Sheriff Gregory nodded and said, "You boys covered about twenty-five miles and took us right to him. I am impressed."

JW said, "I admit, this looks good, but let's wait until we have the guy in cuffs before we celebrate." Gregory nodded.

JW continued, "Does anyone know where this road goes?"

JW put Ares back in the Tahoe to give him a quick rest, and Ben got on the computer. He brought up Google Earth and zoomed into the area. "It looks like it goes westerly for a way and then stops at a large open space. There's nothing there. Hard to tell from this perspective, but it looks like it's surrounded by hills and lots of trees."

Sheriff Gregory said, "Those look like junipers. They can be really thick, but it looks like they're spread out. But then we don't know how long ago these pictures were taken."

JW looked at the sheriff and chief and asked, "How do you want to do this? I would say we continue to follow the trail and see what it gets us. Do you have any tactical guys here?"

Gregory shook her head and replied, "I wasn't convinced this would work. Between the two of us, we have about six officers here."

"The FBI is about twenty minutes behind with five members of their HRT unit with them, if you want to wait," said JW, referring to the Hostage Rescue Team, the FBI's national "SWAT" team that responds to major crises.

Chief Booth looked at Sheriff Gregory and said, "Personally, I would love to wait for the FBI to get here, but I will never sleep another night if that girl dies in the next twenty minutes."

"OK, then I guess we're a go," said JW. "I'll let you guys run this part of the show. It's your jurisdiction and your guys."

JW stood with Ben near the gate and asked, "What do you think?"

Ben looked at JW with deep concern. "I think the devil is waiting for us down that road. I wish we had more than six guys with us, 'cause, pardon the pun, this could be one hell of a fight. But there are over fifty victims standing with us, screaming from eternity for justice."

JW sniffed and then asked, "Do you smell smoke?"

The Truck Stop Killer dropped another log on the fire. The girl was asleep off to the side. He had thrown a blanket over her during the night. He liked killing whores, but he didn't want to see them suffer. He had yet to make up his mind on this one. She said the right words, but that could just be Satan speaking through her. He knew he would need to decide soon. He had an appointment to keep this morning and she would just be in the way. As he stirred the fire, he heard a loud screeching noise. *Someone is at the gate.* He believed it wasn't the person he was expecting as they knew to call before coming in. He roused the girl, cut the ties off her feet, and stood her up.

"You come with me. You give me any trouble, and I'll kill you."

A sheriff's deputy approached the gate with the largest pair of bolt cutters JW had ever seen. He made quick work of the lock and then pushed the gate open. The air was filled with a sound as loud as a dozen eagles' cries. The gate groaned as it opened and got louder as it went wider. Finally, JW said, "Well, if someone is home, they know we're here now."

The officers and deputies quickly deployed, three to a side, with the sheriff, chief, and JW and Ben. JW called Dr. Gaurdia and told her they were going in. She asked if he could delay; they were only fifteen minutes out.

JW said, "Lauralynn, this is their show. We're just here to help. I would love to have you guys with us, but I agree. There may be a fourteen-year-old girl in there, scared to death and praying for salvation. We've gotta go."

JW restarted Ares. It felt kind of stupid, in a way. There was no other way in or out. The suspect was either there or not. However, it could help in a trial if he could testify that the dog went right up to the suspect and alerted. *You knew the job was dangerous when you took it.*

Ares pulled them to the west. The road was composed of loose dirt and their jogging stirred up a lot of dust. As they continued, JW could hear the group breathing heavily around him. JW was hurting again. This thin air was killing him, but they all kept going. Finally, they entered the clearing they had seen on the satellite map; an open area almost one hundred yards across with only light scrub growth. There was an old, rusty travel trailer at the back that looked like it had been there for a long time. On one side were a truck and trailer. There was a fire going in a pit surrounded by river rock. It was noticeably quiet, the only sound the occasional crackle from the fire.

JW asked Ben, "You ever notice how quiet it gets before the shooting starts?"

The Truck Stop Killer stood in the bushes, watching. They couldn't see him. He held the girl tightly, with a revolver pointed at her head. He had told her, "You make a sound; it will be your last." He could see a group of officers moving toward his trailer. There were two others off to the side, talking and pointing. He saw another two men dressed in tactical gear with a dog. They were talking quietly when the dog started to walk in his direction, pulling the handler with him. *Damn it!* He raised the pistol to aim, but the girl struggled, making it hard to steady the weapon with one hand.

"What do you think, Ben? Is he in there?"

"Nope."

JW looked at him and followed his eyes. He was looking down at the ground. Finally, JW saw what caught his interest. A blanket and a zip tie that had been cut.

Ben continued, "He's on the move."

JW felt the leash pull and looked to see what Ares was doing. The dog had his nose down and pulled him toward a hill that overlooked the camp. "Shall we see what he's got?"

"Do we want to tell the others?"

"They look busy; this might be nothing. Let's take a look up top and see what we can see. We can yell down to them if we find anything."

The TSK tried to aim at the officers, but the girl kept struggling. He didn't want his first shot to be at her; it would give up the element of surprise. He watched the two men with the dog and thought, *Maybe I should shoot the dog. The dog probably brought them here. If I kill the dog, maybe I can get away.* He changed his point of aim and tried to focus on the German Shepherd he could see coming his way.

The pistol shot came as a loud boom to JW and Ben, who both ducked. They saw the dirt next to Ares explode, throwing debris into the air. JW had read a book on serial killers, the author asserting that killers rarely were aggressive with the police when caught. JW, now angry, shouted, "Don't you idiots ever read the books? You are not supposed to shoot at the police. What the hell is wrong with you?"

They followed the sound of the gunshot and saw branches swaying as a large form disappeared. Ben shouted, "He's running!" They tried to sprint up the hill after him but didn't want to go too quickly and run into another ambush. Back at the campsite, two deputies ran to help cover them. But unfortunately, they were already one hundred yards behind.

JW and Ben reached the top and spotted the suspect running away, dragging the girl with him. She was slowing him down; they might have a chance to catch him. JW tied Ares' leash to a juniper tree, and Ben turned back to the others and yelled, "Up here, we've got the suspect and the girl. He's running."

They took off, running in pursuit. Ares began barking behind them. If JW thought the elevation was tough on him before, it was severe now. His mind drifted for a moment and he thought of all the women the TSK had killed, suffocating them. They all died, gasping for air. In a small way, he could relate, but he knew he had to fight through it. He saw the TSK stop and look back, raising his revolver again, firing. The shot didn't come near them but had the desired effect. Ben and JW ducked for a moment before looking again. The Truck Stop Killer was still stopped, but he wasn't looking for them at the moment, so they took the opportunity to begin running again.

Hansen looked at the girl. She was going to get him caught or killed. It was time to dump the excess baggage, but something in him just couldn't let her go free. He reached into a pocket and pulled out another zip tie. He looped it and pulled it over her head, tightening it fully and nearly crushing her airway. Hayden gasped and dropped to her knees. She couldn't breathe and her vision was narrowing.

JW couldn't see what the suspect was doing, but he saw the girl drop and the killer turn to run. He and Ben continued running, closing the distance in moments. JW saw the zip tie and said, "Ben, you help her. I'm going after the bad guy." Ben reached into a pouch on his vest for a multi-tool to cut the tie wrap. JW started running again. A fresh load of adrenalin flooded his system, and his breathing evened out. He could see the killer now; he was close. It looked like he was on the phone. *Who is he calling?*

Floyd Hansen hit the speed dial on his phone. It was answered quickly.

"Where are you? I need help; the police are here."

"I'm close. I'll be right there."

JW turned and yelled over his shoulder, "Ben, I think he's headed to the road down there. Call Gaurdia, have them move to intercept."

He continued running down the hill, accelerating his pace. The exertion was causing the perspiration to flow freely. He was drenched and sweat was getting into his eyes, which now burned. He hoped he didn't trip over something. A fall now could be serious. He saw motion to the north; a car was coming. *Oh crap, this could turn into a hostage situation.* He increased his speed, barreling down the hill toward the TSK.

As he reached a slight rise, he paused. The road was below him, and so was the Truck Stop Killer—he was waiting. He looked at JW and raised his pistol. *Not this time, asshole.* JW drew his Springfield Armory Operator in a smooth motion, practiced in hundreds of pistol competitions. The only sound was steel against Kydex as the Operator cleared the holster. The gun felt like an old friend in his hand as he raised it and placed the sights in the center of the suspect's chest. He squeezed the trigger twice in smooth, crisp motions and was rewarded with two reports of .45 caliber bullets leaving the gun. The nearly one-half inch wide, 230-grain hollow points moved slowly through the air at 800 feet per second, which was slow for a bullet. JW had heard it referred to as a "flying hubcap" due to its size and slow speed. He saw the bullets strike the suspect in the chest almost simultaneously. The bullets crashed through his rib cage and burst into his heart. Destroyed by the impacts, the heart stopped, and blood flow ceased. JW watched him collapse. The suspect's pistol fired as if to punctuate the end of the gunfight.

JW climbed down the hill into the cut and walked toward the suspect on the ground. He was aware of a car stopping, a door opening, and a woman shouting, "Why did you have to shoot him?"

"Get back in your car, ma'am. Please wait inside."

He paused and watched the suspect for a moment. He looked for any sign of movement in the chest, breathing. Instead, he saw nothing except blood beginning to pool under his body. He was still wary; he had seen too many horror movies where the bad guy got back up after being "killed."

"You bastard, you killed my Floyd!"

JW felt a sharp pain in his left shoulder. He turned and saw that the woman had sliced his left triceps with a knife and, damn it, that hurt. He holstered his pistol in a natural motion and turned and punched her in the face, right on her nose. It erupted in an explosion of blood, and she collapsed at his feet, the knife slipping away from her. He turned back to the Truck Stop Killer, still expecting him to get back up. *No Stephen King ending this time.*

He heard another car skidding to a stop to his left. He looked up and saw it was the FBI. *Thank God the cavalry has arrived.* He turned back to the woman's car. He looked in the passenger seat and saw a child, a boy, maybe four years old, in a car seat. JW looked at the child and tried to smile. His grin was returned with a look of hatred. The child's stare burned into him. His eyes were black, and there was something evil in them. You typically didn't see this depth of loathing in a young child. *Oh crap, Stephen King ending after all.*

Lauralynn Gaurdia ran to him, "JW, you're hurt."

He looked down at his arm, blood dripping from the incision onto the road, "Oh, it's just a flesh wound." He laughed, "I always wanted to say that." Special Agent Rick LeClair brought a first aid kit and applied a pressure bandage to his arm. "My wife is gonna be pissed that I got hurt again. Well, at least Ares didn't get hurt."

Lauralynn looked at the suspect on the ground as LeClair checked his pulse and shook his head. "JW, why did you have to shoot him?"

"Aardvark, Doctor. God damn it, aardvark." He looked at the woman on the ground, "She stabbed me. I think she's with him. You can interview her. And keep an eye on that kid; he looks like pure evil."

An ambulance arrived to take JW to the hospital. He didn't want to ride in an ambulance, but the chief, sheriff, and Lauralynn told him to get in the ambulance and quit bitching. Ben drove the Tahoe behind him with Ares in the back, taking a well-deserved nap.

Inside the Yavapai Regional Medical Center emergency room, JW sat quietly and talked with Ben. "Well, the good news is we got the Truck Stop Killer. The bad news is Lauralynn is pissed I shot him."

"I saw it; you did what you had to do. It was a good shooting."

"Yeah, sometimes I think she might trade us both for an interview with a serial killer."

Ben smiled, "Then we're gonna have to work on her priorities. She's gonna be busy. I heard her talking to that woman, the one who stabbed you, and I gotta tell you, she is batshit crazy. But she is a gold mine of information. It sounds like TSK always called her on a sat phone, especially after a murder. They found a notebook in her car full of records of each killing. That guy was a lot busier than the FBI knew. So Lauralynn is gonna be busy for a while."

"What happened with the girl? Hayden?"

"While you were chasing TSK down the hill, I cut the zip tie on her neck. I think she'll be fine. She's in a room on the other side of the ER. Her mom said, 'Thank you.'"

JW looked around. "This sure is a nice hospital for a small town. I don't know what I was expecting, maybe a country doctor or something. I think I watch too much television."

"Maybe. I know you like those John Wayne westerns, but that was long ago, JW."

"Ben, do me a favor, hand me my phone. I need to call Bonnie and get my ass chewed." While he was on the phone, a doctor began carefully stitching up his arm.

Bonnie picked up on the first ring. "JW, I've been watching the news. Are you OK?"

"I'm at the hospital getting my arm stitched up. A crazy lady stabbed me. Oh wait, that's redundant. The good news is Ares is OK. So, I'm batting five hundred."

Understanding the baseball analogy, Bonnie said, "Well, that's an improvement, but it would be nice if you could run a trail without getting yourself hurt."

"I hear you. So, here's the plan. Ben and I are gonna stay the night and drive home in the morning. We have some more paperwork to do with the FBI today. So, we'll sleep and be on the road home first thing."

The following day JW met Sheriff Gregory, Chief Booth, and a few of the officers from the night before at a small restaurant near the town square. JW sat and chatted with them, asking questions about the town and the people. He looked around the place, admiring the decorations and signs on the walls. *This is America, right here.*

Outside, he heard Ares start barking and got up to investigate. He looked out the window and saw a thin man standing by the Tahoe's door, yelling, "God damn vicious dog," Then he struck the screen over the window.

JW was pissed and went outside shouting, "Hey, get away from the car and leave the dog alone. That is a police dog, and you can go to jail for bothering him."

"Fuck you, your dog tried to bite me."

JW showed the man his badge and said, "US Marshal, leave now!"

The man started advancing on JW, saying, "Fuck you and your badge."

JW looked at the man; he was emaciated and filthy. *Meth addict.* The man cocked his right arm back and swung at JW, which he easily blocked. JW grasped his wrist, just like he had been taught all those years ago in the academy. He reached across and grabbed the back of the man's hand, twisted it, and then took a step forward. The pressure caused the man's feet to come out from under him and he fell to the ground. JW locked the man's arm and turned, rolling him onto his stomach.

A voice came from behind JW, "Here."

JW felt something in his free hand and looked over his shoulder. One of the deputies from last night was giving him a pair of handcuffs. After JW applied the cuffs, the deputy said, "That was a nice move. You'll have to teach me that one. I'm Deputy Brian Hockler. I was with you last night. That was the most impressive thing I've ever seen."

"Thanks, happy to teach you the takedown. You know this dirtbag?"

"Yep. That's Lamar English. He's a local problem child, meth user, and sometimes dealer. I put him in prison a few years back for vehicular manslaughter. It was a huge accident up near where we were last night. He was wasted and driving way too fast. Killed a whole family in an instant." Brian's eyes lose their focus, allowing him to travel back to a place he would rather not revisit. Then he snapped back to reality. "Not sure what he's doing out already, though. Give him to me; I'll take him down and book him. If he's on parole, I'll see if I can get it revoked."

"Thanks, I appreciate your help. I don't like people messing with my dog."

"Particularly that dog. He's special," said Brian with a smile.

"Sorry to ruin your breakfast."

"Not a problem; I was done anyway."

JW went back inside and told the sheriff and chief, "Sorry about that; I didn't mean to start trouble in your town."

Sheriff Gregory said, "Well, it's his town. Is that Lamar English? What's he doing out of jail?"

Chief Booth said, "If that's English, then he needs to be in jail. But don't worry about it. We have a few like him around, but not many. But somehow, I feel you don't have a hard time finding trouble."

After breakfast JW and Ben took a quick walk around the town square to stretch their legs and give Ares a break. They saw a pair of Prescott PD officers on bicycles, watching them from a respectful distance. As they walked, Ben said, "I see you were outside making new friends."

"Some local tweaker messing with Ares. Deputy from last night took him to jail. He was under the influence."

"You have a way of bringing out the best in people."

They walked for a while and looked at the statues that circled the courthouse, "Hey Ben, look. This is that one we were talking about yesterday."

They looked up at a rider on a horse, a cavalry saber hanging from his side, "That's Bucky O'Neil. He was a local hero who went off with Teddy Roosevelt and the Rough Riders to Cuba. Unfortunately, he was killed there."

JW looked at Ben in wonder.

Ben said, "What? I have to do something while you do all the driving. You know, I can drive too."

"Good, you can drive home; my shoulder is sore."

JW scanned the area. "A lot of history here, Ben. Have I ever told you how much I like history?"

16

"Hey, Bonnie, I think I may have found it."

JW and Ben had returned home from Arizona, and JW immediately called a family meeting. Bonnie came in and thanked JW for the cup of coffee he had made for her. Addy had "yelled" at Ares when he came inside, giving him a piece of her mind for leaving her behind. They were in the backyard playing keep away with a tennis ball. JW watched them out the window. It felt good just watching dogs being dogs.

JW sat down, and Bonnie asked, "Found what?"

"I think I found a place to relocate Big Dogs."

"Where, Prescott? I don't know; Arizona is awfully hot. I don't do hot real well, ya know."

"That's what I thought at first. When we got into Arizona, it was hot. But Prescott is higher up, at five thousand feet. It's not that hot. Ben did some Internet research on the place on the way home. They even get snow there."

Bonnie got a dreamy look in her eyes, "I haven't seen snow in a long time."

JW decided to hit her where he knew she was weak, "Honey, there is a courthouse square in Prescott, full of trees with lots of people walking around. There's a gazebo, benches, and bronze statues memorializing the old west. It looks like something out of a Thomas Kinkade painting. At Christmastime, they decorate all those trees with lights and have a tree-lighting ceremony to kick off the holidays. And they do a boot drop on Whiskey Row at midnight on New Year's Eve. The place has this wonderful small-town feel. I haven't experienced that before, and everyone there is so damn friendly. When they wave at you, they use all their fingers. And they have the world's oldest rodeo!"

"Do you want to be a cowboy, JW?"

"Cowboy, nah. I can't do that. I'd be some kind of poser. I don't even know how to ride a horse. But I think I would look good in a pair of boots."

"OK, let me do some research and see how I feel about it. Then, maybe we can go over there for a weekend, and I can get a feel for the place."

JW called Ben a couple of weeks later and said, "Hey Ben, come over tomorrow afternoon. We need to get the training schedule for Zeus set up, plus Addy is ready to get back to work. We need to get these dogs working. It's quiet now, but who knows how long that'll last. We need to get the team up to strength."

When he got off the phone with Ben, JW turned to Bonnie, "Did you get what I asked you to?"

"Yes."

He rubbed his hands together, "Excellent; I love it when a plan comes together."

The Shadow had been busy. He had already killed five women, but the police had found only three of them. He had purposely tried to change his MO on some of the crimes.

He didn't want to create too much interest too early. If it got too hot here, he would be forced to relocate. He still had so much work to do, but he also had needs. He found that his build-up cycle time was getting shorter. His appetite for fresh souls was increasing, and he was concerned that he would slip up and get caught if he couldn't keep it under control. Going to prison as a sexual serial killer was not an option for him.

He read the newspaper every day and closely followed the cases. The police were too open regarding their investigation and their stupidity made it easier for him to avoid apprehension. One day, there was an announcement in the paper about a volunteer search party. His curiosity overwhelmed him and he decided to volunteer. He felt a little exhilarated as he checked in and they gave him a bright orange vest. What made it even better was knowing the area was miles away from where he had raped and killed the woman. Still, he was energetic and tried to be helpful while fighting the entire day to keep a smile from his face due to the irony of the situation.

As he walked inside his favorite downtown diner, he learned that his regular waitress, Michelle, was off today. It was a good thing because she was getting too friendly with him. He was of two minds regarding her. On the one hand, she was exactly his type and her interest and trust would make her easy to take. But, on the other hand, she was too close to him and it would draw suspicion if she disappeared.

Fortunately, he had someone else in mind. He was trying to wait for a few more weeks before his date with her. He needed some time between his killings. It was hard, though; the hunger was growing and it was so strong.

Ben arrived at the North residence as requested by JW. Lucy came along, claiming she had some things to discuss with Bonnie. JW had also asked Ben to bring Zeus along. It was time to introduce Zeus and Ares. Both being males, there was a chance one would seek to establish pack dominance over the other. Plus, Addy needed to meet her future beau.

As Ben pulled up, he saw JW's black Tahoe in the driveway and another lookalike parked in front of the house. He smiled at Lucy and said, "Looks like you're gonna have to drive home, Honey. Did you know about this?"

Lucy did her best to keep a straight face as she replied, "Who, me?"

They got out of the car, leaving Zeus inside with the engine running to provide air conditioning. Ben got out and started walking around the new SUV. JW came out on the porch and said, "Hey buddy, get away from that car." Behind him was another man that Ben didn't recognize.

"Ben, this is Bill Lombard. He works for Chevrolet as their west coast representative for law enforcement sales."

"Pleasure to meet you, Bill."

JW said, "Bill, you better give him the full tour. He's drooling now and we don't want him to ruin the paint job."

"Right you are, sir. Ben, if you'll come with me, I will give you the full rundown on this fine vehicle."

"Oh, Ben, we're going inside to have a drink. See you in a few hours," JW said with a laugh.

Ben noticed something hanging from the rear-view mirror and took a closer look. It was a small, ornate silver cross. "Hey, what's this?"

Bonnie answered, "Oh, that. It's a silver cross. I picked it up for you, took it to church, and had the priest bless it against werewolf bites."

Ben scowled. "Crosses are for vampires."

She laughed and said, "Not in my world, Ben."

Ben returned to his Tahoe and the group went inside. Lucy looked out the window at her husband and asked Bonnie, "Should I be jealous?"

Bonnie replied, "Well, you know boys and their toys."

When his vehicle orientation was complete, Ben came inside and asked JW, "When do you want to introduce these dogs?"

"Now's as good a time as any. Let's do it out front. Ares will be a bit less territorial there."

JW brought Ares and Addy out and Ben released Zeus. The two males approached one another warily, eyeing each other, and deciding if this dog in front of them was a threat. Their hackles were raised, and for a moment JW thought, *Oh crap, it's on.* Then Addy trotted between them, nipping at Ares, and bumping him out of the way. She turned to Zeus, gave a playful bark, and the dogs began playing in the yard.

Ben said, "Disaster averted."

Bonnie replied, "Once again, the girl comes in and bails you two out."

Ben said, "Hey JW, come look at this."

JW walked over to Ben, who was standing by his car. "What?"

Ben merely pointed at the dash. JW leaned in and saw a metallic plate that read, "This Vehicle is Custom Made for US Deputy Marshal Ben Kellum and K9 Zeus."

JW looked at Bill Lombard with a "Where's mine?" look. Bill laughed and said, "Don't worry, JW. I have one for you too. We just started doing this."

Bill declined the offer to stay for dinner. Everyone else went inside and watched the dogs playing. In and out, back and forth, play fighting and teasing one another with toys. The trio did not need their human partners to provide entertainment. After an hour of intense recreation, the dogs crashed on the patio. Ben and JW went over a training timeline. Bonnie and Lucy were in her office looking at spreadsheets and paperwork. Bonnie and Lucy would need to learn a whole new set of forms, courtesy of the FBI, to get reimbursed for expenses.

JW started to go inside to ask Bonnie if she was ready for him to grill steaks. As he maneuvered around three dogs to get to the door, he turned to Ben and said, "Ben, this gives a whole new meaning to dogstacle course."

"Yeah, and what will you do when you have a litter of puppies to go along with that?"

"Oh, crap."

JW was standing on a pistol range firing line. There were no other shooters on his left or right. The line of targets seemed to extend out of sight. All the targets were turned sideways; he couldn't see the silhouettes. He looked down, his Operator in his competition holster. He was waiting for the sounds of a buzzer and the targets to turn. This was odd; he didn't use this pistol for competitions. It was his duty gun. Also, you didn't shoot by yourself in this type of competition. Something was definitely off.

Without warning, the targets turned. The target in front of JW was the Truck Stop Killer, but it wasn't a target. It was alive. He had a revolver, but not the little one he had used in Arizona. This one was huge; he could see down the barrel and into the chambers. Each one had a bullet with his name on it. Each one calling to him, 'JW, we're here for you.'

JW drew, sighted in, and fired. The bullet pushed through the cardboard target, but the part that was TSK, the part that was alive, just laughed. JW fired and then fired again. When the target didn't stop laughing, he continued to fire. When the weapon was empty, he smoothly reloaded and fired again and again. The Truck Stop Killer raised his pistol and fired one time. JW felt the impact and fell back.

JW felt like he was underwater, but instead of falling back, he struggled to get to the surface. He couldn't breathe; his lungs were on fire. He finally broke through to the surface, gasping for breath but feeling no relief. He opened his eyes and all he could see was a pair of brown eyes looking back. He still couldn't breathe, but now he could see why. Addy was standing on his chest, keeping him from drawing a breath. Her eyes said it all, "What's wrong, Dad?"

Bonnie came to the rescue. "Addy, get off him. He can't breathe."

Addy looked chastened and took a step back. She was off, but she still looked at JW, concerned. JW took a deep breath and coughed, "Thanks, I couldn't breathe."

"What happened? Did you have a nightmare?"

"Yeah, another weird one. This time it was the Truck Stop Killer."

"Well, I guess it makes sense. You have killed two men over the past six months. I know those shootings were fully justified, but still, it has to leave a mark on your soul."

"Maybe I need to play more golf with Mark."

JW's good friend, Mark Powers, had taken on the responsibility of talking to him about his mental health. Mark found he liked the 'work' so much he wanted to do it professionally. He already had his Bachelor of Science degree, so he began working on a master's in psychology, emphasizing getting his counseling certificate. Cops didn't like to talk about how they felt, but experience showed that they would open up to other officers.

"Maybe, or maybe this is beyond Mark," replied Bonnie.

"Bonnie, it's not just Mark. I have talked with one of his instructors, who is still working in the field. So it's kind of a twofer: I get some counseling, and Mark gets some practical experience. You should see some of the papers Mark has written about me. But, of course, the only person who gets to read them is that instructor."

Bonnie hadn't known about the other counselor. Although she was pleased that JW had been talking with Mark, she was relieved that he was spending some time with someone with real field experience. She didn't know how she felt about JW being a lab rat.

"Hey, Honey, I've been doing some reading on Prescott. They have some great golf courses there."

They had both been doing a lot of research on Prescott. So much so that they were starting to pack to go for a weekend visit. Bonnie needed to see the place, to see what JW had and get a feel for it. JW had made a courtesy call to let Chief Booth know they would be in the area. Bonnie had found a couple who worked as real estate agents. She had read about them online and was impressed by their ethics and commitment. Of course, they weren't expecting to buy anything. Still, it would be helpful to establish a relationship and let them know their needs.

The drive to Prescott this time seemed to drag on forever. On the last trip, he was excited about the work to come. And the police escort allowing them to speed hadn't hurt. This time, he had adopted Ben's role of tour guide, pointing out sites of interest as they passed. JW decided to drive the Tahoe and bring the dogs along on the trip. He had two reasons: he wanted to see their reactions to the new place and in case of a callout. The dogs loved to ride, and, as usual, they were sound asleep in the back.

Bonnie asked JW to stop on an overlook on the climb up to Yarnell. She got out and was overwhelmed at the beauty of the desert valley. JW gave the dogs a break on the leash. He didn't want them running off after a rabbit.

Bonnie said, "It makes you feel insignificant when you see how small we are in the grand scheme. I think we lose that feeling living in the big city."

When they got to town, they checked into their motel. Instead of staying in one of the large chains, they chose a small place on the city's south side with cabins instead of rooms. The first requirement was that management was OK with the dogs. After checking in, Bonnie reached out to the real estate agents. They agreed to come and meet them at the hotel.

Jim and Kelly McIntyre were younger than JW and Bonnie. They had transplanted here over ten years ago from the east coast and loved to ride their mountain bikes on all the trails in the area.

Jim said, "If you love the outdoors, this is a great place. I can ride the same trail two days in a row and always see something new."

JW and Bonnie told them what they were doing with Big Dogs and explained their requirements.

Bonnie said, "We need land and privacy. We don't want neighbors on top of us complaining about all the dogs barking."

JW added, "We don't need a huge place, but enough room that we can do some basic training. We believe we will do most of the training in the surrounding area. Also, we want to have enough space to build a few homes for some of the staff living there, plus some guest houses for when others come in for training or to visit."

Bonnie chimed in, "We would like some trees so we can have a mountain feel, so something more on the south or west side of town than the north. We are OK with just land, or if the main house is right, we can look at it."

Kelly said, "That's quite a list. Let me review the listings and maybe we can look at a property or two while you are here."

They looked at several places, but nothing appealed to Bonnie, who explained, "I'm sorry guys, but if we're going to invest this much in a property, we need to get something we really like."

Jim replied, "We completely understand. It may take a while, but we'll keep our eyes open. Now we have a better idea of what you want, making it easier."

"You were right, JW; I can definitely see us living here. The dogs like it too."

It was the next morning. After spending the day shopping for a new home, they had gone out last night and had dinner on the town. They found a wonderful place north of the town square. Bonnie loved the dark paneling and old west feel of the business.

"That's what it is. It's the feel. This place is so welcoming; it feels like home already."

"You nailed it, Bon'. Even when I was chasing the Truck Stop Killer north of town, this place just felt right."

Bonnie finished packing her things and walked out the door to load the Tahoe. The dogs followed and jumped into the back, and JW went to the office to check out. As she loaded the last bag into the back, her phone rang.

"Hi, Bonnie, where are you guys?" It was Kelly McIntyre, the real estate agent from yesterday.

"Hi Kelly, we're just packing up at the hotel. First, I wanted to thank you again. We had a great time yesterday. You and Jim are great ambassadors for the area. Now, if we can find the perfect place...."

"That's why I'm calling. I was up half the night searching. I found a place where the listing is no longer active. It didn't sell, and the owners decided to let it sit for a while. I called their agent this morning, and it is still available. Would you be interested in having a look?"

JW returned from the office, and Bonnie told him what she had learned. "Kelly, that sounds great… OK, we'll see you there in an hour." Bonnie looked at JW, her eyes glowing with excitement. "I'm not going to tell you what she said. I want you to experience it for yourself."

They waited outside the gate to the property. From here, JW couldn't see anything special about the place, but he decided to keep his feelings to himself. After Jim and Kelly arrived, they followed them in. As they passed over a wooden bridge, JW thought, *I hope this old thing can handle the weight.* They continued west along the dirt road and he spotted an old two-story Victorian-era home overlooking the route. They continued and stopped in a clearing.

Everyone got out and Jim said, "JW and Bonnie, this is a special place. I came up here this morning while Kelly was speaking with the other agent. I can't tell you why it's still available, other than the high price and the quirky nature of the current owners. Right now, you are surrounded by the Prescott National Forest. This is almost fifty acres in the middle of a forest. There are no homes here for at least five miles." He pointed through the trees to the north and continued, "If you look through the trees, you can just make out Upper Goldwater Lake. There is a small enclave of private homes to the south and east. As I said before, they are too far away to be bothered by your operation here."

Jim said, "Take a walk with me." He led them along the road, but it was more of a trail now. It opened to the west onto a large field. "JW, you mentioned training fields. How about this?"

JW had tuned into another zone. He could hear Jim talking and he was aware of the others.

"Bonnie, would you please go get the dogs and let them out?"

He then walked out into the field and waited. Ares and Addy came running past him, full speed and fighting over a tennis ball that Addy had in her mouth. She ran to JW and dropped it at his feet. JW reached down and picked it up, then threw it, and it seemed to sail forever. The dogs raced away in hot pursuit. JW stood, but he wasn't watching any longer. His eyes moved across the terrain, but he saw things others couldn't. He looked to his right and saw a large home overlooking the valley. To his left was a kennel with a house beside it. Beyond that, another home. He thought back to the way in and saw another home.

Bonnie asked, "What's up with that old house we saw on the way in?"

Jim replied, "Remember when I said the current owners are a bit quirky? Well, they are the descendants of the original owners. This property was a land grant from the territorial governor for services to Arizona. I haven't been able to find out what that was, but I bet you could find a local historian who could tell you. Anyway, the place has been in that family for over one hundred fifty years."

"What happened? Why did it fall to such disrepair?" asked Bonnie.

"I'm not entirely sure. Some of it was due to the capital moving from Prescott to Phoenix in 1889. When the political power shifted to the south, the family spent less time here. Over time, it just became abandoned.

"Now, here is the weird thing. The current owners have placed a caveat on the sale of the property. The home we saw must not be demolished; it must be restored to its original glory. There is no requirement to live there, just that it be maintained."

"Perfect." JW was off to the side, still looking at things that weren't there, "It's perfect." He was thinking of the dream he had in Las Vegas. Of the picture on the table. It was the same home.

Bonnie looked at him with concern and said, "Earth to JW, come in JW."

JW had a serene look on his face. He continued to scan the area. "What are you seeing that we aren't," asked Bonnie.

"Dreams. I need some paper." JW sat in the car, sketching, erasing, and then redrawing. He was in the zone and Bonnie knew not to bother him. The whole thing, Big Dogs and everything that came with it, had been a dream. As much as she wanted to control things, she knew she needed to let JW do his thing.

Bonnie stood off to the side talking with Jim and Kelly about the potential purchase. JW was in the Tahoe, sketching. Then, finally, he came out and handed her the notepad. She looked at it and saw a rough drawing of the surrounding terrain, with ten structures and training fields drawn in. She looked at JW and then back at the pad, "I often wonder what goes on in your head."

"Me too," he replied.

She looked at the pad again and said, "I need to call Maddox Christensen."

17

Six weeks later, they were back in Prescott. This time they were the proud owners of almost fifty acres of land. Maddox Christensen had introduced them to his real estate attorney, who, along with the McIntyres, had negotiated a good deal for them. Maddox had offered to handle the financing and then simply paid cash for the property. He explained it was quicker and simpler this way. He would be the bank of Christensen and they could make payments to him directly. When Bonnie asked how much the payments would be, Maddox just smiled.

He also introduced them to Storm Laurits, the construction coordinator on some of Christensen's projects. Maddox only asked in return to have his own place on the property. It turned out that he didn't have much family, none of whom were close. The relationship between Maddox and the Norths had become much closer over the past few weeks. He now considered JW and Bonnie his family. JW only asked for one thing—he wanted to ensure they used local contractors and workers whenever possible.

Christensen had set up a large tent with food and chairs. He was wining and dining the local leadership, plus he brought in Dean Chester, the lead local contractor for the job. Based on JW's original drawing, the site plan was still with the architects working on the final drawings. Storm had mentioned that the main issue on every project he had ever been involved with was waiting on inspections. To combat this, Maddox had arranged for the building department in Prescott to hire back a retired inspector for the duration of the construction. Most days, he would sit in a trailer office, waiting to be called. The City was OK with it, as he had been one of their best employees and it would not take away from their regular inspection work.

The tent area was set up with large poster boards showing the layout of the property and the basic design of some of the structures. Landscaping was used to blend the different elements of the project while having the most negligible impact on the surrounding area. From the outside, it would be difficult to tell there was anything there at all.

Maddox pulled JW and Bonnie off to the side and said, "JW, get your dogs and mingle. You're really who they are here to meet. You guys are the celebrities. They may be curious about what we will do here or who I am, but they want to meet the dogs. Our job today is to sell them on having you as a community member and how it benefits them and will not upset their apple cart."

JW replied, "I thought that's why we wanted to be out of town, so we wouldn't have to deal with all this."

At his core, JW hated politics and didn't much care for politicians. He thought there were probably some good politicians; he'd even met one or two. He just didn't understand why people became politicians for the wrong reasons. It was like someone wanting to be a cop because they liked the power. Those people might get in the door but didn't stick around very long. Not so for politicians; once they got the job, it was impossible to get rid of them.

Maddox laughed, "There's always politics, JW, and all politics are ultimately local. The things you do with Big Dogs will eventually come back here, which concerns them. And, of course, what is in it for them. There's always that. Now, shifting gears, let's get this show on the road."

Christensen walked to the front of the tent and introduced himself. "Good afternoon, I'm Maddox Christensen and I am here today to introduce you to our project, 'Big Dog Ranch.'"

JW had to admit that Maddox was in his element. The presentation lasted thirty minutes and told their guests all they needed to know about what Big Dogs intended to do. Maddox had explained to JW that, since they were on private property, and if they stayed within the local codes, there wasn't much they could do to stop them. However, they could get buried in bureaucratic paperwork that could delay them. Therefore, it was simply better to let them think it was their idea and you were merely paying the tab.

After Maddox spoke, JW milled through the crowd and spoke with most of the officials. He already knew the chief of police and sheriff from the Truck Stop Killer incident and both had approached him to talk. As he walked around, a council member walked up to him and said, "Mr. North, I'm Councilman Curtis Merryman. I have to admit I have some reservations about all this."

"Why is that, sir?"

"Won't your being here attract other serial killers to the area and endanger our citizens?"

JW tried to maintain a straight face. He had been warned about this person and told that he was not a strong supporter of law enforcement.

"That is an interesting question, councilman, and I would say that such a thing is highly unlikely. My conversations with profilers and other experts indicate that serial killers do not want to confront law enforcement and it is improbable they would try to come after us. They want to keep doing what they do, not risk being caught. That stuff makes for great movie plots but doesn't happen in the real world."

JW thought to himself, *Of course, those same people had told him that serial killers didn't want to fight with the police, and so far, he had been shot and stabbed.*

"Oh," he replied and moved away to talk to someone else.

Christensen approached, and JW said, "Remind me why we invited him again."

"There is nothing we can say or do to change his mind, JW. Don't think the others here are not aware of him. A small percentage of the population always views the police as a necessary evil. They want to put you away in a glass case with a hammer and a sign that reads, 'In case of crime—break glass.'"

Maddox pulled Storm Laurits and Dean Chester aside as the party started to wind down and asked, "Dean, when will we have approved drawings and plans?"

Dean had expected these types of questions and replied, "Well, Mr. Christensen, I would say two more weeks before we have all the plans drawn up. Because we have so many structures here, we are submitting them piecemeal; that way, we can get approval to start on one structure while we wait on others. Final approval should be two to four weeks after that."

Maddox asked, "How long do you anticipate for the build?"

"I would say nine months for everything. Of course, the indoor range will be more of a challenge with all the regulations, so it may take a little longer."

"OK. Well, the range isn't on my immediate necessity list, and I understand all the requirements may present some issues. But I think six months might be more realistic. If you can get it done in six months, there will be a ten percent bonus. That bonus would be for the complete project, not just your salary. I've been told that you are the best locally, so I'm willing to add an additional percent per week that you can get that under six months." Maddox changed subjects, "Have you found someone to do the Victorian restoration?"

"I have, sir. He lives here in Arizona and is an expert on this type of work."

"Good, I'm not sure yet; I need to speak with JW, but I believe someone will be living there, so we need to make sure everything is up to date."

"I'll let him know, sir."

Maddox walked off, and Chester turned to Laurits and said, "Mr. Christensen certainly knows how to get your attention."

"He's a good man and a great guy to work for. If you do a good job here, he will remember and take care of you. But, as you can see, he is not a patient man. That being said, you and I have a lot at stake here. We need to work together to get this thing done and get it done right. If construction is delayed because we can't get the right air conditioning condenser, then you let me know. If necessary, I will find out who makes it and have the damn thing flown here. We can do this and I believe we will be done in under six months."

"OK, Mr. Laurits. The only other potential complication could be the weather. We are above six thousand feet here; we could get snow."

"Call me 'Storm.' You and I are gonna be best friends for the next six months. We need to anticipate all the things that could go wrong. If we have to, we'll front order everything and store it all onsite in containers. The only day off is Sunday. If we have a sub holding up one phase of work, we pay overtime. If they give us too much grief, we find someone else. I have a team that will be with me here, living in trailers the whole time. You and I will work with them over the next few weeks and lay out a flow chart for every aspect of this project. This will be the smoothest construction project you've ever done."

Chester said, "Storm, it sure seems like Mr. Christensen is spending a lot of money on this."

"I have learned not to question his motivations. He's astute and has a reason for everything he does; money is not an issue. He has taken a liking to the Big Dogs team and wants to do everything he can to help them. You've seen the news; these guys are magic with how they find killers. You spend some time talking with Mr. North and you'll see how he feels. It's like a crusade for him. The only question left is, are you ready to join in?"

"I'm in. Where's my trailer gonna be parked?"

Two months later, JW and Bonnie were back. Bonnie wanted to meet with a decorator to whom Dean Chester had introduced her. She wanted to go over furniture, floor coverings, paint colors, everything. JW had seen the architectural renderings and floor plans and was impressed. He wasn't sure of the style; it looked like log cabin meets mountain chalet, but it somehow worked on paper. JW had been told by Bonnie to keep away from the final design elements. It would be a surprise, whether he liked it or not.

They were about to go out to dinner when there was a knock at the motel room door. The dogs ran to the door and stared at it as if there was a huge pile of doggy treats on the other side. JW opened the door and found Chief of Police Booth and Sheriff Gregory standing there with her cowboy hat in hand.

"Hi Chief, Sheriff. What brings you two here?"

Sheriff Gregory spoke first, "Good evening, JW, Mrs. North. I heard you were in town. We need a favor. I could really use your help."

"Well, OK. Come on in and we can talk," said Bonnie.

"I don't have much time to waste; it's gonna be cold tonight."

"Alright, what can I do?" replied JW.

"I have a lost child in the national forest. She's eight years old and was out hiking with her family. We've been looking for hours already, but nothing so far. We called in the local search and rescue, but the search dog we would normally use is out of town. I'm worried, people get lost in the forest all the time, but this is just a kid."

Chief Booth added, "The thing is, she is the granddaughter of Councilman Merryman. I know this isn't what you'd normally run a trail on, but we could sure use your help."

JW said, "OK, please tell me we're doing this because a little girl is lost in the woods, not because of the councilman."

"There's a little girl lost in the woods, and I'm afraid she won't last the night."

JW turned to Bonnie, "Well, I guess it's about time you got to see how this works for real."

JW followed the chief and drove to a command post in the Prescott National Forest. It was nearly dark and they hurried to get Addy ready. She had been training since she had recovered from her injuries but had not run an actual trail since Las Vegas. Speaking to Bonnie, he said, "I'm gonna run Addy because this trail could be a better match with her skill set. She's better at the neighborhood trails and I think a girl lost in the woods might work the same. I don't know; she may cross back over her trail and walk in circles. Besides, Addy needs the work."

Normally, JW would spend some time explaining the trailing process to whomever he was working with, but he had worked with this group before and didn't feel it was necessary. "I'll need someone to work with me, someone who is familiar with the forest and can stay up with us."

"That would be me." JW turned and saw Deputy Hockler standing there.

JW smiled. "Why, Deputy Hockler, it is a pleasure to see you again. You ready to go to work?"

"Yes, sir."

"Don't call me 'sir,' call me 'JW.'" Addressing the group, "Where was the last place anyone saw the little girl?"

A woman in her thirties stepped forward. "Her name is Maddie, Maddie Merryman. I'm her mom. It was over here; follow me and I'll show you." Recalling the familiar last name, JW looked up and saw the councilman standing in the background.

JW followed her through the woods for about fifty yards. Finally, they stopped in a small clearing.

"We stopped here for lunch. She saw a rabbit and was so excited. I wasn't paying attention; she was gone when I turned around. Please find her."

JW could see tears forming in the corners of her eyes. She was doing her best to keep it together.

Hockler handed him a small jacket. "This is hers. I thought you would need something to scent the dog on."

JW took it and looked at it, a small red jacket.

"I wish she had it. It's getting cold."

JW clipped the trailing lead onto Addy. She looked at him, excited, happy. She loved to trail. He let her sniff the jacket and said, "Geo-say."

Addy worked the trail for a few moments, turning in tight circles, which grew bigger. JW watched and said to Hockler, "She's casting, looking for where she walked away. She's doing the circles because Maddie was here for a while before she left. Her scent has collected here and Addy needs to work through all that."

Hockler nodded and Addy began to pull into the brush. JW asked, "Snakes?"

"I doubt it. It's been getting cold at night and they aren't likely to be out much, if at all."

"Good." JW had researched the area and knew it was home to several types of rattlesnakes. He knew he would need to take the dogs in for a rattlesnake vaccine shot. "I hate snakes."

"Who doesn't?"

The trail went for a while. JW was grateful he had packed a high-powered headlamp in the Tahoe. Without it, he would've tripped over every branch in the forest. After a while, Hockler said, "I can see why the search and rescue teams haven't found her; she went back the way they came in."

JW gave him a questioning look, and the deputy continued, "The trail is off to our left about a hundred yards. She is paralleling the route they took from the trailhead, which is about two miles that way," he said, pointing down the hill.

"OK, it feels like Addy is strong on the trail. I want you to call her name out every minute or so. I need to stay focused on what the dog is doing."

"Maddie, Maddie, call out to me."

It didn't take long before they heard a reply. "I'm here. Over here."

Addy's ears perked up and she turned to JW with excitement in her eyes. They followed her as she worked down the hill. Behind a large bush, they found Maddie sitting on a rock. She had been crying; her face was streaked with tears. Addy went to her and began licking her face.

"I want my mommy."

Hockler said, "Hi Maddie, your mommy sent us to find you. We're gonna take you to her right now. Here, do you want your jacket?"

He got on his radio and advised the command post that Maddie had been found.

"JW, we're closer to the trailhead than the CP. Let's cut back to the trail and walk down there. They can meet us."

"It's your forest, Hockler. You lead and we'll follow."

They cut brush back to a different trail that eventually led them down the mountain and back to the trailhead. It wasn't hard to find; flashing red and blue lights were everywhere. Bonnie arrived in the Tahoe; she had followed the group down from the command post.

As he went to put Addy away after a good neck scratch, he heard a voice, "Mr. North, I'm with the local newspaper. Can we get a picture of you, the dog, and the little girl?"

JW agreed, but only if the little girl and her parents approved and the photographer included Hockler.

"Without him, we'd still be up on the mountain."

Maddie Merryman was excited to have her picture taken and eagerly jumped into the group. The next day, the photograph was on the newspaper's front page with a long article welcoming them to Prescott.

JW went to leave, but this time was stopped by Councilman Merryman.

"Mr. North, my attitude hasn't changed about you, but I want to thank you for finding my granddaughter."

JW turned to face the councilman and saw his extended hand. JW shook it and looked hard into the man's eyes.

"I'm curious, councilman. What is it about me that you don't like?"

"I think the biggest thing is a feeling I get. First, you come in and push your way into town, trying to take over. I don't like your friend Christensen. This is a small town and we like to do things our way."

"OK. Is that our way or your way?"

He paused, pushed back by JW's comment.

"Second, I think your presence will bring more problems than positives."

"Not much I can say about your feelings, so I won't." He looked him hard in the eyes and said, "If you ever need anything—don't call."

Then he got in the Tahoe and drove away.

Bonnie said, "I don't think he likes you."

"Yeah, I've been around politicians like him before. He loves the power and tries to bully his way through when he can't get what he wants. The good news is most of the people around here don't pay him much mind. He's the guy the paper comes to look for when everyone else thinks an idea is perfect and they need a counterargument quote. You know what pisses him off the most about me?"

"That he knows he can't own you," said Bonnie.

"You got it."

"Is he gonna be a problem?"

JW snorted, "Him? No, I imagine he'd like to be, but no. Honey, we've rescued two girls from this town in the past few months. People like us."

JW would find he was only half right.

18

The Norths woke up the following morning in their motel room. Because JW and Addy had gotten a bit of a workout the previous evening, they decided to take it easy. They were returning to Long Beach tomorrow, so a day off sounded good. Rather than lie around the hotel room, they decided to wander around downtown. Their interior designer, Sandra Kyra, was going to meet them. Sandra was petite and slim, in her late thirties. Like many of the young people in the Prescott area, she had moved on after school and tried to make it in the big city. That didn't work out and soon she was back in Prescott. However, she loved the area and seemed to know everyone here.

The Prescott area was populated with numerous artists and numerous art galleries around the square. There was a bronzesmith foundry nearby where local artists could make their dreams a reality. As they went from shop to shop, JW let his mind wander. A few people recognized him from his photo in the newspaper and stopped him to talk. He was OK with it; it let Bonnie and Sandra take their time shopping. Art is personal, and Bonnie would call him over from time to time to get his opinion on different pieces. They went into a shop named Mountain Spirit Gallery and looked around. JW immediately liked the place; it was filled with art honoring the old west. There was also a lot of Native American art. The owner came over and introduced himself as William

Foxworth. He knew who JW was and they chatted about what JW did.

Bonnie called to JW and said, "Look at this one."

He came to her side and looked at a beautiful bronze of a cowboy on a horse with a dog out in front. He loved the detail of the art and how the moment was captured. Next, he looked at the plate mounted on the base, which read, "Lookin' for Sign."

"Huh. I like this piece. The title is appropriate, but not for the reasons the artist thinks." He turned to Foxworth and asked, "Who is the artist? I see a few pieces here that have a similar look to them," pointing to a pair of bronzes on display.

"You have a good eye, Mr. North. Bill Nebeker is a local American West bronze artist. He's extremely talented and has done several pieces around Prescott and at the Phippen Museum."

JW nodded. "Yes, he is. He catches the soul of the moment," and they moved on. Bonnie watched him and then turned to say something to Sandra.

The Shadow lay in the bed in his small room. It was the middle of the night and he was frustrated and angry. Frustrated with his current state and mad that he had wasted so much time. He had selected his next victim, having spotted her in town. She was an office worker named Adora Trinidad. His growing tension had pushed him to speed up his usual process. He knew all his previous victims had been white, but now he wanted to change that. This victim would be perfect for his needs.

He had spent weeks learning about her and where she lived. She used public transportation to get to and from work. It made it harder for him to follow her, which fed the monster and made him hungrier. Finally, he located her home, a nice condominium on the north side of town, and focused in on her.

Finally, he decided this was the night. He had deliveries in that area and could arrange them to go to her place last. He parked a short distance away on a road near the apartment complex and worked his way through some woods to approach from the rear. He was so worked up; he was shaking with anticipation. All the ground-floor apartments had a small, fenced area in the back. He approached her gate and pulled the wire to open the latch. He drew the gate toward him and peered inside. The small yard was dark, but he could make out a couple of chairs and a table. There was just enough light from the moon to allow him to see. Then he caught a glint of movement, and a large dog jumped at him, barking and snapping.

The dog raised such a ruckus that lights began coming on and curtains were pulled back. The Shadow could see people looking out. It was time to go. As he ran back through the woods, he ranted in his mind. *Goddamned woman, what is she doing with a dog?* He hated dogs and had since he was much younger.

He got in his truck and pulled out of the parking area and back onto the road. He quickly made it to one of the many state routes through the area and started toward his home. As he recovered from the run through the forest, his back window was lit with red and blue lights. Realizing the police were behind him, he pulled to the side of the road. He took his driver's license and vehicle registration out and prepared himself, trying to remain calm.

The officer used his radio to run the license plate before he exited his patrol vehicle. As he approached the pickup to talk to the driver, he used his flashlight to check the back. He saw a tarp and some strapping, commonly used to secure boxes together.

As he walked to the driver's side, he again used the flashlight to illuminate the inside of the cab. He could only see one person inside, with a clipboard and backpack. He noted the truck had a sign on the door identifying it as belonging to Collins Auto Parts Delivery.

"What are you doing out so late, sir?"

The Shadow was nervous, but he had prepared for various questions should he ever be stopped.

"I work for Collins. They do overnight parts delivery and I'm the lucky guy who gets to do it. But at least it's a job."

The officer said, "I don't see any parts in the truck, sir."

"Yeah, I'm all done, on my way home. I can show you my manifest if you'd like."

"Please." The officer scanned the forms and then handed them back. "Thank you for your cooperation, sir."

"Officer, can I ask why you stopped me? Did I do something wrong?"

"No. Wrong place, wrong time. We got a call of a prowler in a nearby area. Not much traffic out here this time of night, so I thought I'd stop you and chat. Sorry to bother you."

"No problem, officer. I hope you catch him."

As the Shadow drove back to his room, the officer made a notation on the contact into the department's computer system. His black and white had one of the new mag stripe readers, allowing the officer to quickly take all of a person's personal data. The Shadow had no idea what had just happened and the ultimate ramifications.

Back at his apartment, and now in his bedroom, the Shadow stared at the ceiling. There wasn't much to the place, so the overhead provided as good a perspective as any. The tension was so high that he was shaking. Because of that dog, everything was ruined. He needed that girl, and her damned dog had spoiled all his plans. She was his; she belonged to him. *I hate fucking dogs!* He looked at the scar on his hand and remembered his neighbor's dog from when he was young. He had tried to pet the dog and it bit him. The scar was still there, and the dog, now long gone, was laughing at him from beyond.

The mutt mocked his fear. "Oh, big tough serial killer wannabe, can't even take care of a dog."

After he'd been bitten, he was working his newspaper route and had saved some money. He decided he would go to the pound and get a dog. He thought about what kind he would choose and what he would do with it. Part of him still wanted a pet, but he knew his mother would never allow that. But another part of him wanted to release some of the building anger inside of him on that dog.

When the day came for him to pick a dog, he walked between the rows of cages and listened to the barking. He hated the noise they made. All of them barking, thinking they were coming home with him, to their forever homes, only to discover they were going to hell. He saw a nice-looking German Shepherd and walked toward the cage. The dog wagged its tail initially, then sensed something in him and began barking and snapping at him. It was up on its hind legs, front paws on the kennel. The gate shook with the dog's anger and he took a step back, worried the door would come off. The dog knew who he was. It knew who he was and why he was there and it wasn't going to go quietly. He looked at the dog and knew it would kill him if it got out of the cage. He ran from the kennel and never looked back. He'd spent the rest of his life avoiding dogs.

JW and Bonnie were having breakfast when JW's phone rang. He looked at the screen and saw that it was Ben. *I wonder what's going on.* They'd been in Prescott for almost a week as Bonnie continued working on their new place's design elements. Sandra spent a lot of time with them, working to understand their likes and dislikes. She had reached the opinion that neither JW nor Bonnie really had a style. She was trying to sell Bonnie on a new concept, western eclectic. JW wasn't sure what that meant and he knew he probably didn't want to know. But, on the other hand, he knew Bonnie was having fun and that was all that mattered.

Bonnie had made an interesting decision regarding their new home. Now that her "secret" about having family money was out, she decided to use some of it. Her desire was comfort but not too ostentatious. This gave Sandra something else to struggle with: how to spend money without it looking like it. JW often wondered if she wished she had been on vacation when the Norths first called.

JW answered the call with, "Ben Kellum's answering service; how may I direct your call?" JW could see Ben's face, wondering what was going on. Inside, JW roared with laughter.

"JW, what the hell is that about?"

"Nothing Ben. Just having some fun at your expense."

"Thanks." Switching gears, Ben said, "I got a call from Long Beach Homicide. They had a murder and wanted us to run a trail to see if we could get anything. I know you're in Arizona, but I hate to say no to these guys."

"I understand. We need to maintain relations at the local level, and without Chief Estrada's help early on, we would not be where we are now. I ran a trail on a missing juvenile not too long ago. I get it. Let me work something out with Bonnie and I will get on the road ASAP. I'll call you when I'm on the way."

"Thanks, I appreciate it."

"Hey, this is what we do now. But we have got to get your dog certified soon. So, unfortunately, as the FBI work builds, I may be unable to do this."

"I know. Allen and I have been working while you're in Prescott. It's not like we have been sitting on our hands," replied Ben, referring to Allen Whelan, their trailing trainer.

JW made the arrangements with Bonnie and got on the road. She was going to be with Sandra, who was happy to drive her back to the motel. Since they still had their home in Long Beach, JW had a place to stay when he returned there to work. They had almost entirely moved to Prescott, even though it would still be several weeks before they could finally move in. There wouldn't be much to move in as everything at Big Dog Ranch was brand new.

He returned to their motel, grabbed his go bag and both dogs, and began driving to Long Beach. Although the first part of the trip was the slowest, JW enjoyed it the most. He liked traveling through the small towns of Arizona and wondered what everyone would do that day. The dogs did what they did best in the car, sleep.

JW waited until he was past the steep road outside of Yarnell before he made the call. This part was treacherous enough, with the road close to a long drop-off as they descended from 4,300 feet to the desert floor. The view was spectacular, although JW rarely saw it as he was always driving. Ben told him where he would meet him in the Belmont Heights neighborhood of Long Beach.

"Hey, Ben, you mentioned Allen earlier. How are things with him?"

JW had attended the funeral for Allen's wife almost two years ago. He seemed to weather the loss well, but Ben knew him much better.

"He's OK. I mean, imagine if you lost Bonnie."

The thought made JW feel like he had been kicked in the gut. He hadn't thought of Allen's loss that way, and he was a bit ashamed. Loss was personal, and everyone dealt with it in their own way, but if he lost Bonnie, he would be adrift in an endless ocean of self-pity.

"I hadn't thought of it in those terms."

"I hear you. I'm glad Allen has the program to keep him grounded. He loves the dogs and is the best trainer—dog or handler—I've ever met. But I wonder if he didn't have this, we might have lost him too."

"You're probably right. We'll need to train more dogs in the future, and we could use someone to oversee the training programs. We can't train others properly with both of us fully operational. Do you think Allen would be interested in relocating to Prescott and handling that?"

"I don't know. Allen's wife is gone and his kids are all grown and scattered over several states. He might be interested. If you are going to be in town for a couple days, I can set up a training day for all of us and you can work your pitch in."

After the call to Ben, JW decided to call Dr. Gaurdia at the FBI. He hadn't talked to her in a few weeks and decided the drive to California was an excellent time to catch up.

"Hello, JW. How are you and Bonnie? How is everything going with your new headquarters? Have you healed properly from your injury?"

"Easy Doc, you're starting to sound like a real person. Now, if we can work all those questions into a conversation, we can probably fool most people."

"As you know, I have been working on my interpersonal relations. I just wanted to get all those out there, so I showed the proper level of empathy and caring before we started talking about work."

"There's the Lauralynn I know and love. In answer to your earlier questions, we are both doing well. The dogs are also well."

"That's good. You know I worry about Ares and Addy. You do have a propensity to be around a lot of violence."

JW decided to ignore the last jab. "Big Dog Ranch is coming along well. When it's all done, we will have an open house. We will send you an invitation. Bring SA LeClair with you. He needs to get out more, spend more time opening doors and less time kicking them."

She laughed and said, "We will definitely be there. Oh, the director asked about you the other day. He wanted to know how his favorite gunslinger was doing."

"Tell him I've been practicing and staying sharp. So, anything going on?"

"You mean with killers?"

"Yep."

"Things have been a bit slow, which is a good thing. You don't realize it, but hundreds of hours of work go into an investigation before you can come in and have your fifteen minutes of fun and fame. We are evaluating several clusters that Frankenstein has identified as possibles. We're working with local law enforcement to collect more data to make a better determination. For example, there is a cluster in Kentucky that is rather odd. Several murders have some similar things, but others are very different."

"Perhaps two killers in one locale? It has happened before. For example, the Green River Killer and Ted Bundy in the Seattle-Tacoma area."

"You've been doing your reading."

"Well, you did send me about fifty books on serial killers and profiling. I have plenty of time to read here in Arizona while Bonnie finishes her interior design work."

"Only fifty? I will have to see what else I can send. Bonnie tells me you are going to have quite the library. Anyway, knowledge is always a good thing. But I don't think you will ever be a profiler."

"I hate to ask, but why's that?"

"Well, you have this disturbing habit of shooting the killers before you get a chance to talk to them."

"Easy, Lauralynn. You're drifting back into the aardvark zone."

"You know I hate that word JW. Why couldn't you pick a different code word?"

"Exactly, Doctor. Exactly."

19

JW met Ben and Long Beach homicide detectives Brennan and Jones at the Second Street address. JW got out of his Tahoe and stretched; it had been a long drive. Then, as he walked up to the group, he asked, "Are you two the only homicide detectives in Long Beach? You're the only ones I ever seem to see."

Brennan laughed and said, "You know how cops are. They don't like new things. But Jones and I, being more progressive, are open to this new and innovative investigative tool."

JW started coughing and said, "Yeah, right—progressive. I sense a steaming pile of bovine feces. But to be honest, Ben and I appreciate how you two have been receptive to using us."

Brennan replied, "After my partner's initial reservations were proved wrong, you guys helped us out. Personally, anything that puts the bad guy in jail is a plus."

"So, what do we have here?" JW asked.

"Homicide, single female, forty-two years old." Brennan handed him a few crime scene photos and continued, "She was strangled, been dead for several days before a friend tried to call her. She called us after she found out the victim had not been to work. No sign of forced entry. The back door was locked and the front unlocked when the first patrol unit arrived on the check the well-being dispatch."

Ben said, "I collected a scent article from the victim before the coroner took her away."

JW asked Ben, "What do you think, Ares or Addy?"

"I don't know. Not much to go on, but since we are starting in the house, I would say Addy."

"I agree. Can you get Adeliene ready while I take a quick look inside?"

JW was escorted inside the house by Brennan.

"We found her here in the living room. As you can see, not much sign of a struggle."

JW nodded and looked around. *Nice home, very clean and organized.* JW wasn't sure if this was a home or a museum. Everything was spotless and carefully placed. He looked at the fireplace mantle and said, "Lots of pictures of guys here. Family?"

"Her girlfriend said she didn't have much family. Those are apparently different guys she has dated."

"OK, I ask because one appears to be missing. You see how these are all neatly spaced on this side, but they aren't quite as even on this side? I look around and see how everything is neat and clean to the point of OCD and I wonder."

Brennan said, "Good eye, JW. I could turn you into a good homicide detective if you weren't retired. I'll call the lab back out and ask them to dust these pictures for prints."

JW nodded and, when he heard Ben at the door, said, "Bring her in, Ben. Let's get this started."

Ben brought Adeliene into the house and over to JW. The smell of death was still strong inside and she rolled her ears back in response to the odor.

"Sorry, Addy, I know you don't like smelling dead people. We'll get this trail started, so we can get outside." Addy wagged her tail in response.

Detective Jones asked, "Hey, JW, since Kellum took the scent sample from the victim, how does the dog know to look for the suspect or the victim."

"Because our victim was strangled, we believe there will be scent transfer from the suspect to the victim. Therefore, starting the dog with everyone who had contact with the victim is best. Then, the dog picks up on all the scents and chooses the one that isn't there."

Jones nodded his understanding, and the trail started with Addy working in circles in the living room. She stayed away from where the body had been. Finally, Addy worked her way to the door and outside. Once she was on the sidewalk, she did the same thing. Casting, trying to gain some sense of direction from the scent. Eventually, she worked west and then south toward the beach. Ben had to stop traffic as they crossed Ocean Boulevard and entered Bluff Park. The team worked east and stopped at a bench near a bronze statue of a sailor looking out to the harbor. Addy lingered there momentarily and began working back north, crossing Ocean again.

As they continued north, Addy turned onto First Street this time instead of going up to the victim's home on Second. She did more casting on First as if she was having a hard time localizing the trail. Finally, she returned to the victim's home but went past it this time. Addy looked confused at this point, so JW decided to try Ares. He went the same route, but instead of stopping on Second, he kept going around the block.

Finally, JW looked at Ben and said, "Had enough fun?"

"Yep."

"OK, let's put Ares up, and we can chat."

JW gathered Ben and the two detectives on the porch. "Sure would be nice to have a cup of coffee," JW said half-jokingly. "OK, here is my take, and Ben, you chime in if you disagree or think otherwise. First, I think our suspect was inside the victim's house before he killed her. He probably knows her, maybe even dated her. That's why Addy spent so much time inside. His scent was all over. Once outside, she had the same problem as did Ares. I believe the suspect has been here on several occasions and possibly lives in the neighborhood.

"The trail took us to that bench in Bluff Park. Addy lingered there, and I think he did too. Now, this is complete guesswork on my part, but how about this: the suspect kills his girlfriend, goes to the beach, and thinks about what he did. Even though Addy didn't take us down to the beach, I wouldn't be shocked if he drowned himself and washed up on the beach in a few days. From that bench, the trail came back up to First Street. Now you guys can't know this, but I can tell you Addy wasn't pulling as hard on that stretch. I'm not sure why; maybe the scent was old. On First, she again has trouble following the trail but finally works it out and returns here. With Ares, you have the dog doing laps around the block. It's weird, almost like the suspect was walking around the block trying to decide what to do. That's it. That's all I got, and none of it is based on hard evidence; it's just my thoughts based on the trail and experience working these two dogs."

Brennan said, "Well, it's not much, but there is some stuff we can follow up on. Maybe have patrol do some more interviews on Second and First Streets. Now we can ask some pointed questions. Also, let's go back to the victim's girlfriend and talk to her more. If we get anything, I'll give you guys a call. Thanks for driving all the way here."

Two days later, JW, Ben, and Allen sat on a picnic bench in El Dorado Park. The three dogs were inside their cars, resting after a workout. JW asked, "Allen, how much longer until Zeus is ready to certify?"

"He's ready now, but I want to put another four weeks into him. When we got him, Zeus was almost as good as

Ares. Ben was better prepared than you, and he has learned a lot from working with you. However, I don't want to certify too quickly. It makes us look lazy, and if a smart lawyer ever looked at all three training records, it might be something they could use to attack our credibility."

JW looked at Ben and said, "A month, huh?"

Ben nodded and replied, "Allen has a point. I think Zeus is ready, but I see the reasoning. Another four weeks isn't going to hurt us."

"Agreed," JW said. "Now, Allen, I want to run something by you. Here are the plans for Big Dog Ranch, kennels, training areas, etc. I want to make sure we cover all our training needs. It's easier to change them now before we are finished." JW showed them both the overall plans for the facility. He went into detail describing each building and its function.

Allen asked, "What is this building here? You didn't mention it." He was pointing at the old Victorian house on the property.

"Oh, that's an old Victorian house. Part of the deal when we purchased the land was that we had to restore it. I thought we could use the ground floor as a training room for when we have classes." JW looked at Allen, waiting for the question.

"OK, I'll bite. What's the second floor for?"

"I thought you could stay there, that is, if you want to be our director of training."

"Well, it's about damn time. I was wondering if you were ever gonna figure out that I might be of assistance to you."

"Allen, I have thought about it a lot. Ben and I will be busy working for the FBI, and we need someone with your rare qualifications to keep training dogs. Three dogs are not enough. Besides, we can't break up the team now."

"Quit sucking up, JW. I accept your offer; at least I will once we negotiate my generous salary."

"Salary? I thought that great title would be enough."

"Uh, no."

JW decided he would stay in town for another couple of days. Staying at the old house wasn't too bad; he had lived there for years and it felt comfortable. Bonnie and he had decided to keep the house for now. Long Beach was home to them and it would be hard living out of a hotel for prolonged periods should a case bring him back to town. He knew what that was like now, living in a small cabin while Big Dog Ranch was being finished. Since Bonnie wasn't allowing him to go to the ranch anyway, he might as well spend a few days in Long Beach.

JW reached out to his old golfing buddy, Mark Powers, to see if he could fit in a few days of golf. His regular clubs were in storage in Prescott, but he had a spare set. Mark was happy to hear from him. A round of golf sounded good, and he had a term paper coming up for his counseling class, so maybe he and JW could work in a few minutes of "therapy." Always happy to help out a friend, JW agreed, and Mark told him that he would make the reservations and get back to him with a tee time.

Mark decided to play at the Navy Golf Course in Seal Beach. JW had played there several times over the years. He liked the course as it was challenging but not overly so. JW worked at his game but still sucked at golf. Finally, they made it to a long par five. The group in front of them was waiting for the green to clear so they could make their shots.

Mark muttered, "What a bunch of dumbasses. They can't hit two hundred yards off the tee box, and they have over two-seventy-five to the green, and they're waiting? Layup and stop holding up play."

JW turned to his friend, eyebrow cocked, and said, "Easy, Mark. You sound like you may have some issues there. Maybe I should be counseling you."

"Speaking of counseling, how are you doing? We haven't talked in a while."

"Yeah, I've been tied up in Prescott with the ranch. I'm doing OK."

"JW, that's not a ringing endorsement for your mental health, 'I'm doing OK.' You've shot two guys in less than a year. Does it bother you?"

"I don't know, Mark. Both those guys were trying to kill Ben and me. So I don't have too many issues with it."

"OK, I understand the shootings were justified, but how do you feel about it?"

"Uh oh, we're gonna talk about feelings? Maybe I should call Bonnie."

"JW, you're avoiding the question. How do you feel?"

"To be honest, I don't think about it much. I'm too busy."

"Alright, what about dreams?"

"That's what's weird. I dream about the Truck Stop Killer, but not about the Flynns. I was scared to death during the shootout with the Flynn brothers. But you know that family—they would eventually end up on the wrong end of a bullet. I was just the unlucky one to be there. TSK is different; that guy was about as evil as they come. When I shot him, he was the most prolific serial killer around. So I don't understand why I would dream about him."

"Why do you think?"

"I don't know."

"Neither do I, but since these guys in front of us are so damn slow, how 'bout we talk it through?"

"Sounds good. But I honestly don't have any idea."

"Try this: you said he was as evil as they come. Is your subconscious worried that he might come back? Or is it that you're afraid someone out there is worse?"

JW started to say something, but the group in front finally made their shots and moved on. It was just as well. He didn't really have an answer, but it was something he was going to spend some time thinking about. He did know he was in a hazardous profession, and something worse could always be around the next corner.

JW was on his way back to Arizona when his phone rang. He looked at the number on the infotainment screen but didn't recognize it. He decided to take the call anyway. "JW North."

"JW, Alex Brennan. You sound like you're in a car. Where are you?"

"Driving back to Prescott. What's up? Did you get a break on that homicide we worked on?"

"As a matter of fact, we did. We got lucky and picked up a print on one of those pictures you said didn't look right. It took a while, but we did get a hit on the print. It returned to a male living around the block from the victim. He was apparently dating her. We got a search warrant for his place, but the guy had already killed himself when we went to serve it with SWAT. Looks like he may have done it right after he killed the victim. Anyway, he hung himself. What a mess. He'd been hanging there for several days; his neck was all stretched out. We found the missing picture, which was of him, in the trash. We could never confirm any of that stuff about him being in the park, but it doesn't matter at this point. I wanted to make sure I thanked you, though. No pun intended, JW, but you've got a good nose for this kind of work."

JW arrived at an empty motel cabin in Prescott. He dropped off his bag and called Bonnie, who was at the ranch making final adjustments with Sandra. The main house was basically complete, with only a few people working on last-minute installations of audio-visual equipment and appliances. She told him she was going to be very busy for the next week.

JW knew he needed to start assembling the team for the ranch. He had some ideas, but he needed Bonnie to help with interviews. The one thing he could do now was begin his search for his cover officer. He decided to reach out to local law enforcement to see if they were aware of someone with the qualifications he would need. He called Chief Booth to see if he played golf.

"Hey, JW, good to hear from you. Yes, I have a weekly game with the sheriff. Are you interested in joining us?"

Two days later, he met the chief and sheriff at The Club at Prescott Lakes. Their fourth had backed out at the last minute, so it was just the three of them.

JW asked, "OK, I've never played this course. Any hints?"

Chief Booth replied, "It's not too difficult of a course. Some holes are challenging, but we'll warn you when we get to them. The big thing is to keep the ball in the fairway. Out of bounds here is gone."

JW looked and saw what they meant. There were homes around the course, but most of the fairways were lined with natural local desert plants and trees. If you went out of bounds, you weren't likely to find your ball, let alone have it in any kind of playable lie.

It was a beautiful day as the group approached the tee box on the first hole. While they waited to tee off, JW asked, "How is the COVID virus treating Prescott?"

"We've been pretty lucky here. We've had our share of cases, but not the big numbers they have in the larger cities. We have an older population here, so that's a good thing. It could be much worse," the chief answered.

"California is on a pretty tight lockdown; you can't really do much there," JW continued.

"Our local politicians decided not to be too aggressive on that. As a result, people here have been good about following guidelines, which has helped keep our numbers down. But, of course, there are always those who think they know better," said Chief Booth.

Sheriff Gregory added, "We've had a few arguments between the maskers and the no-maskers in the stores. But, all in all, people have been civil during a highly stressful period."

They snaked through the first few holes of the course until they reached five. As JW stood at the tee box of the fifth hole, he looked out past the golf course to some beautiful rock formations to the north. The hole was a par three, and the tee boxes were elevated.

JW said, "I can't imagine a much more beautiful view than that."

Sheriff Gregory said, "Those are the Granite Dells and Willow Lake next to it. Off to the left is where you started that trail you ran for us. Way off to the north is where it ended."

JW looked off in the distance and said, "When you look at it from up here, it sure looks like a long way."

After finishing five, there was a delay on six. The group in front of them was looking for a lost ball. Thinking this was perfect timing, JW said, "We're almost done building and will be ready to move in soon. I'm looking for a couple guys, retired cops, or maybe ex-military. My partner, Ben, is going to stay in Southern California and I need some people here to work with me, cover officer and such."

The Sheriff looked at JW and smiled. "What about Brian Hockler? He was there for the first trail and went with you on the second when you found the Merryman girl. He seemed pretty excited and just had his twentieth anniversary with us. He might be interested. I'm not looking to get rid of him or anything. He's a good man. But I feel he might be ready to move on and this could be a good fit."

20

Brian Hockler seemed like the best prospect of any the chief or sheriff had suggested. JW thought he would be perfect as his cover officer and had called him the next day. JW now sat in an old west bar on Whiskey Row, waiting for Brian to arrive. The bar was located along the downtown courthouse square. It was a touristy place but still had an old saloon feel that JW loved. A group of four men dressed in 1880s clothing played cards at one table. It was busy and a little noisy, but it would have to do as the ranch was off limits until Bonnie and Sandra were done with the house.

JW waved as Brian walked in to catch his attention. It was unnecessary. Brian spotted JW the moment he entered; he had scanned the room, looking for threats. Some people might think this was paranoid, but cops worked in three stages: Green, Yellow, and Red. Green was for when you were at home, relaxing. Yellow was for when you were in public; a threat was unlikely but could appear. Red was obvious and was reserved for those most dangerous occasions, such as an arrest. You were a lawman 24/7, and experienced officers were always aware of their surroundings. Some never moved out of green and were quietly ushered out of the profession as they were a danger to themselves. Others never left red and died early of a heart attack or drank themselves to death. The best moved up and down the scale as demanded by their surroundings and the situation.

"Brian, thanks for coming. Have a seat," JW said.

He replied, "Hard to turn down lunch and free beer. The sheriff told me you wanted to talk to me." They quickly reviewed the menu and ordered food and beer.

"This is a great place. I love the old west feel. Do you get a lot of tourists here in town?"

"I work in the more rural areas around the county, but I have lived in town most of my life. Whiskey Row has a tourist flavor; it plays off the western history of the area. Of course, it wasn't always like this. The first bars weren't much more than shacks and then wooden structures. There were three different fires, but the one in 1900 burned down four blocks. The story goes that the bar here was carried out into the town square, and everyone drank and watched the fire. Then, there's all the stuff about the Earp brothers and Doc Holiday. They all spent some time here."

"I love history. I'll have to get some books on this place."

"I read a lot," said Brian, "I have a number I can recommend."

JW took on a more serious look. "How much do you know about what we do at Big Dogs?"

"I was curious after we ran that trail up north and you killed that guy. I was impressed by the work your dog did. And that was a nice shot you made too."

"I was shot almost two years ago, and ever since, I cannot seem to avoid trouble."

"If you don't mind me saying, you seem to put yourself directly in the path of danger."

"The idea for this came over ten years ago. We had a bloodhound program in Long Beach. We did a lot of work to see if we could transfer that technology from the hound into a patrol-type dog. That project died off for many reasons, but that is a subject for another day." JW then explained how this new program would work more independently on a contract basis. "After I was shot, I had a lot of time to think as I recovered. I knew I had to take my life in a new direction, but I needed to stay in touch with law enforcement. The old trailing program came to mind, and here we are."

Brian listened intently and then said, "The first trail was very impressive, but it was a whole different world up close watching your other dog, Addy, find that Merryman girl. I had no idea what was happening, but you seemed to be tuned into each other. I know what I did when I went with you to keep you from getting lost, but what does the other guy do?"

"Ben?"

"Yeah."

"What he was doing was different from what you did on the mountain. But it was also a very different environment. The mountain was a no- to low-threat, and the other trail was obviously high. When we deploy, the dog is the team's most important member. Without the dog to help us find what we are looking for, there is no point in being there. My job is easy. I keep the dog on the trail, look for subtle clues of what the dog may be sensing, and try to determine whether the dog is truly on trail, or looking for scent. The second most important guy there is Ben."

"He's your cover officer."

"Exactly! He doesn't need to watch the dog, but that is what happens if you bring a novice into your search team. The cover officer keeps the dog and me safe. He handles many of the administrative details before we run and serves as a back-up to the handler if needed."

"There's a lot more to that than I imagined."

"We do a lot of training. Practice makes perfect and allows you to make what seems complex, simple. We can teach you."

Hockler looked at JW with a question in his eyes. "You can teach me?"

"Here's the deal, Brian. Ben is staying in Southern California and building his own team as part of Big Dogs. There is plenty of work; eventually, we may add even more teams in other parts of the country. The operation here will be our headquarters and training center. I need someone to work with me as my cover officer. I think you would be a good choice for that. I can see your enthusiasm and interest. I have one question: why would you want to leave the Sheriff's Office?"

"First off, I love my job. But there are a lot of reasons why I would be interested in this job. I love dogs. I've had them since I was a kid, and now that I don't, there's a hole in my life. I divorced a couple of years ago and she took my dog as part of the settlement. She only did it because she knew I loved that dog. With my odd hours, I just can't give a dog the attention it needs. That's not fair to the dog. So, being around dogs would be great. I've met your wife, and you seem like good people, and you're doing something that I find noble, for lack of a better word.

"You had the pleasure of meeting Lamar English the other day, the tweaker at the restaurant." JW nodded. "Well, I think I told you he had been in jail for vehicular manslaughter." JW nodded again, sensing that it was best to keep silent for now. "Well, a couple years back, I was working the North County area on the overnight shift and I got dispatched to an accident." JW watched Hockler's eyes as they drifted out of focus, reliving that night, and he went into the dream with him.

Deputy Brian Hockler arrived at the accident scene, but it looked more like an explosion. What remained of a minivan was off to the right. It was torn open like a giant reached down and ripped it apart. There was no longer a vehicle there, just pieces. He radioed dispatch, told them what he'd found, and requested fire rescue and ambulances. He knew it would be too late by the time they arrived, but he had to try.

The van's contents were strewn everywhere, including the family of five that was once inside. He checked the driver, but he was gone. His chest looked like it was crushed against the steering wheel. For some reason, the airbag did not deploy. He moved to the passenger side; the woman, maybe his wife, was halfway through the front window. No seat belt. She wasn't able to move, but he heard her asking about her children. He didn't know; he hadn't seen them yet. He told her to hang on, help was coming, but he knew his words were hollow. She was on her way to meet her husband in the afterlife.

He shined his light into the back and saw a boy; he couldn't tell his age, maybe ten or twelve. His body was pushed forward. The seat had been torn from its anchors, and he was wedged between it and the front bucket seats. His neck was wrenched sideways, broken. His face was twisted into a grimace of pain that lasted only a moment. There was no one else left in the car.

Deputy Hockler walked around looking for any others. He could hear the sirens and knew other deputies were coming to help. It had been a quiet night until now. He found a young girl, her body off the side of the road. He spotted the smear of her blood from where she landed, almost a hundred feet from where she was ejected. She was missing her right leg. Her face was peaceful. He realized he will see all these faces, like so many others, for the rest of his life.

He walked to the other car. A large, one-ton pickup. The front was crushed, but the driver was sitting on the side of the road, dazed. Hockler could smell the alcohol, even from ten feet away. He looked at the man; he knew him. It was Lamar English. Hockler had known him for most of his life. He was always in trouble, an embarrassment to his family. He had been arrested for driving under the influence or being under the influence so many times that Hockler had lost count. And now he had murdered an entire family.

Deputy Hockler's training kicked in. He handcuffed English and read him his rights. There was no point, though; he had no intention of asking him any questions. He was afraid that if he started talking to him, he would strangle him to shut him up. He walked English to his car and put him in the back. Then, all of his self-discipline washed away, as if a summer monsoon just dumped its contents on his head. He leans into the car and asked, "Lamar, do you think anyone would miss you if I killed you and dumped you in the desert?"

Several other deputies arrived at the scene. They were all shocked into silence by the devastation in front of them. They walked amongst the wreckage, thinking of their own families, trying to make sense of what they saw. One stopped, bent over, and examined a car seat over two hundred feet from the accident. He reached in and tried to find a pulse, but this last family member is also gone. He called Hockler over to see, and he walked as if in the dream he is in now, seeing but not believing. The emergency lights bounced off the landscape, providing a surreal atmosphere. He stopped and saw a baby girl in the car seat. The skin on her cheek was worn to the bone from sliding on the unforgiving asphalt. There was little blood as she likely died quickly. Tears streamed down Brian's face and he turned to go back to English. The other deputy stopped him and said, "No, Brian, he isn't worth it."

Hockler shook his head. "No, he isn't, but they are."

The cloud lifted and JW looked at Hockler; there was a single tear on his cheek. He looked away, ashamed, and wiped it away.

"Brian, we all see horrible things on the job—things the public never sees—and that's why they don't understand. If the average person saw what you did, they'd throw up on themselves. Us, we get to go back to work. Maybe they make us go see a counselor, who probably doesn't understand us either. Look, I can't promise you that you won't have to see something worse than that. The people we hunt are the worst of mankind. They are evil and what they do to their victims is horrible. It turns my stomach to think of it. But I believe this is a job that needs to be done. We are part of an incredible team with the FBI. It's a tough job, but who better than us to do it. Now, I don't want your answer right now. Give it some time and give me a call." JW handed Hockler a business card and got up.

They both left, but at the door, they turned and walked in different directions. JW enjoyed walking here. Even with all the bars, it was orderly and people greeted one another as they passed. As he reached his vehicle, his phone rang. JW answered and heard, "When do I start?"

"Meet me tomorrow at nine a.m. at the ranch. I want to show you your new house."

"House? I live in an apartment, JW."

"Not anymore."

21

JW woke the following day at seven a.m.. He was still living in a motel room, but today would be his last day. Bonnie was over at the ranch, making sure everything was just right. For some reason, she was focused on impressing JW with the results of this project. He had been impressed with her focus, planning, and creativity. She and Sandra were a perfect match: Bonnie knew what she liked, but Sandra brought the western flavor that they both wanted. It looked like Bonnie had found her new Prescott best friend forever.

JW had arranged to meet Bonnie and Sandra at the first structure on the property, which would eventually become Brian's home. The homes were somewhat spread out to provide privacy for the team members, but they were all within a hundred yards of the main house. Careful use of landscaping created a sense that everything was much larger than it was.

At nine a.m., Brian Hockler arrived at the gate. JW met him there, having walked down earlier. He found these walks to be perfect for his troubled soul. His injuries, the pressure of building Big Dogs, and forging the relationship with the FBI all weighed heavily on him. The construction project had gone so well that it scared him. When would Murphy's Law kick in and create new problems? So far, the comprehensive planning by Maddox Christensen's construction crew had kept it at bay.

JW sighed as he felt the pressure lift from his shoulders. Bonnie was very religious; she went to church regularly, although she had yet to choose one here. JW also felt close to God, but he didn't feel the need for fellowship. His beliefs were very personal to him. He found God here, in nature. He was in everything JW saw around him, and he felt the comfort of His presence.

The bridge at the entrance to the property had been rebuilt and was now a tall, covered bridge. An electric gate and intercom had been installed to control access, and a worker was there applying the finishing touches.

"Good morning, Brian Hockler. Are you ready for the first day of the rest of your life?"

"Wasn't that a TV show long ago, like before I was born?"

"Yep," said JW as he sat in the passenger seat of Brian's SUV. They drove down the main road and stopped at a beautiful, two-story house. It was painted a light blue with white trim and had a bit of a Victorian flavor without looking too dated. As they exited the vehicle, a landscape crew planted flowers and bushes around the front.

"This is nice, JW. Is this your new place?"

"Nope."

They walked inside and were greeted by Bonnie and Sandra.

"Welcome home, Brian. I'm Bonnie, and this is Sandra Kyra. She will help you pick out furniture for your new place."

Brian looked around the room, taking in the great room with a fireplace and a small kitchen off to the side.

"Nice to see you again, Mrs. North, and it's a pleasure to make your acquaintance, Sandra. Wait, so I'm gonna live here? It seems awfully big to me."

"Don't worry, when we put your furniture in here and a few touches of color, it will feel much more like home," Sandra said.

Bonnie looked at JW; she had picked up on the spark between them. JW nodded. He had noticed the quick glance by Brian to see if Sandra had a wedding ring.

"OK," JW said, "Bonnie and I are going to head up to the main house. After you two finish here, come on up. Maybe we can go out to dinner tonight in town?"

Outside, Bonnie said, "Nice move there."

"I don't want you playing cupid with those two. If it happens, it happens, but they are our friends, and if we push something that isn't there, we could ruin things."

"Buzzkill."

"Fine."

"Fine." They both laughed and held hands as they walked up to their house.

JW's first impression was a simple, "Wow." As they finished their stroll, they entered an open courtyard separating the main house from two other similar-looking buildings. All the buildings had a log cabin flavor, but more finished and less like they were roughing it out in the woods. Each of the buildings was two stories tall.

Bonnie assumed the role of tour guide.

"Alright, let's start small. The building across from the main house is a guest house on the upper level and a garage on the lower." As they climbed the stairs, Bonnie said, "I call these cabins, even though they're not really. They just feel that way inside." There were two cabins upstairs, and Bonnie walked him through one. "The other side is the same, and this door can be opened to connect if they want." The interiors were nice, but not overly luxurious. The theme seemed to be comfortable. "There is one bedroom per cabin. The idea is that these will be for non-family guests. The couch can be opened into a bed if needed. Throughout the entire project, the floors are heated. Each residence has a fireplace for ambiance and backup heat."

JW looked at his wife and said, "This all looks very expensive, Bonnie." Of course, he knew his wife came from money and she had a sizeable fortune. Still, they had always lived a relatively simple lifestyle.

"It is, but I only want to do this once, so I put a little extra into everything. The main house is a little nicer. I didn't want to make these too nice, or we would never get rid of people." They both laughed at that.

"OK, I'm calling it. Alien abduction. Where is my wife, and what have you done to her?"

Bonnie turned to him and gave him a deep, passionate kiss. "Convinced it's still me?"

"Maybe, I might need some more convincing."

"Easy, cowboy. You're mine tonight. We're gonna break in the new bed properly."

"Woohoo. Coitus."

"Shut up, Sheldon," referencing a character from *The Big Bang Theory* television show.

The next building was to the left of the main house. The main floor was set up as an open space office, except for one office on the left. This space had two large French doors that could be closed for privacy.

"I wanted more of an open office so we can talk to one another."

There were two other desks and an area to the side with some chairs and a table.

"This is the main office for Big Dogs. We have three distinct work areas, plus that large table on the side where we can do group projects. I don't know if I want that many people, but it gives me room to expand. I think I will need someone to help me process all the paperwork; believe it or not, I do not want to work hard all the time. It would be nice to be semi-retired and enjoy this place."

Bonnie said as they exited through the front door, "Upstairs are two more cabins, just like across the street." Bonnie led JW, not to their house, but in the opposite direction, up a street that intersected the square on the south side. She gestured to her left at a building that looked like a barn.

"This is a special present to you, JW. I know how you like to work with wood, so I asked the carpenter if he would help me out."

She opened a set of barn doors and they walked into a large woodshop. There were windows everywhere, including the ceiling, letting in natural light. Work crews were busy installing a dust collection system on several machines.

"No more cramped space in the garage for you."

He looked at her, leaned down, and kissed her. He had no words.

Next came a kennel building on the right. They went inside and JW saw ten kennels on one long wall. On the opposite side were an office, a food preparation space, a restroom, and a veterinary exam room.

"This space is almost done. We have an exam table on order; it should be here later this week. I thought we could meet with the recommended local vet and see if he could give us some ideas about what we will need here. Then, if we get enough dogs, maybe we can arrange a deal with the vet to come here for regular exams, and we go there for the things we can't do here."

Next door to the kennel was a house similar to Brian's that JW had toured earlier.

"I had them make all the house interiors the same. We don't want house envy among the others. The architect changed up the exterior design elements and landscaping so they don't all look the same.

"Oh, I forgot to mention the training fields. Behind the kennel house are several dog break areas. Beyond that are two large fields; one is set up with an obstacle/confidence course for the dogs and the other is open field space for now. You can't see it from here, but each area is surrounded by a low cinderblock wall to help keep snakes out, topped with wrought iron so the dogs can't jump out.

"OK, this next building on the left is the range," she said as they walked in the door. "I was pleasantly surprised by this. Everyone was worried about the air exchange systems and getting all the inspections passed, but it was actually the first building finished."

There were four rooms inside. First, a lobby with tables to prepare to go into the range with a restroom on the side. Next is a large workspace with three double-wide safes in the back to store weapons and ammunition. There was also a desk, a large workbench, a pegboard for tools, and a large tool chest.

The range itself had five lanes.

"You probably won't need that many, but better too many than too few."

Each firing point had its own computer-controlled target system. Downrange was open and could be set up with different target types and obstacles.

"I asked Mark Powers for his suggestions on this. He just drew it all up, including a list of all the tools we would need. I snuck him in last week, and he was here for a few days finishing it up."

"Amazing," was all JW could manage.

As they left the range house, Bonnie pointed to the left.

"We have one more place up there for staff. You mentioned having two guys work on running trails with you. That will be where they live. The road turns right there and, if necessary, there is room to add a few more buildings. At the end is where Maddox's house will be. He insisted that construction not start on his house until everything else was done.

"Another thing we didn't think of is a gym; it's a long way to town just for a workout. We have a couple spots, but I'm thinking something similar to my office, except entirely open. On top would be a couple more cabins."

JW looked down the road and asked, "What are all those trailers down there?"

"Oh, construction offices and such. Maddox had the key people live on site. That's how we were able to finish early. I had no idea how much there was to build a house, much less all this. Thank God those guys were here to make it happen."

JW looked to the left and saw a large open space. "Lots of space over there, Bon. What're you gonna put there?"

"Nothing for now, although Sandra is trying to talk me into a stable. She likes to ride horses and wants to talk me into it."

"That might be fun for you. You deserve something special here too."

"I don't know. Horses are a lot of work."

"Everybody needs a hobby."

"We'll see how I like riding. You ready to go home?"

"Yep."

They arrived back at the main house and stopped outside.

"Before we go in, you may have noticed a driveway that turns off the road between here and Brian's place. That leads to a lower-level three-car garage. There is space for our personal cars, and perhaps one day that mythical Corvette will arrive." Bonnie referred to JW's decades-long desire to own a slightly used Corvette. He had been saving for years and every time he got close another emergency came up and drained the fund.

"Now, don't be disappointed when you go inside and see an empty space."

JW put a pout on his face that lasted a few seconds and then started laughing.

"OK, we can skip that for now."

Bonnie led them to a front porch that ran across the length of the house.

"We didn't put too much effort into this area because we figured everyone would spend more time in the back. Still, it's a nice place to hang out."

They entered through double doors into a large entryway. In the center was an antique table with the bronze statue that JW had seen when they were shopping, "Lookin' for Sign."

"See, I pay attention," Bonnie said.

To the right were stairs leading up to the second floor.

"We can go up there later and look around, but it's basically two guest rooms with their own baths and a small common area. It's meant more for family than the cabins.

"Next, off to the right, is your space."

JW walked through a pair of French doors into a library. The room was lined with bookshelves, his entire Stephen King book collection and all the other books he owned. Dr. Gaurdia had recently added more books to his collection. Spaced throughout the room were different pieces of art from the local area. Directly in front was another antique table with a bronze on it. This one was called "Lest We Forget." It was a fund-raising replica of a full-sized monument downtown. JW looked at the two-piece set that featured an 1890's lawman holding his hat in his hand looking down at a pair of empty boots.

"Prescott has so many artists here, it was hard to make selections. Thank goodness for Sandra. She has remarkable taste. That one is also by Bill Nebeker. Did I tell you I got to meet him?"

"No, you didn't."

"Well, good news, I invited him to the housewarming and he and his wife are coming."

"Speaking of Sandra, where are she and Brian? I'm placing my bet now; that house will be decorated with two people in mind."

"JW, stop! Now, as you can see, there is room for you to add either books or art."

At the end of the room was a large desk with a computer. To the left were a fireplace and a flatscreen television on the opposite wall. There were two comfortable leather chairs in front of the desk.

"I don't know, Bon; this looks pretty fabulous as it is."

"I know you; you'll find something to fill the spaces. OK, now follow me. This next room is mine. You can come visit, but it has been designed for me."

They entered the great room from the side. The ceilings went to the roof's peak, and the beams were all-natural wood and looked as if they'd been carved by hand. The ceiling itself was bleached knotty pine.

"I can adjust the lighting here to match my mood."

In the center of the room was a huge stone fireplace made of local river rock. It was open on both sides to heat each part of the space.

"All the fireplaces are gas. Being in a national forest, I just didn't want to take a chance with burning real wood."

JW nodded, and Bonnie continued the tour. Thomas Kinkade's painting, "Reflections of Family," was on the wall above the mantle, downlit to highlight the scene's beauty. JW thought, *Bonnie created herself a little slice of heaven right here.* In front of the fireplace was a leather couch with two matching chairs; pillows and throw blankets highlighted the area and provided color.

At the end of the room, a door led either outside or to a set of stairs to a lower level.

"Your choice, JW, finish this floor or go downstairs."

"We're here; let's finish the main floor."

They went to the other side of the fireplace and entered the kitchen. The cabinets were in a darker knotty pine and provided a western touch. The room was modern with high-end appliances. A cook's dream. A center island contained a grilling surface with side burners and a breakfast bar for informal dining.

To his right was a large dining room. The space from the outside was a round turret. Inside, the room seemed a little less circular. There were French doors leading to the outside flagstone patio. The table dominated the room; it was a beautiful piece that seemed pieced together from different types of wood. A matching china cabinet on one wall held Bonnie's mother's china.

Next to the dining room was a butler's pantry. Inside, JW found the most essential item in the house, the coffee maker.

"Go ahead and make yourself a cup; we still have a ways to go."

JW fired up the cup at a time and made himself his favorite brew.

"Please try not to spill. The dogs aren't here yet to clean up after you."

She pointed to a hallway and said, "That leads to the laundry room and our lower-level garage, and this leads to our master bedroom." Above a massive bed was a painting of a single lawman on horseback in a beautiful river valley. "That one is done by an Arizona artist." There were closets on the right and a master bath on the left.

"I gotta say, Bonnie, I am stunned. I am at a loss for words."

The master bedroom had a sitting area with a small fireplace and more doors leading to the patio. Outside, JW spied a hot tub with the cover on. They walked out onto the patio. In the center was an outdoor dining area with an adjacent fire pit with seating. On the far side was an outdoor kitchen with a grill, smoker, burners, and pizza oven. A set of stairs led to a lower level. The view from the patio was amazing. It was the same scene Jim McIntyre had pointed out when they first looked at the land. Everything had changed so much, but the vista was still gorgeous.

"OK, last but not least. We could go inside and use those stairs, but these lead to the same place." Finally, they reached the bottom of the stairs, and Bonnie directed him to a lovely garden area to the left. "That has artificial turf for the dogs and is fenced against snakes and other critters."

"Critters?"

Turning and looking at the house, it appeared the patio above was resting on two massive boulders. In between them was another small terrace with a multi-tiered Spanish tile fountain. "This and the spa won't be all that useful during the winter, but they will be nice for the rest of the year."

They went through another set of French doors into a large game room with a small fireplace in the corner. To his right was an eighty-inch 4K flat screen television with a couch and chairs set up for viewing. "This is your man cave, although I may come to visit." A pool table and a couple of tables and chairs were opposite a bar. "The bar is an antique. The builder, who is doing the Victorian, found this in a ghost town and restored it. Isn't it beautiful?"

JW ran his hand over the wood, feeling the grain and character of the piece. There were a pair of beer taps and a nice back bar containing various liquors.

"So, we got a brand-new house and imported our own ghosts?"

He looked at the mirror in the back bar, and as he turned away, something caught his eye. He shook his head; he swore he saw someone looking back at him, smiling.

Bonnie scowled at him and said, "Yeah, something like that. Don't make me hurt you, JW North."

As Bonnie and JW climbed the stairs back to the main floor, they heard a knock at the front door.

"Anybody home?"

"Come on in, Sandra," Bonnie replied. "Are you guys ready to go out to an early dinner?"

"In a bit. First, I wanted to show Brian how we decorated this place."

"Great idea. Brian, come on, let us girls give you a quick tour."

JW laughed to himself as he saw Brian look at him with a "Help Me!" expression. *Nope, you're on your own now, big boy.*

JW went to let the dogs out for a break. They had been in his Tahoe for a while. But, of course, they were asleep in the back. The kennel was done, but the outside break areas were not ready yet, so he took them around to the back of the house and led them down the stairs to their designated break area. Addy immediately chose a spot and christened it. Ares, not to be outdone, marked over where Addy had gone. JW laughed; *good thing Bonnie had them put in artificial turf; otherwise, all the grass would be gone soon.*

Bonnie selected a different restaurant downtown for dinner that night. Sandra had insisted she needed to stop by her place to clean up a little before they met. Brian went ahead and drove to his place and changed too. Bonnie led JW to his closet and showed him it was full of his old things and some new clothes she had picked. He decided on a nice pair of jeans, boots, and a sports coat. Bonnie had one of her little black dresses on.

"Nice choice, Bonnie."

"Oh, you like this? Wait until you see Sandra; hers is even littler."

"Poor Brian, the man is doomed. Two against one isn't even fair."

They all arrived at the restaurant about an hour later. Brian had picked Sandra up, so they came together. Obviously, she really wanted to impress him. JW had only seen her dressed for work: either slacks and a jacket or sweats. But, hidden inside was a lovely woman. Brian looked a little uneasy and JW pulled him aside.

"What's wrong, Brian? Have you not seen how gorgeous Sandra looks?"

"She's really something, that's for sure. Well, have you ever seen a wild horse who is about to be corralled?"

JW laughed and said, "Don't look to me for sympathy, man. You can always say 'no.'"

"What, do you think I'm crazy?"

Over dinner, JW asked Brian, "Hey, I think we need one more guy on our search team. I always believe in having backups. What if I twist an ankle and you're running the dog? We need a third."

"I got a guy who might fit the requirements. A friend of mine. We went to high school together. Guy's a hell of an athlete. Instead of playing college ball, he joined the Army. I think he was a Ranger. He's out now—he got hurt somehow. I don't know what happened, so that may disqualify him. But, when he was in the Army, he started lifting weights and got big. He's a gun guy, like you. So, you'll have that in common."

Sandra chimed in, "Are you talking about 'Booker the Bruiser'?" She was also from Prescott, although a few years younger than Brian.

Brian laughed. "I haven't heard that name since we played football together. Yep, Big Booker Moss. He and his wife are working at a nice place in Chino Valley. She's a great cook and Booker is tending bar."

JW asked, "Can you set up a meet?"

"I can, but I think he is out of town for a couple weeks. So, after he gets back?"

JW and Bonnie returned home and let the dogs in for the first time. They wandered about, going through each room several times. JW knew it would take them a while to fully adjust to the new place. He and Bonnie grabbed coffee and followed them in case they tried to get into trouble.

JW said, "Hey Bon, one nice thing about this house. There is so much room, no more dogstacle course."

"JW, your naivety sometimes is overwhelming. I give you three days before they find all the chokepoints and know exactly how to blockade you. I give you a week before you step on Addy."

"That's not my fault; she literally throws her feet under mine as I walk."

"Yeah, right."

Finally, the dogs accepted their new home and settled down for the evening. JW and Bonnie snuck into the bedroom for a few moments of intimacy. Later, JW opened the door to find both dogs sitting in front, staring at them. "Perverts." The dogs looked away and found a new place to settle.

The Norths refilled their coffee cups from earlier, walked out onto the patio, and took seats at the fire pit. Bonnie opened her iPad and tapped it several times. He could hear the fountain below activate, and then the fire pit flared up, warming them. Next, she opened another app, and music played from hidden speakers. It was the Farm Aid version of *Tennessee Whiskey* by Chris Stapleton. JW liked how it started slow and then built to the strong voice of the singer. The song spoke to him and his feelings for his wife.

JW leaned back and thought of a time in his past when things were very bad for him. He'd fallen into the depths of a bottle and almost drowned there. Then, a friend introduced him to Bonnie and his life forever changed. He started to go down that dark road and then stopped himself. He reached over and grabbed her hand and sipped his coffee.

The dogs stretched out on each side of them, ever vigilant. They knew something was coming and were ready to protect their pack. They were not bound by the rules of man. They understood these two were part of the pack and would do whatever it took to keep them safe. What else was there? There was nothing more important than pack. The two dogs understood this instinctually and would obey the call from their past.

22

The following day, JW woke and found things were as they should be. Bonnie was asleep beside him, Ares at her feet. Addy was back against his calf, radiating heat onto him. He was grateful the night had turned cool as he and Addy ran hot.

He got up and made some coffee in the butler's pantry. Then, he walked into his office and sat at his desk. It was cool in the house, so he returned to his closet and pulled on his favorite USC sweatshirt. Once back at his desk, he turned on the fireplace with a remote. He knew he could do it with his iPad, but he needed to learn all that.

He opened his email and scanned through it. Nothing was interesting; most went in the trash. He opened his secure FBI email and read through the daily briefing. Things were building in Kentucky. There still wasn't a strong enough lead to have JW and the dogs respond, but there were more killings that Frankenstein had identified as likely related. When JW had visited with the FBI team in Quantico, he met Dr. Fischer, the computer genius behind Frankenstein. He'd asked the doctor, "Why 'Frankenstein?'"

His response made complete sense. "I chose the name because of what the program does. It takes things from many parts and makes them one. Frankenstein gathers data from all over, studies it, and makes sense of it for us. We take those results and, hopefully, point you and SA LeClair in the direction of a killer. Then we do it all over again. They never stop, and neither do we."

JW discovered his coffee cup was empty. Time for another. He walked back to the pantry and ran into Bonnie. He hugged her and told her she looked lovely.

"Mountain air must be agreeing with you."

"I look like hell, and I know it. I need some coffee. Where's my mug?"

JW always accused Bonnie of hiding his coffee cup and found this statement incredulous.

"What is this, role reversal? Try the kitchen sink. I wish I had thought to wash it for you."

She scowled at him, knowing he had caught her in the same trap she often used. She began to feel better once she had her first sip.

"Wow, it must be the elevation. I slept like the dead."

"You don't think it was the fantastic lovemaking?"

"No, I'm going to stick with elevation. What's on your calendar for today?"

"I'm not sure. We need someone to take care of the kennels, but I don't know where to start looking. I already asked Brian."

"And I checked with Sandra," added Bonnie. "We're going to meet with the new vet this afternoon. They have a full kennel service; maybe they have a part-timer or something."

They arrived at Prescott Animal Hospital early, anticipating filling out lots of forms. Instead, when they arrived with Ares and Addy, they were surprised. Their Long Beach veterinarian had transferred their records here and generated most of what they needed from them. Bonnie stood at the counter chatting with the receptionist, answering the occasional question as they filled in the blanks. This hospital was brand new, as the founder had recently decided they needed more room and an updated facility. It seemed half the staff came out to meet the dogs. Everyone knew one of the two girls they had rescued, so both dogs were now famous and local celebrities. It was a small town, after all. The dogs ate so many treats that, when it came time to weigh them in, JW remarked, "Oops, you two may need to go on a diet."

The group was ushered into one of the many exam rooms and waited. Within moments a clinician came in and began asking them questions and answering theirs.

"Rattlesnake vaccine, which is given in two doses. We can do the first today. It looks like their other shots are all up to date, but the doctor will look all this over and talk with you."

Dr. Hunter Pierce came in a few minutes later. He was younger than JW expected, about the same size as he was, dressed in jeans with a white smock. Bonnie had anticipated they would have many questions, as would the doctor, and had asked for a longer appointment. First, he looked over the records and then the dogs. Each eyed him suspiciously when the thermometer came out and relaxed as he listened to their hearts.

"OK, so this is who everyone is talking about. The dogs look great, and their records and shots are all in order. You asked about the rattlesnake vaccine, and we have that here. Now, what questions do you have for me?"

Bonnie broke out pen and paper and started at the top of her list.

"Dr. Pierce, I'm sure you have heard or read about what we do by now, so I won't go into that unless you have questions. We have a nice kennel facility at our property, but we are looking for some staff members to oversee it. Do you know anyone who might be qualified? We are looking for someone with experience caring for large dogs like these two. Eventually, we will have several more."

"Yes, I can recommend someone, actually two people. The Ward sisters might fit your needs. We use them here to backfill for vacations and such. They both were born here, but the one sister, April, I think, left for a while. That happens with kids here a lot. They grow up here in small town USA and long for the excitement of the big city. But eventually, they realize what they left behind and come back. I know they do house and pet sitting, and I have not heard anyone complain. They are the first ones we recommend when someone asks for a referral. But I have to warn you, they are a bit quirky."

Bonnie laughed, "We love quirky, Doc. Who else would want to join our crazy enterprise? The other thing we are looking for is a part-time vet. We built our kennel with a small exam room. As I mentioned, eventually, we will have a lot of dogs there. We thought maybe we could hire one of your staff to come up and do the routine veterinary work onsite. We would pay Prescott Animal Hospital for any expenses, and they would be your employee. It seems like bringing a parade of dogs through the lobby might be more disruptive than usual. Obviously, we would come here for the more serious matters."

"Your request isn't as unusual as you might think. We deal with many large animals—farm, and wild—and bringing them in is not practical. However, I have a newer doctor, Melissa Ames, who could fill that role for you. Let me see if she is busy, and if not, I'll introduce you."

A few minutes later, Dr. Pierce returned with a short, dark-haired woman in her early thirties.

She was warm and energetic and said, "Hi, I'm Dr. Ames. Dr. Pierce explained what you're looking for. I think that would be exciting, considering who my patients would be. I would like to come by and look at your facility and decide what we need."

It was Monday morning in Quantico, Virginia. Dr. Lauralynn Gaurdia was summoned to a meeting in Washington, DC, with the director of the FBI, Alexander Murphy. He had explained to her that she was only as good as her most recent success, which meant the death of the Truck Stop Killer, Floyd Hansen, months ago. The day before, the director had been summoned to the White House to meet with staff first thing in the morning. In addition, the governor of Kentucky had called. Another murder of a young woman in the Bowling Green area had occurred. The citizens were apoplectic and demanded action. The local media informed them that the FBI had been called in for a consultation.

Director Murphy wanted a briefing on the killings and what steps could be taken to assuage the public's concern and capture this unsub. The first words from Dr. Gaurdia were, "I am not aware of this new murder, but I have a briefing based on the previous crimes and what actions we have taken to date. She explained that the computer analysis confirmed what they already knew—that one suspect likely was responsible for the previous crimes. She noted that there were several missing women the media had already declared dead and taken by the same suspect. She advised they were possibly related, but they might be standalone crimes. It could be another copycat serial killer or an opportunist taking advantage of the other crimes to obscure them as a suspect.

Lauralynn explained that members of her staff had been in contact with state and local authorities in Kentucky and provided as much assistance as they could; however, to date, there was no evidence or other leads that pointed them in a specific direction. They had some partial footprints and tire tracks that had been identified, but both were so common as to be almost worthless until they had a suspect.

Director Murphy asked, "Has JW North been involved?"

"No, sir, nothing actionable would call for deploying JW."

"OK, well, we may need to bring him in anyway. The press is killing the local law enforcement, and now they are aiming at us. Apparently, they are calling your unsub the 'Misty Knob Ripper.'"

"Sir, Unsub 20-03 is very smart about his crimes. He is selective of his victims and careful with the crime scenes. Unfortunately, we have no prints, hair, or other trace evidence or DNA. If I were to guess, I would say he had done some reading about forensics and other criminology methods. He is going to be difficult to apprehend."

"Sometimes the smartest criminal gets tripped up over the simplest things, Doctor."

When she returned to Quantico, she held a quick staff meeting with all her section heads. They went over what they knew, and Lauralynn asked the forensics and profilers sections to send representatives to Kentucky to meet with the different agencies with victims. She wanted the reports and evidence reviewed again, especially for the latest victim. She told them, "We need some leads to investigate. Right now, we have nothing, and that is unacceptable."

As she was about to wrap up the meeting, her assistant, Mandy, handed her a file folder.

"I'm sorry to interrupt, Doctor, but I thought this was important, and you would want to see it right away."

She reviewed the papers and told Mandy, "You were right. Thank you." She then turned to the group and said,

"OK, you all have your assignments. Please get the away team en route and let me know if anything changes. The director is under a lot of pressure and is counting on us. I want an update meeting at five o'clock. We're working late tonight, people. I want information on that new killing.

"Louise," speaking to Louise Gallagher, the head of the profiling group, "Let's meet back here in one hour with everyone from your group that isn't going to Kentucky. And let's reach out to Julio Hernandez from the main group across the street."

Louise looked at her with questioning eyes and said, "Sure thing, boss. Can you tell me what it's about?"

"Yes, Jack the Ripper."

23

"Alright, everyone, thank you for coming, especially you, Special Agent Hernandez. We've had an interesting development with Unsub 20-03."

She turned on a big screen displaying a document covered with red handwriting. The group scanned the screen, taking in the message.

Lauralynn continued, "The sheriff in Kentucky, who is coordinating the investigations, received this document in the mail this morning. Fortunately, this message has not made it into the media yet. But, trust me, if it does, and it comes from someone within the FBI, their career is over.

"Julio, as the FBI's leading expert on Jack the Ripper, I would like you to head up a group here to evaluate this document. But, first, look at our existing profile on Unsub 20-03 and give us your take on him."

Special Agent Hernandez replied, "Dr. Gaurdia, I'm happy to help with this effort, and I will let my section head know what you need. However, I hardly think I qualify as the leading expert at the FBI."

Lauralynn laughed. "Julio, I appreciate your modesty, but please. You have researched the Ripper for over thirty years and written two books. You've spoken at countless conferences, so I believe we can safely call you our expert." Then, gesturing toward the screen, she asked, "What do you think of this?

Dear Doctor Gaurdia,

I have been reading the newspapers and following your poor efforts at catching me. I laugh when I read about how clever you all think you are, especially when you talk about being on the right track. I especially like how you believe I may be a cannibal. Please. That is beneath me. I will hunt and take my girls until you catch me. That means I will be killing for a long time. My last date was a special one. I did not give her a chance and took her quick. How can you have a hope of catching me. I love my work and want to start again. You will soon here of me and my fun. Do not worry, I did not use the red stuff for ink. It does not work. Next time I will keep a little sumthing from the girl and send it to you. Do not send this letter to the press. It will prove I am real. My knife is nice and sharp. I want to get to work right away if I get a chance. Good luck to you.

Yours truly
Misty Knob Ripper

PS: About my last girl. You will need to work harder to get a leg up on me.

After reading, Special Agent Hernandez said, "Well, that certainly is interesting. I will need some time on this, but here are my first impressions, which could change. Obviously, he likes the attention. This is his version of the Jack the Ripper 'Dear Boss' letter. He has changed it a little, using words more appropriate to our time. That shows a bit more intelligence than the original letters did. Also, there are fewer misspellings here. I'd like to meet with a handwriting expert to get a better feel for this unsub. I think he is smart but not necessarily intelligent."

Dr. Gaurdia, looking at the screen, asked, "What do you think the PS comment is about?"

"Unknown at this time, but I think we will have an idea when we get the crime scene data in."

"OK, we are meeting at five and have a briefing with the director at six, so it would be great if we could get a bit more in-depth by then," said Dr. Gaurdia.

FBI Director Alexander Murphy sat at his desk and shook his head. He had just hung up the phone after speaking with his old friend, Simon Berg. Berg and Murphy had gone to the Academy together. They were of similar character and the experience created a bond between them. They spoke weekly and exchanged gifts at Christmas. Berg was currently the special agent in charge of the Denver office and lived in a nearby suburb. He and his wife, Olivia, had one daughter, Grace, who was nine years old.

Berg had told him that Grace was missing. At first, they thought she was at a friend's house, but that was wrong. They spoke with the principal of her school, who confirmed that Grace walked home after school with several girls. Olivia called every mom she could think of and no one knew where Grace might be.

At their wits' end, they finally called the Castle Rock Police Department. Berg knew they might not do much; most agencies require more than a few hours of absence before they expend any resources to find a missing person. They checked the location of her cell phone, but it was in her bedroom. That worried him more than anything else because his daughter, like many girls her age, was always connected to her network of friends.

After his call, Simon Berg was surprised when several police cruisers arrived along with a sergeant. Apparently, Berg was well known in the area and they provided VIP service to his family. He was told the chief was on his way but had been in Denver for a meeting. The officers were very professional, and the sergeant quickly organized a search. They first checked the Berg house, even though Simon had already told them he had done it. Then, armed with photos, they began a door-to-door search throughout the neighborhood and adjoining blocks. The local media was quickly called in, and Grace's face was soon on TV. Incredibly, no one had seen her that day. However, several neighbors had reported spotting her a few days earlier as she was selling wrapping paper for a school fundraiser.

Rusty Wheatley was panic-stricken. When the girl had come to his home a week ago trying to sell him holiday wrapping paper, she must have mistaken his desire for her as interest in her product. Young girls had always interested him. He had never acted on his hidden desires except for the occasional trip to the dark side of the Internet. That is, until earlier today. The girl had returned, this time still dressed in her school uniform.

It was too much for him. He invited the girl into the entryway and told her to wait; he needed to get his wallet from his bedroom to pay her. When he returned, he had a battery-operated stun gun in his back pocket. He asked her if she could make change, and when she turned to reach into her backpack, he zapped her. She dropped hard to the floor, and he jumped on her, quickly zip tying her wrists and ankles and then taping her mouth shut. That was when he realized what he had done. His actions had been impulsive and he needed to deal with the consequences. He quickly pulled her into a spare bedroom and pushed her into the closet.

The girl, having fully recovered by now, began kicking the door. A couple of quick and painful electrical shocks ended that. Rusty started to think, *What the hell am I gonna do? Maybe I could make her promise not to tell anyone and then let her go. But, NO, that won't work.* Besides, even though he was terrified, a part of him still wanted her. He thought for over an hour and then finally decided he would go for a walk. Maybe she would escape while he was gone, and when he came home, he could kill himself.

Inside the closet, Grace was also terrified. The electrical shocks had persuaded her that she should stop trying to escape. She wasn't sure what she would do, except the one thing her father had told her if anything strange like this ever happened to her: Stay Alive! Stay alive and he would come for her. She knew he was an important police officer who worked for the FBI. *Maybe if I tell the man who did this, he will be afraid and let me go.* That was proving hard right now as her mouth was taped shut. Her wrists and ankles hurt from having the circulation cut off. She was thirsty and scared. Afraid she would never see her family again, she began praying.

When Rusty returned, the damn girl was still there. *Now, what am I going to do?* He had it worked out in his head, right down to the small details of how he would hang himself. *The stupid girl had to complicate things by not escaping.* He was afraid that if he went to let her out, his desires would take over the little reason he had left. He knew he would end up in hell but didn't want the horrible things he had in mind for her to add fuel to that fire.

He decided to turn on the TV. Perhaps the first good decision he made this day. He turned to a local news station, and there was the story. *THE GIRL'S FATHER WORKS FOR THE FBI! The fucking FBI!* He closed his eyes and imagined drones overhead and FBI agents in black circling his house. He stared at the TV, resigning himself to the fate of life in prison. Prison—where he would be abused by the other inmates.

This was his own particular hell, one from which he had suffered many nightmares. As he stared at the TV set, he realized he had let his bladder go. There was a large, wet stain on the front of his pants and the room now stank of urine. Now angry, he stormed to his bedroom and changed after a quick shower. Disgusted, he took his clothes and tossed them in the trash can by the garage. He looked at the can and wondered if the girl would fit inside.

Director Murphy was still at his desk. He was expecting a video briefing from Quantico about the Kentucky murders, so there was no sense in going too far. On those few occasions when Murphy had a few moments to himself, he liked to wander the hallways and pop into offices. He found these informal visits went a long way in improving morale in a thankless job often made up of long hours away from family. Unfortunately, he didn't have that luxury today.

He was still faced with the dilemma of what to do about SAC Berg, his friend in Denver. When he had listened to him earlier, it tore his heart apart. Although he was childless, he loved Grace, and the thought of her away from her father, perhaps dead, ate away at him. He had offered every resource the FBI had at its disposal. Many of those assets were rushing to Denver right now, so it hadn't surprised him when Simon Berg inquired about JW North and his dogs. They were already becoming legends within the Bureau.

Now his friend was asking for North. Not really asking, but actually begging. He had never heard Simon so desperate. Perhaps if he had a child, he could fully understand his friend's despair. When Director Murphy hesitated, Simon pressed harder. Finally, the director told him he would have to think about it. He knew this might ruin his friendship with the Bergs, but he had made North a promise.

When JW and the director had spoken earlier in the year, they had agreed that JW was not going to trail after every lost child in the United States. There was no way JW could do that and still be available and effective when called upon by the FBI to search for serial criminals. When the director agreed to this stipulation, he did so because he knew North was a good man, and it would pain him to say no. The director was now faced with going back on that promise and sending North to Colorado. He thought about that night with North at dinner and how they had also agreed that JW would have the discretion to support local law enforcement with these searches to further relations. *Maybe, just maybe.*

"JW North."

He looked at the caller ID, and it identified the caller as FBI, Washington, DC. *Huh, I usually talk to Dr. Gaurdia in Quantico, not DC.*

"JW, this is Director Murphy. Do you have a minute?"

North mouthed "FBI, Director Murphy" to Bonnie, Brian, and Sandra as they sat around the fire pit.

"Sir, I always have time for you."

"Thank you, JW. I hate to do this, but I need to ask you for a large favor."

JW cocked his head thinking, *Favor?*

"Whatever you need, sir."

"I'm in a bit of a pickle. We both agreed on the conditions of your deployment, but I have a predicament."

He then explained the circumstances of the situation in Colorado.

"Sir, there is no dilemma here. You call your friend and tell him that JW North is going up that way for some fishing and may stop by and take his dogs for a walk in the neighborhood. I may even bring my friend, Brian Hockler, with me. Funny thing, sir, I've been meaning to talk to you about Brian. He's a good man retiring from the Yavapai County Sheriff's Office and joining my team. He will probably need that US Marshal's credential sooner than later."

At his desk, the director nodded, made a note on a pad, and said, "If you can get me his information, I will personally put the paperwork in."

"Sir, I'm gonna go pack. I'll put Bonnie on. She has all that information. Tell your friend we'll be there in the morning."

"JW, thank you. Are you sure you can be there by the morning? That's a twelve-hour drive for you."

"Piece of cake, drive all night and walk the dogs in the morning."

"This means a great deal to me. Oh, and good luck fishing."

JW handed the phone off to Bonnie, who greeted the director and walked into the Big Dog office. North turned to Brian and asked, "You got your 'go bag' packed?"

"Yep. I just need to know how many days we'll be gone."

"I would say, plan for four days."

"OK, what was that about fishing?"

"We're driving to Colorado, then we're gonna go fishing for perverts that like to kidnap little girls. Oh, and Brian, be sure to pack your gun."

The video screen lit up with the faces of Dr. Gaurdia's team.

"Good evening, Dr. Gaurdia."

"Good evening, Director. I believe you know everyone here, except perhaps Special Agent Julio Hernandez."

"Although we have not met, I am familiar with SA Hernandez. Thank you for joining us."

Hernandez nodded and Dr. Gaurdia continued, "Sir, I have the entire team here, so we can answer any questions that might come up during the briefing. We would like to first talk about the latest murder and then our revised impressions based on that information and this new 'Ripper Letter.'"

"Very well."

"As you know, there was a murder on Saturday. It was discovered early Sunday morning by a friend of the victim. The victim was Elizabeth Harden, forty-four."

A photograph of the victim was projected to the side of the conference screen.

"She was five-foot-five and approximately 140 pounds. She was attacked in her home, south of Bowling Green, Kentucky. We are working with local law enforcement, and I have other team members on the ground there.

"Miss Harden was killed in a manner similar to the others. Although the formal autopsy is not complete, it appears she died of exsanguination. Her head, arms, and legs were severed from her torso post-mortem, and she was posed as the Vitruvian Man, as were the others. As we have seen with the previous murders, the unsub decided to pick one appendage to move away from the body. This time it was a leg, and it was hung from a wall in place of a picture. At this time, we are not certain of the significance of that pattern; however, Special Agent Hernandez will provide his opinion."

"One thing that is different and possibly promising to the investigation is that the unsub bit this victim on her shoulder. We have requested multiple swabs of that wound for analysis. As with the other cases, there was a significant lack of forensic evidence at the scene. The unsub is very careful and appears to have some knowledge of our methods.

"A detailed analysis of this crime is being forwarded to your office. I asked Special Agent Hernandez to assist us because of the letter that was received by the local police but was addressed to me. We believe the unsub got my name from the local media as we have made no secret of our involvement. I was interviewed regarding one case. I believe SA Hernandez's analysis adds a little more depth to our understanding of this killer."

Seeing this as his cue to take over the presentation, Hernandez said, "Director, I have reviewed the previous profile developed by the team and concur with their findings. The letter our unsub sent says several things to me. First, he enjoys the attention provided by these murders. Some killers may feel a sense of shame or a desire to hide their crimes to avoid detection. This unsub enjoys the limelight. I believe when we find him, he will have a scrapbook of newspaper articles related to his crimes.

"This letter may indicate a pause in his crimes. The crimes have been accelerating in both time and violence. Since I believe this unsub does not want to be caught, he may pause to allow the investigation to lose focus or relocate geographically. We can't be certain of this as he is a bit of a risk taker; this can be seen in his taking of his victims in their homes. There is a much greater chance of being caught by taking this action, but it also makes the crimes more spectacular for him. The one victim found by the road was most likely a crime of opportunity. As I said, he can be a risk taker, but I believe he may pause to avoid apprehension.

"I believe it is likely that the unsub may have inserted himself into the investigation. He may have phoned in a tip or have volunteered for a search team. I know they collect names, so it might be worthwhile to follow up on those 'volunteers.' If there is a bar in town that the police frequent, he may try to associate himself with officers there in order to find out information about the investigation.

"His crime scenes show an organized killer. It appears he stalked most of his victims, except the one, and is very prepared. He brings things with him to secure his victim while he sexually assaults her, and the same is true for whatever he uses to dismember them. His method of operation is specific from planning through execution. The only signature trait we have identified to date is his staging of the victims. We do not believe he is collecting 'souvenirs' from his targets.

"The letter itself is a copy of the 'Dear Boss' letter from the Jack the Ripper investigation. In that case, it may have been from the killer or a member of the media. This current letter, I believe, is from the unsub. He clearly sees us as his adversary here, not the local police. I believe he has purposely selected his victims from different jurisdictions, as he may think that the agencies do not share information with one another.

"As Dr. Gaurdia mentioned, the unsub chose to hang one of the latest victim's legs from a wall. This was likely done for the shock value the killer seems to crave. This highlighting of a body part could be a signature element, but it is inconsistent. It may be done to obfuscate other things from the crimes. As far as the mention of the leg in his 'Dear Boss' letter, I believe this is either another type of attention seeking or some sick form of serial killer humor.

"So far, we have identified seven possible victims of this unsub. There are several missing women in the area, four of which match this unsub's victim profile. He is particular about his choices and probably prefers them sexually. He refers to them as his dates in the letter. The violence directed toward the victims indicates a deep-seated hatred of whoever they represent. That may be a maternal figure or perhaps a woman who rejected him. We have notified the local agencies about this victim profile, and they are considering whether to go to the media with it.

"Finally, because of the sophistication of these crimes, I believe the unsub has researched our methods and could even work in law enforcement, although I do not place high confidence in that. Most of this information is available on the Internet. While he exhibits a high degree of intelligence and cunning, I believe he will have completed only high school. This is seen in his letter; the spelling and structure are better than the 'Dear Boss' letter. It shows a degree of sophistication that he could model his letter using the original as a template rather than merely copying it. Still, his word choices and structure are very basic.

"One other thing, Director. The unsub has shown a level of sophistication in his crimes, and I believe he has likely killed before, perhaps not in this jurisdiction. Unfortunately, I believe the crimes will continue until we stop him. That's all I have for now, sir."

The director said, "Thank you, Special Agent Hernandez. Dr. Gaurdia, what are your plans?"

"The evidence I mentioned is coming to us via overnight delivery. We will run Rapid DNA on it and a full DNA profile using Gel Electrophoresis. As you know, Rapid DNA has been shown to be reliable in identifying saliva samples from the skin. Still, since this may be the only physical evidence we have other than possibly a bite mark casting, we want to make sure. Several members of my team have relocated to the area and are meeting with local law enforcement. I am considering bringing in JW North and his team.”

“Lieutenant North is on another mission for a few days. Does your staff there have a scent collection device? If so, have them collect some samples for when he does deploy.”

“We do not have a scent transfer unit there, but I will put someone trained on it on a plane tonight.”

“Very well, you seem to have it well in hand. Thank you all for your briefing. Please let me know immediately if anything changes,” the director said as he disconnected from the video conference.

24

JW and Brian stopped for gas in Trinidad, Colorado. Brian located a large truck stop and they quickly refueled and grabbed coffee and snacks. They were three hours from their destination south of Denver and wanted to be ready to work when they arrived. They had been on the road to Colorado all night and, although fatigued, each was exhilarated at the prospect of the search.

JW decided to use the driving time for two things. One, to have Brian do as much research as possible on the victim's family and the area where they would be working; and two, to go over his responsibilities as the backup officer. He wished he had access to Dr. Gaurdia's resources. JW wondered if this was a one-off event or if there was a pattern he needed to be aware of. Brian didn't have Ben's computer skills, but he showed promise.

They learned that Castle Rock was a small, upper-income bedroom community on the southern outskirts of Denver. It had its own police force, although it was small. JW wondered if there would be other law enforcement resources to assist them or if the locals were it.

As the sun crested the eastern horizon, they stopped in Kit Carson Park to give the dogs a quick break and then breakfast. That would give them plenty of time to digest their food before going to work. As the dogs were stretching their legs after a long night in the Tahoe, JW examined a large statue of Carson in the park. Although JW recalled reading a book about Carson when he was young, he found he really didn't know much about him. *Another hole in my knowledge of history. I guess I'll have to read another book or two.*

Both dogs had voracious appetites and ate quickly. JW was glad to be on the Interstate again in fifteen minutes as the neighbors had begun to come out and give them odd stares. He decided to call the local police to let them know they had been there in case anyone called about a suspicious vehicle.

When he talked with the dispatcher and explained they were US Marshals on the way to Denver and had stopped to give the dogs a break, she said, "Well, I hope you cleaned up after the dogs."

JW laughed. *Small town priorities.* He always marveled how, as a police lieutenant, he had gone to community meetings in one part of Long Beach. One neighborhood would be concerned with shootings, while another was upset about skateboarders in the park. Each concern was valid for them, but they were light years apart on the JW North scale of importance.

JW went over Brian's trailing responsibilities for the tenth time, and his look in response told North it was enough.

"Sorry, Brian. I've never had to break in a new cover officer. This would be a lot easier if we were training; we could just talk about what we were doing and why. But soon, we will be doing this in a possible life and death situation. Even if there is no threat, if we mess up the trail and fail to find the girl, it could still be deadly for her."

Brian nodded. "I hear you. I'm really nervous right now. I guess I'm just one of those learn-by-doing guys. Sorry if I'm showing attitude."

"No worries, Brian. I understand completely. I remember the first time I ran a trail with Ares. My heart was pounding, and I felt like the whole world was watching me. I almost cried with joy when the trail worked out. My best advice is to try and minimize expectations or you'll put too much on your shoulders. Believe it or not, all that pressure travels down the leash and can affect the dogs. We fail if they spend time worrying about us instead of doing their jobs."

Lauralynn Gaurdia was in the main FBI crime lab building with one of her forensics technicians. She had a cooperative working relationship with them. Although she had a small version of this facility, there was no need to completely duplicate everything. It just wasn't cost-effective.

"OK, Doctor, we have extracted two different DNA profiles from this sample obtained from the bite on the victim. We can exclude this one because, as you can see, it matches the profile from the blood sample taken directly from the victim. This other profile is from an unknown source and I will enter it into the Combined DNA Index System (CODIS) to see if we can find a match. I can monitor that from my office back in our building."

"Great! Let's hope that we get a hit from CODIS. Any guesses as to how long it will take for something to come back?"

"It could be anywhere from a day to a couple weeks. There isn't really a standard pattern. It takes as long as it takes."

Lauralynn scowled, "I hate that saying. I don't like feeling as if my life is controlled by the whims of a machine."

"Yeah, me either. But it is what it is."

Lauralynn thought *I hate that saying too.*

JW climbed out of the driver's seat and, after a short stretch, turned to walk to the front door of the address the director had provided. There were several police cars on site, and a couple of police officers with coffee were guarding the home. JW flashed his US Marshal credentials at them, and before he could start toward the door, a large man walked out and inquired, "JW North?"

JW nodded and walked toward him, "Yes, sir."

"I'm Simon Berg. Thank you for coming. Would you like some coffee or something? I know that was a long drive for you."

"Sir, I never turn down coffee and perhaps a cup for my partner, Brian Hockler? I have some questions about your daughter, Grace. By the way, you have a beautiful front yard; would you mind if Brian gives the dogs a quick break before we go to work?"

"No problem, JW. How long do you think it will take to get ready?"

"Oh, about ten minutes."

Berg looked surprised, and JW said, "We came to work, sir. No sense standing around talking about it."

"I understood you were on some kind of fishing trip?"

"Yup."

He led JW inside the home, where he was quickly introduced to Berg's wife, Olivia, Castle Rock Police Chief John Ellis, and several FBI agents. Everyone except for Olivia Berg looked at JW with a degree of suspicion. Who was this outsider and what was he doing here? JW thought, *I guess they haven't read our press clippings.*

Berg noticed this and said to the group, "Mr. North works with the FBI Serial Criminal Task Force. He is responsible for the case's conclusion in Las Vegas and recently located the Truck Stop Killer. His arrival is a bit of a surprise, as I wasn't sure if he was available." After that, the tension in the room lessened somewhat.

JW accompanied the Bergs into the kitchen, where they gave him a cup of coffee. He sipped it and sighed.

"That is excellent coffee. Thank you."

"You're welcome. I'll have one of my agents run some out to your partner."

JW nodded and took on a more serious tone. "Alright, I need to ask you some questions about your daughter's pattern of activity before you discovered she was missing. I know you've been over this before with the others, but I would like to hear it directly from you two."

Mrs. Berg looked on the verge of tears.

"If you need to sit this one out, ma'am, I understand."

"No, I'm OK," she said.

"Where was Grace before you discovered she was missing?"

Mrs. Berg said, "She was at school."

"OK, two questions: Did she walk home? And did she often stop at a friend's house on the way?"

Special Agent Berg answered, "She walked. The school isn't far from here."

Olivia added, "If she wanted to go to a friend's house, she always called and asked. But we have checked with everyone and no one has seen her since school."

JW asked, "Do we know she made it home?"

Both parents nodded, and Mrs. Berg said, "Yes. Her books are in her room. She had them with her when she left this morning. I am positive of that."

"Good, that gives me a starting point. Is there any place your daughter likes to go nearby, maybe a place to think?"

Again, Mrs. Berg replied, "Not really. She is always on her phone, talking or texting with her friends. That's in her room too. So that makes me think if she did leave, she didn't go far or plan to be gone very long."

"So, there's no reason for her to leave the house?"

It was silent for a few moments. Then, finally, Olivia said, "Her school band is raising money by selling holiday wrapping paper. She's been canvassing the area; she's very competitive. But she knows not to do that by herself."

Simon and Olivia looked at one another and JW knew what they were thinking. *Did she go out trying to sell wrapping paper?*

JW thought for a second and said, "OK, that gives me a place to start. I'm gonna grab a dog and start fishing."

JW went outside and approached Brian, who was drinking coffee and talking to one of the local officers.

"What have we got, boss?"

He quickly briefed Hockler on what he knew and asked, "What do you think, Brian?"

"Well, based on the little bit I know about trailing, I would say this is a neighborhood trail and Addy is the dog we want."

"Excellent choice. Would you get her out, please? I want to ask the local chief if he has someone he can loan us to follow along in the Tahoe. We may need to bring Ares in if Addy gets tired."

"I can do that, sir," offered the officer Brian had been chatting with. "There's not a lot of us here, but I'm going off shift now so I can follow you guys. I'm sure the chief will be OK with it."

"Thank you, officer?"

"Hastings, sir. Samuel Hastings."

"Sam, you call me JW and him Brian. Welcome to Big Dogs."

"Thanks, JW. I'll run in and let the chief know."

While JW waited for Brian to get Addy in harness, he looked around the neighborhood. These were very nice homes in what appeared to be an exclusive area. *Well, I guess there isn't any place genuinely safe from evil. Always be vigilant, JW.*

Addy nuzzled JW's hand, breaking him from his momentary reverie. "Well, hello, Princess Adeliene. Are you ready to go to work?"

She looked up at JW and smiled while Ares scratched at the screen on the side window of the Tahoe.

JW noticed people were starting to collect in front of their homes and turned to Brian. "I got another job for you. As we run this trail, if people start to come up like they want to pet the dog, and they will, tell them we are working and ask them politely to step back."

"Got it."

Officer Hastings returned and Brian gave him his keys. As he got in, he turned toward the back and looked at Ares.

"He isn't going to eat me, is he?"

"No, we fed both dogs a couple hours ago. He's not hungry," answered Brian with a deadpan face.

JW said, "You're gonna fit right in, Brian," and turned his attention back to Addy and walked her up to the porch. The Bergs had come out, so JW asked them to stand on the side. He had asked Olivia for a piece of Grace's clothing and now she handed him a T-shirt. He scented Addy on it, handed it back, and then commanded, "Geo-say."

Addy began working in circles on the porch, around and around, occasionally eyeing the front door like she wanted to go inside.

"She's just trying to isolate an individual scent trail. Since this is the home's main entrance, there is a lot of your daughter's scent here."

As he finished, Addy began pulling him down the steps. JW hoped that, with just he and Brian, plus the Tahoe, he might avoid too much attention.

As Addy turned onto the sidewalk, JW overheard a helicopter. Behind him, Simon Berg asked, "Can we get those guys out of here?"

JW looked over his shoulder and said, "Too late now. If they're live, whoever has her most likely knows we're coming."

25

Rusty Wheatley woke in the living room of his home. He had fallen asleep there the previous evening while watching the late news. Pictures of the girl were all over the television, along with her FBI agent father. Her mother was interviewed, pleading for her daughter's life with tears in her eyes. It hurt him to watch it, but it hurt even more when he thought of what would happen to him in prison. He would become the bitch for some large man covered with tattoos named Bubba.

He hadn't heard anything from the girl in hours. Last night he could hear her crying in the closet; his crying on the couch matched hers. He considered letting her out, but he hadn't decided what to do yet. He still considered suicide his best option, but he wasn't sure he could do it. He had a gun in his room, a Glock 9mm, but he was worried that if his courage failed him, he would only wound himself. Finally, as he watched the news this morning, a solution occurred to him. He went and grabbed the Glock.

In the closet, Grace had cried herself to sleep the previous evening. She woke early; the house was quiet. The girl wondered if the man had left, abandoning her. She was already thirsty and wondered how long it would take to die of thirst. She had reconciled herself to her own death. Her logical mind could think of no way out of this problem. She knew the cavalry wasn't coming, that was how it was in the movies, but her dad had told her that it was rarely like that in real life. All she hoped for now was that her death would come quickly and her parents would not miss her too much. That is what made her cry last night. Imagining her own funeral, her parents seated in the front row, her mom crying.

Wheatley continued to watch the TV and saw a dark vehicle pull up in front of the girl's house and more men got out. Ten minutes later, the men got a dog out and started walking it on a leash. *They weren't walking; the dog was leading them to him.* For a man who was about to die, Rusty was calm. He opened the front door and stood there to wait for them. He knew it wouldn't be long until they came for him.

Addy worked up the street slowly yet deliberately. JW was used to being dragged behind the dogs and having to apply a lot of back pressure to slow the dog down. For some reason, this time, she was taking her time. *What does she know that I don't?*

They continued along the sidewalk. JW imagined the little girl walking the same way. He imagined slapping himself on the face. *Get your head in the game, JW.* People were silent and respectful along the way, and everyone kept back, not wanting to get in the way. JW imagined most people were aware of the situation and knew what he was there for. He was starting to get anxious with the helicopter overhead announcing their arrival. Damn media, another thing to add to his checklist of things to do at a scene.

They approached an intersection and Addy turned left. Her pace continued and she showed no signs of tiring. JW was grateful that Prescott was at a high elevation and he had adjusted or else he would have already been gasping for air. Addy made another quick right turn and Hockler jogged ahead to block any traffic. People could see they were both wearing exterior body armor and had guns. JW's vest said "FBI Task Force" on it, so even drivers yielded to them with no problem.

Addy stopped mid-block and then cut across the street to the other side. He thought they might be getting close when she stopped in front of an older brick house. JW knelt by her to see if she was OK, but she seemed fine. She was not alerting, just standing there. JW looked and, at the end of the walk that led to the front porch, saw a small lawn jockey statue depicting an African American man holding a lantern. *Now that's culturally insensitive. What idiot would have something like that in front of their house?*

As he stood up and prepared to restart Addy, JW heard a voice.

"Excuse me, sir, are you the police?"

JW started to turn and said, "Yup." Standing on the porch was a middle-aged white man with red hair. He had a pistol in his hand, and...*He has a pistol in his hand!*

"Gun, gun, gun!" hollered JW as several gunshots broke the silence. JW heard the rounds striking a car behind him.

Officer Hastings, driving the Tahoe, saw the windshield spiderweb as several rounds struck it.

"Fuck," he said and dropped over in the seat to avoid further shooting.

JW dropped to one knee and pivoted toward the door. He ordered Addy to lie down, "*Platz!*" and then drew his

Springfield Armory Operator. The redheaded man was turning, running inside. JW fired twice and saw one round strike the man in his lower back. He could hear Hockler to his right also returning fire with his handgun. JW looped Addy's leash around the lawn jockey and advanced toward the door, his gun pointed into the dark interior. He felt Brian on his right, but he only had one thought in his head. *If the girl is alive, I have to stop him before he kills her.*

Rusty panicked. He hadn't intended to shoot anyone. He was hoping to make the officers shoot him by pointing the gun. But, of course, they had shot him; what else were they going to do. Except it wasn't like in the movies, he didn't die, and it hurt like hell. He was shot in his lower back and left shoulder, and he was bleeding a lot, making a mess of his clean floor. His pain made him angry, and he decided if he died, so would the girl.

He struggled to his feet, knocking over a small table. Then he staggered down the hallway leading to the closet where the girl was. Again, he felt something hard hit him in the back, knocking him into the room. He crawled on the floor, trying to get to the closet door…only a few more feet.

JW ran through the door. *Bad tactics*. He knew if the suspect was waiting for him, he was dead, but he didn't think that was the case. The suspect was going for the girl. He heard Brian behind him, but more importantly, he listened to the suspect moving down a hallway just off this room. JW "pied" the doorway quickly, using the angles he created by moving sideways to provide some cover for himself and reveal whatever was there. He saw the suspect; he was staggering, bouncing off the wall. One hand was on his lower back, where there was a lot of blood, and the other still held the gun.

Not wanting to lose sight of him again, JW raised his pistol and fired once, striking the suspect in the mid-back, knocking him into a room. JW continued after him. As he reached the door, he pied the opening again and saw the suspect on the ground. His hands were empty and JW saw the gun a few feet away.

"Do not reach for that gun. I will kill you."

The suspect looked up at him and said, "I can't. I can't move. Do you think I'm dying?"

"Not yet; you aren't."

JW moved into the room, picked up the gun, and placed it in his back pocket.

"Where's the girl?"

"I want a doctor."

"Where is the girl?"

JW looked the man dead in the eyes. He didn't say a word, but it was clear there would be no doctors yet. The man didn't say a word but looked toward a closed closet door.

"Brian, check the closet."

Hockler opened the door cautiously and saw a pair of legs. He shined his light up and saw Grace looking at him.

"It's OK, Grace. We're with the police. We're here to take you home."

He carefully pulled the tape away from her mouth.

"I can't feel my legs," was all she said.

"She's got tie wraps on her ankles, probably cut off the circulation. You got a knife, JW?"

"Rule nine, Brian, never go anywhere without a knife. Here, take this. It will be better for cutting those."

Brian took the offered multi-tool and cut the plastic restraints. He then twisted her sideways and cut those on her wrists.

"I'm going out front and get this young lady a drink of water while you chat with your new friend."

Finally, Brian picked Grace up in his arms and carried her out of the room to the front of the house.

JW leaned out the door and said to Hockler, "He ain't gonna die, Brian. Go ahead and order up an ambulance for him."

Returning to the room, JW said, "Well, friend, it looks like it's just you and me." JW removed his phone and opened a recorder app. "I have another friend; she likes to talk to people like you. So, I guess this is a good opportunity to get all the bad things you have done off your chest, you know, before you meet your maker."

"So, you do think I am going to die."

"Maybe, if you're lucky. A pretty boy like you won't do well in prison." JW looked at the floor and the pool of developing blood. "Well, I guess I need to get to this; that's a lot of blood there. What's your name?"

"Rusty. Rusty Wheatley."

"So, how many girls have you killed?"

"Killed? What? I've never killed anyone in my life."

"I hope you'll pardon me if I find that hard to believe. OK, how 'bout we start with Grace here. Tell me what happened."

Wheatley then told North how the girl had shown up, looking to sell him something. He didn't even know what it was. He went on to relate the whole story.

"Well, I'm sorry, but I don't buy any of that. That just seems too easy for you to have been the first time. No way I believe any of that crap. Try again."

"Beginner's luck?"

"Rusty, you're really not doing your part in this interview. Do you want me to believe you are that fucking stupid? You grab a girl at your home and think you can get away with it. How long have you been thinking about young girls?"

"All my life, I guess. At first, I didn't think there was anything wrong with it. Later, I discovered people don't like you looking at their kids. I was never gonna do anything about it, but she was just there and I lost it."

"You just lost it? That's it. No plan? What were you gonna do with that girl, Rusty?"

"I wanted to let her go, but then I saw on the TV that her dad works for the FBI. So when you guys showed up and shot me, I was angry at her; this was all her fault. I might have killed her. I got scared."

"Scared? You've left a mark on that girl that will be there for the rest of her life. None of this is her fault. This is all on you. Rusty, you are a disgusting piece of garbage and you make me want to vomit! People like you have no place in this world."

"I guess this means we're not really friends then?"

"No, we're not."

JW was thinking, his right hand resting on his pistol, his thumb resting on the holster release. He stared at Wheatley with anger in his eyes and animus in his heart.

At this point, JW heard others coming into the house. First, an officer came in, followed by paramedics.

JW said, "Looks like it's your lucky day, friend; you're gonna live."

The paramedics began to tend to Wheatley and JW turned to the officer, "Well, he's all yours."

"Hey, wait. Where are you going?"

"Hi-Yo Silver!"

JW walked out the door and to the front, where he found paramedics treating Grace. She was petting Addy—who was smiling the smile of a happy dog.

Hockler was leaning against the Tahoe, talking to Ares, who was OK. All the bullets had struck the windshield and a house across the street.

JW stood there, taking it all in. A whirlwind of activity was all around him while he stood in a sea of calm.

"You seem pretty calm for a guy who was just in a shooting," said Hockler.

"Yeah, well, remind me to call my wife in a few minutes and let her know we're OK. You might want to call Sandra too, earn yourself some points. You OK?"

"I think so. I believe we did what we had to do in there, though it wasn't what I expected."

"It never is. Where's Officer Hastings?"

"He's over at the ambulance, getting the glass pulled out of his cuts. He got a few cuts on his face from the windshield. He'll be OK."

As the two chatted, Simon and Olivia Berg ran up. Olivia went to her daughter, and Simon came to JW.

"I don't believe I can ever thank you enough. Do you know what happened?"

"I talked to the suspect. I think he was trying to commit suicide by cop. He grabbed Grace and then didn't know what to do with her. I believe he would have let her go, but then we showed up."

"Thank God she is going to be OK. If you ever need anything, let me know."

"Well, right now, I think Brian and I will need a referral to a good hotel. I imagine we'll be here for a day or so giving statements and such."

"There are a couple of nice places to stay in town. I'm not sure how they'll feel about the dogs, though. Regarding the statements and such, I'll do what I can to expedite that, but yes, they will want to interview you about the shooting."

"Hey, sir, do you know any place I can get a new windshield? It's gonna be hard to drive home like that."

26

Bonnie had been working while JW was in Colorado. The Victorian home was complete and Allen was busy in California packing his things. He would move in the following week. She and Sandra had reached out to a few acquaintances in Prescott in hopes of finding some possibilities for kennel staff. Since she didn't know the Ward sisters, she wanted to be able to interview several people.

So far, she'd had no luck. She decided to contact the sisters and set up an interview for the day after JW's return. Also, Booker Moss had called and was scheduled for an interview on the same day. Brian had recommended him, so she didn't feel the need to research other candidates. Moss had sounded pleasant on the phone, and his wife, Etta Baker Moss, had asked to come along. She wanted to meet the dogs and see the ranch too.

JW and Brian were finally on the road again. The interviews in Castle Rock had seemed endless. First, local law enforcement, then state officers, and finally, the Feds. It was a never-ending stream of the same questions, asked over and over, with the same answers. JW felt bad for Brian; they hadn't had a chance to discuss a shooting policy. He wasn't even sure what the FBI's shooting policy was or if it applied to him since, technically, he was a US Marshal.

"Brian, we should talk about a shooting policy. I apologize that you were thrust into a position where you had to shoot at a suspect without that being clear in your mind."

"We were a bit rushed to get there, so I don't see it as anyone's fault. But you're right; it seems like we may be faced with that decision again, considering who we go after."

"The policy at my agency…." The conversation was interrupted by the chime of an incoming call. JW glanced at the infotainment screen and saw it was Dr. Gaurdia.

"Good morning, Doctor. How are things in the land of the FBI this morning?"

"Hi, JW, I heard there was another shooting. Is everyone OK?"

JW decided to give her a little jab, "If by everyone, you mean the dogs, yes, they are fine."

"That is not what I meant, and you know it, JW North. So how are you and your new associate, Mr. Hockler?"

"We both survived the encounter without injuries, although I believe Brian may have suffered substantial emotional trauma. I was wondering if you could give him a couple of counseling sessions."

Lauralynn, not liking being the subject of one of JW's jokes, turned serious, "I see from the after-action report that you both were involved in another shooting. JW, do you believe a bullet is the answer to every problem?"

"Well, bullets are cheap, Doc."

"Perhaps they are, but the volume of paperwork you generate with every one of those bullets represents a forest."

JW paused for a moment and said, "Well, we are in a digital age, Lauralynn. We don't have to print every report."

"OK, I'll give you that one. I listened to your interview with the suspect. I must admit that you have a unique interrogation technique. I'm curious, why didn't you Mirandize the suspect?"

"No need, in my opinion. Wheatley initiated the contact with us and then shot at us. Therefore, he represented an immediate threat, and we returned fire. We made entry under exigent circumstances in pursuit of a felony suspect who had just shot at us. Also, there was a reasonable belief on our part that the victim would be in the residence and could still be alive. The fact that he did not attempt to flee the house but went into another area provided me with the further belief that the victim could be in that room, and there was a substantial risk of immediate harm from the suspect. Once we deescalated the force situation, we were still concerned with the safety and well-being of the victim and asked about her whereabouts, only to ensure her welfare. Everything after that was for you and your ever-inquisitive mind."

"Wow. That was very lawyer-like, so unlike the JW North, I know."

"Thanks, Doc; I like to sneak one in now and then to keep you off balance."

"You never cease to amaze. Oh, and in case you hadn't guessed, the director is delighted with your work on your fishing trip. I wasn't aware that you provided such favors."

"Speaking of favors, Doc, can you send me the shooting policy for whoever we fall under? I want to check and see if I need to file a complaint with human resources for all your harassment regarding my use of force."

"Aardvark, JW."

"Sorry, Doc, that only works one way."

"Damn it."

When they arrived in Prescott, Sandra pulled Brian off into one of the many alcoves of the home and began asking questions about Colorado. You could tell by her tone she was concerned about what happened but also very proud of him. Finally, Brian said, "Sandra dear, please, before you conduct a complete interview, may I have a cup of coffee?"

"Of course, you can have a cup of coffee, and you know where you can find one."

Bonnie and JW stood off to the side and chuckled. Then Bonnie said, "Aren't they a cute couple?"

"I wonder if we should start a lottery for the lucky day. That poor boy's life is over."

"What do you mean, his life is over? I'm the best thing that ever happened to you."

"I won't dispute that, Bonnie, but he's not marrying you."

"What are you saying? Sandra isn't a nice girl?"

"She's lovely and a great decorator too." Sensing he was about to go down the rabbit hole, JW changed the subject. "So, how are we looking for interviews? Did you get ahold of Booker Moss?"

"Yes, I did. Actually, Booker called me. I spoke with him and his wife, Etta. She is coming along with him tomorrow afternoon. I get the feeling he is interested in the job but also somewhat reluctant. I think she is pushing him along. It may have something to do with his time in the Army."

"PTSD?" asked JW, referring to Post Traumatic Stress Disorder.

"No, not that, something different."

"Well, if he doesn't want to be here, then I'm not sure we want him, even with Brian's recommendation."

"I don't think it's like that. You will have to talk to him to understand. Oh, and I was able to contact the Ward sisters. They are coming two hours after Booker. You're gonna love them—they're not quirky like Dr. Pierce said—

they're crazy like you. Just imagine, JW, they could be the two daughters we never had."

"Bon, with all the craziness in my life, Lauralynn, a batch of serial killers, a reluctant veteran, and now a couple of crazy daughters, I was hoping for a bit of peace around here."

Bonnie snickered, then laughed, and finally began a series of snorts until she bent over at the waist, barely able to breathe. She reached out to JW, who steadied her, and pulled herself upright. Tears streamed down her face, and she said, "Oh, Honey, this party is just getting started."

"I didn't even think what I said was funny."

This started Bonnie laughing all over again. Finally, JW decided it was time for coffee.

They opted to do the interviews in the Victorian. The once large dining room had been converted to a conference room. The furniture was still period-appropriate but not antique. A large sideboard had been converted to a televator TV cabinet. A large flat screen monitor was concealed within the rear of the cabinet and could be raised using a remote. The room looked like a photo from a Victorian-era dining room when it was down.

Allen Whelan had parked his Jeep to the rear and was unloading the last of his personal items upstairs. The upper level had been converted into a private living space for him. The first time he walked through the home, all he could do was smile. However, he did like to complain about walking up and down the stairs to cook. Unfortunately, the sales agreement limited what they could do on the remodel.

When the Mosses arrived, Bonnie greeted them and walked them to the Victorian. JW walked out onto the porch and was amazed. Booker Moss was big; perhaps the more appropriate term was large. The Black man stood six-foot one inch tall and probably weighed in at two hundred fifty pounds. However, it did not look like there was a pound of fat on him. He had a round, cherubic face with a happy smile. Booker walked with a bit of a limp. Even though JW could tell Booker was a little nervous, he did look happy to be there.

When they shook hands, JW felt like his hand had been swallowed by the other man's.

"Brian said you were a big guy, but I think he may have downplayed it. You are a mountain of a man."

"Brian and I played ball together in high school. Then, I was a running back. After I joined the Army, I started lifting and grew a little bit. I went to school while in the Army, studying exercise physiology. I actually got my degree."

"Yes, I read that in your resume. You have a very impressive background. You were in the Army for what, over twenty years?"

This question perked Booker up. "I was in the Rangers, 3rd Battalion, of the 75th Regiment. That all seems like a lifetime ago. I loved my time in the Army, but I guess all good things come to an end."

They walked into the house, and JW offered, "Coffee?"

Booker replied, "Always."

"A man after my own heart."

Allen, who was upstairs, heard them in the kitchen and said, "I hope you two aren't making a mess in my kitchen."

JW laughed and said, "Booker, this is Allen. He is an old, angry man who, if you end up on our team, you will learn to ignore."

Allen shook hands and went back to his work upstairs. Booker said, "I hope angry and old are not job disqualifiers?"

"Nope." JW led him into the dining room and offered him a seat.

"I called Brian after I heard about the job." He looked around the ornate room. "I have to say, this is not what I expected. Where is Brian, by the way?"

"Oh, he's downtown talking to the sheriff, explaining why he had to get into a shooting in Colorado. You passed his place on the way in."

"That beautiful new house is Brian's?"

"Yep, we try to treat our people right here at Big Dogs. But we work hard, and we go when we are called. But I have to warn you, if you take the job, you may not be around here very much."

"Sounds a lot like my old job."

"What did you do in the Army?"

"Well, since I was in for a long time, I did lots of things. After Basic, I went to Airborne, then Ranger school. Been to a bunch of schools in the Army. Rangers like to work in small teams, so you have to learn to do a lot of things that might normally get spread out in a regular Army unit. Plus, you're often outside the wire with no support services. I've had a lot of medical training, been a weapons armorer, sniper, and just about everything else. As I rose in rank, I started getting Army leadership training. I spent a lot of time overseas, in Iraq and Afghanistan. You know, the Army always sends you to the best places."

"Sounds a lot like the Marines."

"You were in the Corps? Well, then you know."

"If you don't mind me asking, why'd you get out?"

"I got hurt, took some shrapnel in my knee. Nothing life-threatening, but lots of surgeries. They got it about as good as they could, but my knee's still not right. It's funny, I walk with a bit of a limp, but I can run. I'm still working on that, though. I work hard to keep my body fit, and if a part isn't up to snuff, I just work it harder."

JW found himself liking the man. His smooth, effortless style was nice, but there was a quiet confidence there too.

"So, the Army forced you out?"

"No, nothing like that. The Regiment was good to me and did all they could. We both knew that I couldn't be one hundred percent in the field. You know how it is; you have to lead from the front, and if you can't do that… Well, they're not going to put you in a position where your disability might get someone else hurt. They offered me a position running the teaching and training the new kids. I thought I might like that because of my love of guns and shooting, but it didn't feel right. When you've been at the tip of the spear for over twenty years, it just doesn't work when all you're doing is support work. Not that those things aren't important, I guess I just didn't feel important anymore. It was time for me to get out and come home."

JW nodded and thought for a few minutes. An old clock on the wall ticked the moments away.

"You know, I'm tired of sitting on my ass. You up for a walk?"

"Sure thing."

They left the house, yelling up the stairs at Allen that they were going. JW and Booker walked down a path and entered the courtyard of the main house. JW pointed out the different buildings and what they were for. He opened the front door to the main house and Ares and Addy bounded out.

Booker laughed at the sight of the dogs running around him. He bent down and began rubbing the two behind the ears. His smile would have served as a beacon in the night if it were dark.

"I love dogs. These two are beauties. Are they the ones you work with?"

JW introduced them and then stepped back to watch. Booker was a natural with the dogs; they took to him immediately. *You can tell a lot about a man by how he interacts with dogs.*

"Let's continue up the road here."

JW pointed out the kennels and then walked to the ranch armory. The dogs followed along, each sniffing and marking as if it was their first time there. Booker's eyes lit up again when they entered the otherwise nondescript range building.

"Wow. You really did it right when you built this place. Five-lane range? What's it rated up to?"

"We can shoot 7.62 or 5.56 in here. Sorry, no fifty caliber."

Booker laughed, "I don't imagine you have much of a need for fifty caliber. But I tell you, they sure are fun to shoot."

JW let Booker walk through the facility, examining the work area. He looked at the safes and asked, "What's in these?"

"Nothing yet. I'm looking for a guy to give me some solid recommendations."

"OK. Well, that is something I can certainly do."

They left the armory and continued to walk.

"That house up ahead would be yours if you decide you want to join our team."

They took a quick look through the home.

"We decided to leave these homes empty for now. We have a designer to work with you if you need one, but it seemed nicer if we let people decorate for themselves rather than just pick stuff out.

"Next door, we were thinking of adding another building like those down by the main house but putting in a small gym on the ground floor. But, of course, we would need someone to help us set that up. Bonnie is talking about putting some stables over there," pointing to the left and then, back to the far right, "Another big house is going in back there. That one is for another friend who helped make all this possible. That's a story for another day."

They walked back down the road to the main house. Bonnie and Etta were in the kitchen, Etta looking around at the space like she was in heaven.

She said, "Mr. North, I don't entirely understand what you do here, but this is the most amazing place I have ever seen. This kitchen is to die for."

"Brian mentioned you were working up in Chino Valley as a chef. How do you like it?"

"I love to cook. I could cook all day and still be up for a late dinner. I feel most at home when I'm in the kitchen."

JW replied, "My magic place is with dogs. There is just something about a dog; they can make whatever is wrong, right."

Bonnie chimed in, "Oh, now I'm jealous."

"Sorry, Babe, second place."

Bonnie promptly hit him on the arm. JW turned to the Mosses and said, "You saw it, spousal abuse."

"I didn't see shit. Oops, sorry," Etta said.

JW laughed and said, "I like her. But, Honey, let's go outside and admire the view. These two may want to talk."

Once outside, Bonnie asked, "Well, what do you think?"

"I like him a lot. He's got a lot of skills and knowledge that could benefit the team."

"I sense a 'but' in there."

"It's not a 'but' on my part. Booker seems hesitant. I think it's why he got out of the Army. He was injured—his knee—and they moved him from an operational to a support role. I think it was as much his idea as the Army's. He didn't want his injury to be a liability and probably feels the same about us."

"I guess I can understand that. I'm picking up on another JW North reclamation project here," said Bonnie.

"He doesn't need reclamation. That man has it all. He may lack the confidence, but I think his military experience will bring that out with some time here. The only issue I see is he has no law enforcement background. The FBI may want him to attend an academy and earn a certificate or something. He's smart and got a degree already. It shouldn't be too tough."

Bonnie said, "Let's go back inside. I've got an idea."

Inside the house, Etta asked, "Well, Booker, what do you think?"

"I don't know, Etta. I mean, I like them, and it would be nice to work with Brian, but I just don't know."

"Booker Moss, what do you mean 'you don't know?' I can read you like a cheap dime store novel. You want to do this so bad; it's already eating at you. Where else do you think you're gonna find something like this, as close to what you did before? I chatted with Mrs. North, and I can tell these are good people doing good things. I know you have your doubts, but I can read that Mr. North pretty well, too. He wants you, but he wants it to be your choice. He's a good man, Booker; you can trust him."

"Well…"

"Well, my ass! You need to get off the bench and get back to work. You've been lazing around long enough."

"I did like tending bar, though."

Etta smiled. "Have you been downstairs?"

"Well, Mr. North, if you'll have an old broken-down soldier, I think I'd like to join your team."

"Excellent! I think you will fit right in, but there may be one caveat. Since you don't have a law enforcement background, the FBI may want you to go get some training. I think there is a program at the local college."

Booker smiled. "I guess that'll be OK, as long as you don't mind me embarrassing those young pups a bit."

Bonnie said, "Etta, I'm finding, with running the business and such, that I am a bit short of time around here. Would you be interested in being the head chef at Big Dogs? I think it would be nice if we could have some of our meals here, it would add to the family atmosphere and all. But I completely understand if you like what you're doing."

"So, all this would be mine? I could cook in this beautiful kitchen."

"Yes."

"Would I be able to tell Mr. North to get out of my kitchen?"

"Definitely."

"And I would get to live in that beautiful house up the road?"

"Yes."

"Since you put it like that, I believe you have made me an offer I can't refuse. It would definitely shorten my commute," Etta said with a grin. "I can also help out with managing the household if you like. I know a few people that do housekeeping. They do good work."

"That sounds good. I hate cleaning but love a clean house. Oh, but I have to warn you, JW hates to have his coffee cup cleaned."

"Well, if he leaves it in my kitchen, it's gonna get cleaned. Cleanliness is next to godliness."

Bonnie smiled.

27

The Ward sisters arrived five minutes early for their interview. That was fine with JW because if you were on time, you were late. They dressed nicely in blue jeans, cowgirl shirts, and boots. April was the older of the two, with short brown hair. She seemed a bit reserved. Julie was two years younger, with long blonde hair. She was much more vivacious. Bonnie brought them both into the Victorian house and seated them in the conference room.

JW stood and greeted both young women and asked if they wanted coffee. Both declined, but April did accept an offer of bottled water. JW decided to eye them for a moment, give them a chance to say anything they wanted. Both just chatted and told them what a lovely home they had. Bonnie laughed and said, "This isn't our house. We live down the path a little further."

Julie said, "Oh, then who lives here?"

JW replied, "An angry old bridge troll."

Allen, who was in the kitchen, said, "I heard that, JW North. Don't go giving those girls the wrong impression about me." He then came into the room and introduced himself. "And if anyone is angry around here, it's that guy." He was pointing at JW. The two girls looked at one another and thought, *This is the strangest job interview ever.*

JW looked over their resumes and said, "It seems like you both have a lot of experience working with dogs. Have you ever been around German Shepherds?"

Julie nodded and said, "Sure, we've worked at several kennels, and they have all sizes and breeds of dogs. We both also volunteer at the local animal shelter. They have some hard cases there. That's what happens when you grow up without a home. I mean, look at us."

April looked like she was going to burst and finally blurted out, "I just want to say that I'm gay. I know that makes some people uncomfortable. I don't know if that will affect how you feel about me with your dogs, but I want to say it now, and if it matters, I understand."

JW paused and looked at her, but before he could continue, Julie said, "If it does matter, I just want to say that I'm not gay. I could really use a steady job because, with COVID-19, the pet sitting jobs are few and far between. No one is going on vacation."

JW took a deep breath in and looked from April to Julie. "Everyone finished? Because I have something I need to say, OK? First of all, April, I don't care if you're gay. It doesn't matter to me. I was a cop for twenty-eight years in Long Beach, California. I have worked with a lot of good officers, men and women, who were gay. So, let me say this, so everyone is clear. I don't care. I didn't care then, and I don't care now. I'm not hiring you for your sexual preference. I am interviewing you to run the kennel and care for our dogs. OK?"

Both ladies nodded, and April said, "I'm sorry if I made you mad."

"April, I'm not mad, and I'm sorry if I seem that way. It's just that those things aren't important to me. I just need you to do two things: take the best possible care of our dogs and help with the training and everything related to that. You guys have excellent references; I have no doubt you would be great members of Big Dogs. Even Dr. Pierce said good things about you.”

“Oh, he loves us,” said Julie.

“Well, he did say you were quirky,” replied JW.

April said, “He thinks we’re crazy.”

“I’m inclined to agree with him,” said JW.

Bonnie watched the three of them talk, her head turning left, right, and center, and then it would start over again. Finally, she said, “I’m getting a crick in my neck.”

April immediately jumped up and started massaging Bonnie’s shoulders and neck. Finally, she closed her eyes and sighed, “She’s hired.”

Julie, ever competitive, said, “Oh, I give better neck rubs than her.”

April looked at JW and said, “You said there were two things.”

“Yes. You guys know what we do here, right? I believe you said you read some articles about us. It’s hard work, sometimes long and tedious hours. But it’s not about us; it’s about the dogs. Everyone here is important, whether trainers, handlers, or dog poop scoopers. That all contributes and works toward our goal of trailing serial criminals. The work is hard, the pay is good, plus you get a place to stay. But to do all this, you must be of one mind and work together. We are a family, so you must join our family to work here.”

April had a small tear in the corner of her eye. “You want us to join your family?”

“Yep.”

She looked at Bonnie, hope in her eyes.

“Yes, April, we want you and Julie to join our family.”

April looked down at the table and said in a very small voice, “It’s been a long time since Julie and I were in a family besides ourselves. I’m not sure if I know how to do that.”

“We’ll work on that together,” said Bonnie.

Ares and Addy danced around the girls, barking, and chasing each other. They had been cooped up for most of the day and had a lot of energy to burn off. They were on the exercise field, and the dogs and girls were well on their way to being best friends. Addy ran to April with a tennis ball and dropped it at her feet.

April turned to JW and said, "They speak German, right?"

"Yep."

"Addy, 'sitz.'" The dog sat in front of her, and Addy's eyes focused closely on April. "Addy, 'fuss.'" She moved to a sit position on her left side. When April sent the ball downrange, Addy went off at a tear, Ares in hot pursuit.

JW said, "Nicely done. Once they know you, you won't need to preface your commands with their names."

Julie came up by his side. "April is magical with dogs. She is going to be so happy here. Thank you, Mr. North."

"Call me 'JW,' and I want you to be happy here too."

"Trust me, if April's happy, I am too."

JW said to them, "Let's go check out your new digs."

When the Ward sisters entered their new place, they began running from room to room, arguing over who got which bedroom. Finally, Bonnie explained that their friend Sandra would help them pick out furniture. Both girls were overcome with emotion and ran to JW and hugged him.

Afterward, as they walked back to the main house, JW said to Bonnie, "Well, you always said you wanted daughters."

"I think Dr. Pierce was right; they are crazy."

"More like batshit crazy."

"I don't care. I think we did a good thing today."

"Yeah, I hope we survive."

Dr. Lauralynn Gaurdia was sitting at her desk. It was late afternoon in Virginia, and the leaves were starting to turn. It was cool outside and the chill crept through the walls. As she read the reports on the Kentucky murders, she drew the sweater she was wearing even tighter against the cold. This was an interesting case; the unsub did so many intelligent things, but his urges got the better of him and then he did stupid things. His mistakes would be his undoing, and she would be happy to be there when they clicked the cuffs on.

Dr. Cecelia Mercado ran down the halls like the devil was chasing her. It was late in the day, but she hoped Lauralynn was still here. Mercado was confident she had not left yet, as Lauralynn often worked late into the night. She burst into the outer office and saw that Mandy, Dr. Gaurdia's personal assistant, was already gone. The door to the inner office was open, though, and Lauralynn was at her desk. She looked up, concerned, and asked, "Cecelia, are you OK?"

She was panting from the run but managed, "Lauralynn, here...." She reached out and handed her a computer printout. "Frankenstein, he found him...."

"Cecelia, please sit down before you fall. You should start doing power walks with me in the afternoon." She took the paper and began reading. Whatever it was, it certainly had Cecilia worked up.

"We programmed Frankenstein with a search based on the saliva test results from Kentucky. As you know, Frankenstein reaches out to all databases, including CODIS.

However, sometimes CODIS can be slow, so this result is from a local agency search."

Lauralynn reached the end of the page and said, "Oh my God. We've got him. I need to make a phone call."

It was early evening when JW's phone chirped at him. He really needed to change the ring tone to something less obnoxious.

"JW North."

"JW, it's Lauralynn. We found him."

"Hi, Lauralynn. You found who?"

"We got lucky—we got a small saliva sample from the most recent murder in Kentucky. We ran searches against it and the results just came back. The unsub in Kentucky is the same suspect who killed the woman in the rest stop in Wyoming and the same person who raped those women in Long Beach. Unsub 20-3 is the Shadow."

"What's his name?"

"The name isn't in the results. I don't think any other searches will return a name either. We never attached a name to the Long Beach suspect, so it's unlikely we will get one now. JW, pack your bags. Get your team ready. We will be deploying to Bowling Green soon. Is Ben's new dog certified yet?"

"Yes, last week. Allen certified him before he moved here. Do you want Ben too?"

"Yes, I want everyone. I'll be on the phone with the director next. I'm sure he is going to authorize a full deployment. There is a lot of pressure on us about this case."

Bonnie walked over to JW; she had heard half of the phone call and knew it was serious. She could see JW was looking far away to the east. Before she could ask, he said, "That was Lauralynn. A DNA search came back on the Misty Knob Ripper in Kentucky. The unsub is the Shadow."

"The Shadow, from Long Beach?"

"One and the same," his voice sounding hollow. "Can you get everyone together? Lauralynn is not sure when, but we will deploy to Bowling Green. We need to be ready. I have to call Ben; he's going too."

"Of course. JW, are you OK?"

"Me, I'm good. I just need a second to think this through. I'm good now, but I'll be even better when the Shadow is out of our lives."

EPILOGUE

The Shadow sat in his favorite seat, reading the paper. He was concerned but not overly worried. He had made a mistake with his last victim and he knew it. By biting her, he had given them the possibility of a DNA sample and physical evidence of his bite. He knew his DNA profile was not in the system, but it still caused him some anxiety.

He was looking for something in the paper about the case. "New discoveries" or anything else that might say they were on to him. There was nothing. He thought it might be time to move on, but he was not finished with his plans here. He didn't want to push his luck too far, but he knew he was smarter than the police or the FBI. They had been involved for months, yet he was still free to take more of his girls.

Part of him wanted to abandon his plans, but he had put so much work into them. He really wanted to see this through. His ego would not allow him to know that he was tempting fate. What he wanted had become paramount and nothing else mattered. He had two more dates planned in this area and then it would be time to move on. He wasn't sure where he was going next. He would think about that at work tonight. He would consider the new options after he had killed again. He needed something to send to the FBI to convince them that the author of the first "Ripper" letter was, in fact, the killer of all these women. They would know soon enough and they would recognize his genius.

End…for now

ACKNOWLEDGEMENTS

Greetings, and thanks for reading *Gasping for Air–Book Two in the 'Big Dogs Series.'*

I'd first like to say thank you to the fans of the Big Dogs series. As I mentioned at the conclusion of Big Dogs, I would have written these books whether anyone read them. That's still true, but it certainly helps to know that people are reading these stories and enjoying them. With that in mind, if you enjoyed this book, please leave a review on Amazon or Goodreads.

I was a police officer in Long Beach, California, for twenty-eight years. I worked as a patrol, narcotics dog handler, and unit supervisor for nine years. It was one of the best jobs ever, and I had many great jobs and worked with many incredible people. I wanted to create a story that combined the life of a police family working in a dangerous and stressful job. This book is the result of that dream.

I try to be accurate but, hopefully, not dull. This is not a training manual. It is a story, and I have chosen to leave much of the tedium and repetitiveness out of the book. Accuracy and correctness were crucial to me with this project. I read a lot and occasionally watch cop shows on TV. I hate it when they are inaccurate and create an incorrect impression in the minds of their viewers or readers. Those writers do all law enforcement and their community members a disservice.

Police training varies greatly across the country, as does the language officers use. There is no national standard; however, being safe is universal.

Next, I'd like to thank my beta reading team. Half of this group comprises experts in firearms, police K9, human scent detection and trailing, and medical and veterinary services. The other half have little connection to law enforcement. They aim to ensure the books are not too laden with technical detail or jargon. They help ensure that someone unfamiliar with police work can read and enjoy the story.

They are, in no particular order: Laurie and Floyd Enault, Sue Westbury, Kerry and Eric Ditmars, Paul and Sheryl Sanford, Long Beach PD Sergeant Billy Kift, retired Long Beach PD Lieutenant David Cannan, retired Long Beach PD Sergeant Marc Cobb, retired Los Angeles Sheriff's Detective Bobby Taylor, Dr. Kenneth Skinner and Dr. Raenell Killian of Prescott Animal Hospital, and retired medical professionals Dawn and Geoff LaGary.

I have added two new members to my advanced reader team with this book. Kevin Fryslie is a retired FBI agent. As JW North becomes more involved with the FBI, getting the little things right becomes even more important. Kevin provided me with insight into the technical aspects and some of the terms and procedures of the FBI. It's all about making it real for you, the reader.

Bob Sisley is a retired police officer and current volunteer with the Yavapai County Sheriff's Office. Bob was an eager reader of the first book, and when I asked him to become an advanced reader for this one, he jumped on board enthusiastically. In the law enforcement world, it seems no one does things the same way, and Bob was very helpful in weaving through the complexities of JW's new home.

My final thanks go to my wife, Barbi. She reads the rough work and puts a polish on it that makes it an enjoyable read. It's a hard job, but I appreciate it. Without her as my first reader and initial editor, the stories wouldn't be the same.

This is our second book with WildBlue Press of Colorado. Without reservation, it has been a pleasure working with this team of professionals. I want to thank Steven Jackson and Michael Cordova, partners in WildBlue Press, for continuing to work with us. If you can imagine the volume of books published yearly, it is even more gratifying for their faith in Big Dogs. In addition, it has been a joy working with WildBlue's Stephanie Lawson Johnson, Abigail Stark, and our editor, Tanya Mravik, who have been fantastic. All of the above and many others were invaluable in their assistance in releasing Gasping for Air. If there are any errors in this book, they belong solely to me.

Again, thank you to all my readers and my advanced reader team. Thanks for joining me on this journey. It has been long and hard work, but I hope the results are worth it. I look forward to entertaining you all with *Ghost Stories–Book Three in the 'Big Dogs Series'* sometime soon.

*For More News About S.L. Ditmars,
Signup For Our Newsletter:*

http://wbp.bz/newsletter

Word-of-mouth is critical to an author's long-term success. If you appreciated this book please leave a review on the Amazon sales page:

http://wbp.bz/gaspinga

www.ingramcontent.com/pod-product-compliance
Lightning Source LLC
Chambersburg PA
CBHW060904210726
48293CB00006B/1948